dust

Ann McMan

Bywater
BOOKS

Ann Arbor

Bywater Books

Copyright © 2011 Ann McMan

Print ISBN: 978-1-61294-127-1

Bywater Books First Edition: April 2018

Printed in the United States of America on acid-free paper.

Cover Design by Ann McMan, TreeHouse Studio

Dust was originally published in 2011 by Nuance Books, a division of Bedazzled Ink Publishing Company, Fairfield, California

Bywater Books
PO Box 3671
Ann Arbor MI 48106-3671
www.bywaterbooks.com

This novel is a work of fiction.

For Domina, who told me to get over it—
then held my hand while I did.

Chapter 1

Andy Townsend. There he was again.

The populist former governor of Delaware had won the recent senate election by one of the thinnest margins in the First State's history, but you'd never know that by the media frenzy that now followed him around. Every time you blinked, there he was—being interviewed on some morning talk show or making the rounds of the Sunday TV news magazines. Today, it was *Meet the Press*—and Evan thought Townsend was a little out of his league.

David Gregory had the junior senator facing off against conservative pundit Jamie Baker, and, so far, Baker was doing all the talking. The topic was climate change, and Baker was all over Townsend about his participation in the recent Clean Energy Summit in Nevada.

"I think it's ironic that the former poster boy for Delmarva Power is now crowing about the need to conserve energy." Baker warmed to her line of attack. "Isn't your state one of the biggest chemical polluters on the Eastern Seaboard?"

Townsend sat quietly, listening to Baker's tirade. Then he smiled that million-dollar Kennedy smile.

Here it comes, Evan thought.

"The only chemistry that matters in my state is the kind that pours millions of dollars each year into researching and developing alternative and renewable sources of energy. If I'm lucky enough to be tagged as the poster child for an industry that serves as a national role model for innovation and progress in the effort to relieve us of our dependence on foreign oil—and clean up our environment—then that's a cross I'm willing to bear." He winked at her. "Thank you, Jamie, for the vote of confidence."

Gregory cut to a commercial break, and Evan snapped up the remote control and muted the volume. *Every time I think he's had it, he rebounds and nails a three-point shot at the buzzer. Amazing.*

The phone rang. Evan stared at it for several seconds before deciding to pick it up. It was Sunday, for Christ's sake. Who in the hell would be calling on Sunday? The phone rang again. Sighing, Evan picked it up.

"Reed."

"Evan? It's Dan."

Evan sat up and leaned forward on the sofa. "Dan? What's up? Is Stevie okay?"

"Stevie is fine. I'm calling about Andy."

"*Andy?* What about him?"

"Don't tell me you're not watching it."

Evan sighed. It was useless to lie. Dan knew her too well. "Of course I'm watching it."

"What do you think?"

"I think Gregory should get a haircut. He's starting to look like Davy Jones."

"Don't fuck around, Evan. I've only got ninety seconds. How do you think he's doing?"

"Why do you care what I think?"

"Why do you *think* I care?"

She looked back at the TV screen. Archer Daniels Midland was droning on about its efforts to feed the world. "You can't be serious about him, Dan. He's a lightweight."

"He's a lightweight who's polling in the seventies. Marcus thinks he's got a good shot at winning the nomination in two years."

"That's crazy. He's a blank slate."

"I agree. That's why we need you."

"You can't afford me."

2

"I can't—but the party can."

"Gimme a break. Townsend's an Independent. They couldn't pay my bar tab."

Dan laughed. "What if I told you he's switching parties?"

Evan was silent for a moment. "When?"

"In about two and a half minutes."

She thought about it. "Call me after the show."

Dan hung up.

Evan held the phone against her forehead.

Shit.

She tossed the phone down on the coffee table, then picked up the remote and sat back to watch the rest of the program.

Dan ordered another glass of the Owen Roe petit sirah and glanced for the fifth or sixth time at his watch. Where the fuck was she? Evan was supposed to meet him for lunch at 1:15, and it was now ten minutes to two. He'd already texted her twice. No response. He'd asked for a table near the front window—more so he could keep an eye out for her approach than because he had any desire to watch all the pedestrian traffic on Pennsylvania Avenue. He'd picked the Sonoma Wine Bar because it was only a block away from the Library of Congress, and Evan would be able to walk there.

She had told him on Sunday that she'd be in D.C. the last few days of the week, finishing up some background research on the president's short list of candidates for attorney general. The last nominee had withdrawn under a cloud, and the administration couldn't afford another snafu. That's why they called Evan. She was the best in the business.

The server arrived with his glass of wine just as he caught sight of Evan making her way across Independence Avenue. She was crossing the street with a crush of people, and he only noticed her because of her outfit. *Jesus.* A lime-green jacket and black cargo pants. He shook his head. She often said that the real reason she didn't sign on with one of the bigger PR firms was because of the wardrobe requirements. She wasn't kidding. As she approached

3

the restaurant, she saw him through the window and rolled her eyes. In another minute, she was at the table, pulling out a chair and dropping her bulging messenger bag onto the floor at her feet.

"Sorry I'm late. I got hung up with some piss-ant debutante in the microfiche duplication office. She wouldn't take my AMEX."

"Really?"

"Yeah. Apparently, the U.S. government only takes Visa." She chuffed. "And probably Exxon—I should've thought of that. I could've been here half an hour ago."

Dan held up his cell phone. "I texted you twice. Why'd you have your phone turned off?"

"Been a while since you were in a library, hasn't it? They have rules about that sort of thing."

"Whatever." He picked up the wine list and held it out to her. "Want something?"

"What are you drinking?"

He held up his glass. "Some overpriced Washington state wine." He shook his head. "You'd think they'd get cheaper the further up the coast you go."

She laughed at him. "If you ever read any of those white papers on climate change your boy Townsend is so fond of waving around, you'd know that Napa is rapidly turning into a desert. They now have to harvest grapes in the dark, just so it's cool enough. That's why all the best wineries are now found in the Northwest."

"Whatever."

"You say that a lot."

He smiled at her. "Whatever."

She rolled her eyes. "Okay then. Just get me a glass of *whatever*."

He looked around the room until he caught their server's eye, then held up his glass and pointed back and forth between it and Evan. "I should've just bought the whole damn bottle."

"What are you griping about? Have you maxed out your expense account?"

4

"Not yet. But I expect to, shortly. Did you have a chance to review the numbers I sent you?"

"Um hmm. Pretty generous offer. I was surprised."

"You shouldn't be. We want the best. We're willing to find the money."

"We?"

"Okay. Marcus is willing to find the money."

"Marcus couldn't find his own ass with two hands."

Dan shook his head. "Jesus. Don't hold back."

The server arrived and deposited Evan's glass of wine. She picked it up and sniffed it before taking a sip. "You didn't offer me this job because of my ability to make polite conversation. Marcus is nothing more than a two-bit hustler in handmade suits. You know what I think of your involvement with him."

Dan took a deep breath as he regarded her. *Christ.* The woman could be so infuriating. Why did she have to be so goddamn attractive? Even in her ridiculous ensemble, she was sexy as hell. At least, she was to him. But there was no going down that road again—not for them.

"The good news is that you wouldn't be answering to Marcus—just to me."

She raised an eyebrow. "Would Marcus be the one signing my checks?"

"Why do you care who signs your checks as long as you get paid? You've never cared in the past."

She sat back in her chair and pushed her sandy hair away from her forehead. "Maybe I'm getting soft in my old age. Maybe I want to be able to sleep at night and not feel like I have to hide what I do from my kid."

They fell silent. He could feel a vein in his head throb. "She's my kid, too."

"Remembered that, did you?"

He knew she could see him tensing up, and that pissed him off. "That's not fair, Evan. I interact with her as much as I can."

"Interact with her? Jesus, Dan. She's your *daughter*—not your tax lawyer."

He took another deep breath. "Look. Let's have this conversation on our own time, okay? We're not here to talk about Stevie."

She met his gaze. Her gray eyes looked green today. He figured it was probably because of that obnoxious jacket.

"You're right. We're not here to talk about Stevie." She picked up her wineglass again. "So. You want to pay me an obscene sum of money to find out if your up-and-coming Horatio Alger has an Achilles' heel?"

"In a nutshell."

"What makes you think that Mr. Clean has any skeletons hiding in his penthouse closet?"

"I don't. I just want proof that I'm right."

"Pretty expensive proof, if you ask me."

"Look, Evan, this guy is the real deal. He can go all the way. I want to do everything I can to clear a path for him. That's my job."

"So, let me get this straight. You're just playing John the Baptist to this latest messiah of the liberal left?"

"Townsend's a centrist."

"Oh. Right. *I forgot.* He only changed party affiliations because the dental insurance was so much better."

"Fuck you."

"Sorry. Been there, bought the diaper bag."

He chewed the inside of his cheek. "Let's just cut to the chase. Are you interested or not?"

She crossed her arms. "I don't know yet."

"What will it take to convince you?"

"I need to meet him."

"Townsend?"

She rolled her eyes. "No. Daffy Duck. Of *course* I mean Townsend. And I want unrestricted access to everyone—*everyone*, Dan. No exceptions."

He nodded. "Okay. I can set something up for next week."

"Great. Now. How about some lunch? I'm starving."

He picked up one of the two menus on their table. "They have

6

great mixed cheese and charcuterie boards here. Wanna split one of each?"

"That depends."

He looked up at her over the rim of his menu. "On?"

"On whether or not I'm on the party's expense account yet."

"And if I say that you are?"

"Then fuck the cheese plate. I want a steak."

He waved their server over. "Some things never change."

Chapter 2

Townsend lived in a three-story row house on a cobblestone street in Old New Castle, about three blocks from the waterfront. At least, that's where he lived when he wasn't in residence at his fashionable digs in the Watergate complex. That was the first thing about him that piqued Evan's interest. The luxury apartment complex was too synonymous with scandal to be listed on any serious comer's resume. She knew that if Marcus was interested in taking over Townsend's career, his Foggy Bottom address would be the first thing to change.

She parked her rental car in a public lot near Battery Park and walked down Delaware Street past trendy shops that sold overpriced boogie boards and six-dollar cups of coffee. To Evan, the seventeenth-century town was a lot like Townsend. It had a base coat of refinement, but had been overlaid with so much lacquer that any real merit it had was hard to find.

Dan had initially arranged for Evan to meet Townsend at his senate office, but she rejected that idea and suggested instead that she take the train from D.C. to Wilmington, and then rent a car for the ten-minute drive down to New Castle. She knew that Townsend commuted to Washington from his Delaware home a lot, and that he had done the same thing during his four years as governor. There wasn't anything especially odd about that. Hell, the entire state was only ninety miles long. Still, she was curious about his obvious attachment to the townhouse in New

Castle, and she wanted to see it for herself. According to Dan, Townsend agreed to the change of venue without question. If he had anything to hide, he wasn't doing much to hide it. She didn't know if that meant he was clumsy or smart. Or whether it just meant he didn't have anything to hide.

Not very likely.

She smiled as she walked past another coffee shop—the fifth one she'd seen in the ten minutes since she left her car.

She was fifteen minutes early, and that gave her plenty of time to find Townsend's house and scope it out from the opposite side of the street. It was a beauty all right—only a few doors down Fourth Street from the Amstel mansion and tricked out with lots of polished brass and handmade red brick. Eight steps led up to the imposing front door. Fourth Street had a fair amount of on-street parking available, but an alley next to Townsend's house led to what looked like a small gatehouse over a single-car garage. A black Saab 9-5 sedan with Virginia tags was parked behind the house. Evan pulled a crumpled ATM receipt out of her messenger bag and wrote the tag number down, knowing she'd never remember it otherwise. Those days were long gone.

She already knew that Townsend had purchased the New Castle house six years ago—two years before he ran for governor. Prior to that, he had lived with his wife, Julia Donne, in her Upper East Side apartment in New York. As far as Evan knew, Ms. Donne had never actually lived with Townsend in Delaware—although she had made regular appearances at official functions in and around the state throughout his tenure as governor. They had no children.

Evan walked the rest of the way down the block, crossed the street, and headed back toward Number 8. This time, she climbed up the steps and knocked on the shiny black door. To her surprise, the senator opened it himself. He had a mug of something in his hand.

"You must be Evan Reed. I'm Andy. Come on in. You're right on time, just like Dan said you'd be."

He was wearing dark jeans and a tailored blue shirt. He looked more handsome in person. Someone had spent a small fortune on his smile. Evan had never seen such white teeth.

"Thanks for agreeing to meet me here." She shook his extended hand. His nails were short and very clean. He had a good handshake. "I thought it would be less formal than meeting in your senate office."

"Oh, no problem. I jump at any excuse to come down here."

"I can see why."

"Have you ever been to Old New Castle?"

"Not before today."

He looked her over. "You're younger than I thought you'd be."

She was used to that reaction. "Really? I was just thinking that you look taller on TV."

He laughed. It seemed genuine. "*Touché.*" He waved her into the house. "Want some coffee? I just made a pot."

"Sure." She followed him down a wide center hallway to an enormous kitchen that dominated the back of the house and looked like it wasn't part of the original structure.

"Need cream or sugar?" he asked.

"Black. Thanks."

He gestured toward a small table in front of a pair of tall windows. "Have a seat." He took a ceramic mug out of an overhead cabinet and poured her coffee.

Evan looked around the kitchen. It was impressively equipped. Someone liked to cook—a lot. The last place she'd seen this many stainless-steel appliances was at Best Buy. Townsend even had a tandoor, and she couldn't remember the last time she'd seen one of those in a private home—except her own, of course. She loved Indian food.

She sat down and took the mug of coffee from him. "This is a great kitchen. You must like to cook."

He smiled. "Not really. It came with the house. I think the former owners were self-styled gourmands."

"I guess with your schedule, you don't have much time for hobbies."

He sat down opposite her. "Not anymore. When I'm not

10

working or doing interviews, I'm on the train between here and D.C."

"Not New York?"

He seemed surprised. "Julia's work keeps her pretty busy. We try to make time for each other one or two weekends a month."

"That sounds like a custody arrangement."

"Something I guess you'd be familiar with."

Ah, Evan thought. *A nerve.* She had got under his veneer with that one.

"Dan told me about your daughter," he continued. "I hope that's okay."

"Sure. But I already know the details of my own past."

"But you don't know mine?"

"Not yet."

He sat back and regarded her. "You don't mince words, do you?"

"I can if you want me to. But I get paid by the hour, and it would just end up costing you more."

He laughed. "So. What do you want to know that isn't already public record?"

"I want to know anything that has the potential to *become* public record."

"Like?"

She tilted her head. "You do read the papers don't you, Senator Townsend?"

"Call me Andy."

"Okay, Andy. For starters, let's think for a moment about Edwards, Spitzer, and Foley—and I'm not talking about the accountants who prepare my tax returns."

He sighed. "I'm afraid you're going to be disappointed."

She crossed her arms. "I don't have a dog in this fight. It's Marcus you need to impress, not me."

"Then Marcus is going to be disappointed. I'm happily married."

"To a woman you make time for once or twice a month?"

"That's not unusual or immoral."

"It is if you're running for president."

11

He sipped from his cup of coffee. "I'm not running for president. I'm a United States senator from the great state of Delaware."

Evan sighed. "Look, Andy, let's agree on a division of labor here. I'm a dustbuster. I'm not your antagonist. I don't give a flying fuck about how deliriously happy you and your wife are or aren't, or how you choose to define your career aspirations. I make no judgments. I just find and report the facts. You can help me out with that and save your party some coin—or not. It doesn't matter to me what you decide, because either way, I'll find what there is to find, and I'll make my report to your campaign team. Then I'll walk away. End of story." She met his gaze. "So. I'll ask again. Is there anything you want to tell me about that will shorten this process?"

He met her level gaze. He seemed unfazed by her comments. "I have nothing to hide."

"I'm glad to hear it." She pushed back her chair and stood up. "Thanks for the coffee."

He belatedly got to his feet. "You're leaving?"

"Yeah." She glanced at her watch. "I've got a train to catch."

"Going back to D.C.?"

"Nope. New York." She picked up her messenger bag. "I'll be sure and give your regards to Mrs. Townsend."

Evan drove her rental car back to Wilmington and took the train into New York. She took advantage of the two-hour ride to review what she knew about Andrew Townsend.

He was the only child of solidly upper middle-class parents, who still lived in Lewes, Delaware. Andy's father had worked for twenty-five years as a chemist for DuPont, and his mother was a successful real estate broker. The Townsends had managed to send their son to the prestigious Archmere Academy in Claymont, where he excelled both on the soccer field and in the classroom—and earned a named scholarship to Yale.

At Yale, his successes continued. He majored in business management, and, as far as Evan could tell, minored in marrying for money. His wandering attentions seemed to shift from one wealthy debutante to another, until—finally—he landed a prize worth keeping.

His political aspirations appeared to evolve in sync with his financial objectives. Almost from the outset of his college experience he was active in the Yale Democrats society and in the Yale Political Union. It was only after he had earned his MBA at Columbia—while he was working on Wall Street for a hedge fund—that he drifted more toward the political center and changed his party affiliation to Independent. Since both Delaware and New York had open primary systems, Townsend's lack of major party allegiance didn't present any real roadblocks to political success. But once he leapt onto the national stage, all of that changed in a hurry.

Two years after his marriage to publishing heiress Julia Donne, Townsend accepted a position with DuPont Capital Management, relocated to a small apartment in Wilmington, Delaware and commuted to New York on the weekends. He first became interested in alternative energy technologies during his tenure at DuPont, particularly those related to solar power—one of DuPont's emerging market successes.

A year later, he bought the house in Old New Castle and began to lay the groundwork for his successful gubernatorial bid.

Townsend was good-looking and charismatic, and seemed to adapt well to the shifting sands of national political trends. He catapulted seamlessly from the governor's mansion in Dover to the floor of the U.S. Senate, while managing to scrape past lesser-known major party contenders for the open seat.

It was then that he caught the eye of the national Democratic Party, and they hired Marcus to see if Townsend had what it took to go the distance.

Marcus hired Dan, and the rest was history.

Or, if she did her job right, it would all be history soon enough.

Chapter 3

Donne & Hale was one of the oldest North American publishing houses. Founded in 1825 by Lewis Donne and Samuel Hale, the firm's roster of authors read like a *Who's Who* of American literature. After the Civil War, the small, Boston-based firm expanded nearly overnight into a thriving literary powerhouse as educational opportunities increased for a booming population, and the public library movement became firmly entrenched in American culture. In 1935, the firm moved its offices to New York and staked its claim as the leading literary publishing house in North America.

The contemporary heir apparent to the company's prestigious business and social fortunes was Townsend's reclusive wife, Julia Lewis Donne.

Evan had Dan to credit for the ease with which she got an appointment to meet with the publishing magnate. Professionally, Donne was held in high esteem, but personally, the woman was an enigma. Evan found that perceptions of her ranged from cold and aloof, to quirky and mercurial. But the few people reputed to know her well were intensely loyal—divulging little and circling around her like junkyard dogs.

The more Evan learned about the populist Townsend, the less his marriage to the patrician Donne seemed to fit. She guessed she'd be able to make her own assessment soon enough.

The firm's offices took up two floors of a forty-five-story limestone and black marble high-rise on Madison Avenue, designed in 1931 by architect Kenneth Franzheim. Evan walked across the art deco lobby with its rose-colored French marble floors and tried not to gawk at the crystal, triple-star-shaped chandelier that monopolized the massive space.

She hated places like this. She hated New York. For the first time in eons, she worried that she might be underdressed. And even having to think about that pissed her off. More than one Lady Gaga clone on three-inch heels had given her the once-over as she made her way toward the elevators.

Yeah. She hated New York.

She punched the "up" arrow and waited on a car to take her to the thirty-eighth floor. She had thirty minutes with Donne, and then a quick trip to Penn Station to catch the Ethan Allen Express to Albany.

Tomorrow, she'd be with Stevie, for parents' weekend at Emma Willard. Evan had promised she'd be there. Dan was traveling with Townsend, who was delivering the keynote address at a Renewable Energy Summit in Denver. He had promised to call her on Saturday night, but Evan knew that Stevie wouldn't be holding her breath.

A bell rang, and the big steel doors rolled back. Evan walked across a walnut-paneled hallway and entered the understated but elegant offices of Donne & Hale. A receptionist with an exaggerated British accent and the loudest herringbone suit Evan had ever seen was seated behind a massive desk. She phoned Ms. Donne's personal assistant, and within moments, Evan was being escorted down a long hallway toward a suite of offices that overlooked Central Park.

Evan was right on time, but it appeared that the normally punctual Ms. Donne was not quite ready for her. The assistant showed her into a surprisingly small but tastefully furnished corner office with panoramic views and a chevron-patterned parquet floor, and told her that Ms. Donne would join her directly. Then she departed, closing the door behind her.

Evan walked to the windows and looked down East 60th Street toward 5th Avenue and the park that spread out beyond

15

it. New York from this vantage point wasn't quite so offensive. She looked at the modest desk and Herman Miller chair that sat at a right angle to the windows. The physical arrangement was odd for the office of someone in such a position of prominence. Apparently, Donne enjoyed the view more than she enjoyed the opportunity to intimidate her visitors.

Evan noted the absence of any personal photographs. There were several paintings—one a Mark Rothko that looked original. Books and papers were tidily stacked on shelves that lined one wall. She glanced at Donne's computer—a silver Mac Power-Book. Scattered around the office were a few pieces of what looked like antique Islamic pottery. She thought she recognized some similarities to pieces Dan had collected during his fellowship in Jordan. She made a mental note about that and wondered if Donne, who had met Townsend at Yale, had also traveled to the Middle East during her college years.

Classical music played at low volume from a Bose Wave radio that sat on a credenza behind the desk. Several well-cared-for plants in massive pots were strategically placed around the room. A small sitting area with a loveseat, coffee table, and two upholstered chairs sat on the side of the room opposite the desk. A faded kilim rug covered most of the floor. A leather jacket hung on a hook just behind an open door that appeared to lead to a powder room. Craning her head, she could also see a small espresso machine atop what looked like a dorm-sized refrigerator. It appeared that Julia Donne spent a lot of time in her office.

Behind her, the door opened and closed.

"Ms. Reed? I apologize for keeping you waiting."

Evan turned around and got her first real look at Delaware's former first lady. Her photos had not done her justice.

"I'm Julia Donne." She crossed the room and extended her hand. "Dan has spoken very highly of you."

Evan looked up at her as they shook hands. She had to be at least five-ten. That was a surprise, too. "I'm afraid you can't believe too much of what Dan has to say, but I'm glad you're inclined to value his opinion. Otherwise, I think it would have taken me six months to get this appointment."

Julia smiled and gestured toward the sitting area. "I'm sorry about that. But you're here now, so let's make the best of the time we have. Please sit down." She walked to her desk and deposited the notepad and pen she had been carrying. "Would you like some coffee or a cold drink?"

"No, thank you. I'm fine." Evan dropped into one of the armchairs. "I confess that I stopped about three times for snow cones on my walk here from the train station."

Julia sat down across from her on the small sofa. She crossed her long legs. "What flavor?"

"Cherry."

"Personally, I like the lime ones." She smiled.

Evan sighed. "Where would we be without our guilty pleasures?"

"Isn't that what you're here to find out?"

Evan noticed that her eyes were very blue. "Did Dan tell you that, too?"

"No. *Andy* told me that, when he called me in a panic about four hours ago."

Evan was intrigued. "In a panic?"

"There might be some room for interpretation, but, yes. I'd say he was in a panic."

"And why do you think that?"

"If I had to guess, I'd say it was because he had no confidence in what I might reveal to you about the real status of our relationship."

"Which is?"

She sighed. "Have you ever read a novella, Ms. Reed?"

"It's Evan. And, yes. I have."

"So you know that it's a literary form that's longer than a short story, but shorter than a novel?"

"That's my understanding."

"Well, that same description can apply to relationships, too."

"So, you're saying that your marriage to Andrew Townsend is not about to get a sequel?"

17

"Correct." Her response was unemotional.

Evan was silent for a moment as she regarded Julia. "I'm curious."

"About?"

"About why you would volunteer information like this to me within the first five minutes of our conversation."

Julia turned toward the windows that ran along the back wall of the office. "Andy and I had a bargain, and I held up my end." She shifted her long, brown hair back over her shoulder. Evan noticed that she wasn't wearing a wedding band. "I've done my stint as first lady. Let's just say it's not a role I'm willing to reprise," she brought her eyes back to Evan, "no matter how much Marcus Goldman wants me to."

Evan thought she saw a flicker of something in Julia's eyes. The hair stood up on the back of her neck. "Wait a minute. Exactly why do you think I'm here today?"

Julia looked surprised by her question. "I assumed that Marcus sent you here as his emissary."

"It that what Dan told you?" Evan was becoming agitated and was trying hard not to show it. Goddamn *fucking* Marcus.

Julia shrugged. "Dan didn't say much of anything—other than to tell me that the party had hired you to help out with vetting Andy… and improving his odds at becoming their next nominee."

Evan tapped her foot in agitation. "So you thought that meant I was here to strong-arm you into signing on for another tour of duty as Townsend's doting wife?"

"In fact, I don't think I've ever actually *doted* on anyone—but, yes. That's more or less what I thought." Julia paused. "Was I wrong?"

Evan stood up and paced across the office. She looked out the big window at the traffic on East 60th Street. Cars were crawling along now. Rush hour was heating up. She shook her head and turned back to Julia, who watched her with what appeared to be calm indifference.

"Yeah. You were wrong." She walked back and reclaimed her seat. A thought occurred to her. "Do you like to cook?"

Julia looked at her with a puzzled expression. "No."

"So, you eat out a lot? Restaurants, take-out—that kind of thing?"

"I suppose so."

"Like Indian food?"

"Not even a little bit." She met Evan's eyes. "Why? Are you asking me out?"

Evan was startled by her directness. Embarrassed—and surprised. "No." She felt anxious again. What the fuck was going on here? She dropped her gaze, and then was pissed at herself for looking away. "I'm sorry if I offended you."

Julia was quiet for so long that Evan thought she had just made things worse.

"I'm not at all offended." Julia's voice held a trace more warmth.

Evan gazed at her. *Jesus.* Her blue eyes really were hypnotic. They stared at each other for a few seconds before Julia glanced down at her watch.

"I'm sorry to cut this short, but I've got a five-thirty conference call." Julia stood up. "Could we continue this conversation another time? When will you be back in New York?"

Evan stood up as well. "That depends on your definition of another time. I *could* be back as early as Monday." She deliberated about how much to say. "I'm spending the weekend in Troy with my daughter."

"That's right. Dan said she was a student at Emma."

Evan didn't quite succeed at hiding her smile. "She's a freshman. It's her first year away from home."

"I see. And how is that going?"

"I think she's doing great."

Julia smiled. "I meant for you."

Evan was nonplussed. "I'm ... okay." She smiled shyly. "In fact, it sucks. Scissors." Julia laughed. "But I'm managing."

Julia walked to her desk and tapped a key on her laptop. Her calendar popped up on the screen. "How about lunch on Monday?" She met Evan's eyes again. "You can even try to make me eat Indian food, if you like."

19

Evan shook her head. "I've got a better idea. What's the most expensive place in the Upper East Side to eat lunch?"

"Why?"

"Because Marcus will be paying."

Julia smiled. "David Burke Townhouse."

"Do they take reservations?"

"Of course."

"Great. What time?"

Julia looked back at her monitor. "One-thirty?"

Evan nodded. "I'll see you there."

Chapter 4

Every time Evan set foot on Emma Willard's manicured campus, she spent the first ten minutes regretting her decision to send her daughter there. But that was one argument about Stevie's future that she had let Dan win. His sister, mother, and grandmother were all alumnae of the historic prep school for girls, and they waged a full-court press to have Stevie take her place in line with the rest of the Cohen women. Evan's initial opposition to this scheme took a nosedive when Stevie fell in love with the school during an open-house visit two years ago. That forced Evan to rethink the whole scenario.

So she did what she did—literally. She spent weeks researching the pros and cons of single-sex education for girls. And the realities surprised her. Teenage girls, it seemed, got a whole lot stupider when they were grouped together with teenage boys. Hardly a news flash, if she thought about it. Her own public school education in and around southwest Philly was a prime example. She learned more in the backseat of a Chevy than she ever did in a science lab.

The simple truth was that girls deserved a better shot at life than that. They needed the tools and the time to make good decisions. If most of them were destined to fuck up over some guy sooner or later, then at least it could be *later*—after they'd had a chance to figure out who they really were.

But this was Parents' Weekend, and it gave Evan the chance to meet with Stevie's teachers, attend a class or two, and watch an evening showcase of student talent. What mattered more to her was the opportunity to spend a weekend with her daughter. She hated to admit how empty the house in Chadds Ford was without the fourteen-year-old.

Stevie had been living at the private girls' academy near Albany for over two months now, and this would be Evan's first visit since she'd left her there in August, loaded down with clothes, bed linens, her bike, and fifteen rolls of quarters. Stevie had to do her own laundry.

For this weekend, she had booked a two-room suite at the nearby Morgan State House B&B, thinking it would be the most homelike place for them to spend the time together. She dropped her bags off and drove her rental car the short distance to Mt. Ida and the Emma campus so she could sign Stevie out for the weekend. *Sign her out. Christ.* This was worse than trying to take a reference book out of a library. She thought back over her recent encounter with that Valkyrie at the Library of Congress. *Nope.* Even escaping from this joint with somebody else's kid would be a helluva lot easier than *that.*

She parked her car in a visitor's lot near Kiggins Hall and made her way toward the freshman dorm where Stevie now lived. There were cozy-looking family groups all over the place. Most of the adults were wearing nametags. Evan rolled her eyes. *Great.*

A makeshift reception area had been set up inside the hall. Evan approached a table that held a stack of fat file folders. A frizzy-haired girl in a red Emma sweatshirt looked up at her as she approached.

"Hi. Are you a parent?" She held a clipboard that contained what looked like a list of names.

"Yes. I'm Stephanie Cohen's mother."

The girl looked down at her list. "Got it." She checked off a name and then sifted through the pile of folders. "Here you go." She held one out to Evan. "This is your schedule and information packet." She smiled. "I hope you enjoy the weekend."

Evan looked down at her folder and at the nametag taped to its front. *Evangeline Reed. Shit.* She knew that someplace, her mother was laughing like hell. "Thanks. I'll try."

22

She turned away from the table and started toward the stairs when she heard Stevie's voice.

"Mom!"

Evan looked toward the lounge and saw Stevie making her way across the lobby. She was dressed in dark jeans and a purple sweatshirt, and she was the spitting image of Dan. Evan thought she looked thinner.

Stevie ran the last few steps and hugged her. Evan was surprised. Her daughter wasn't usually so demonstrative. Evan hugged her back. Stevie smelled like cinnamon.

"Have you been eating Altoids?" Evan asked.

Stevie dug into the front pocket of her jeans and pulled out a small tin box. She shook it back and forth like a rattle. "Yeah, and I'm almost out."

Evan smiled and pushed a loose strand of blonde hair back behind Stevie's ear. "Well, then, it looks like my timing is perfect."

"I'll say." Stevie shoved the tin back into her pocket and looked down at the file folder Evan was holding. She smirked when she saw the nametag. "I had *nothing* to do with that."

"Yeah. Right." Evan flicked the edge of the nametag with her index finger. "Know where I can get a blank one?"

"Nope."

"I don't believe you."

Stevie shrugged. "It sucks being you, then."

Evan agreed. "Sometimes it does."

They smiled at each other. Stevie gestured toward the lounge where she had been waiting.

"Can we go? I've got my bag, and I'm already signed out."

Evan was surprised. "You don't wanna show me around first?"

"Not really. I figured we'd do all of that tomorrow."

"Hungry?"

Stevie nodded. "I'm starving."

"Where do you wanna go?"

Stevie started walking toward the lounge. "Zaika. It's in Albany, and they have great pakora."

"Sounds good to me." She studied Stevie. Her daughter was

23

already as tall as she was, but that wasn't saying a lot. Evan was barely five-five. "You don't look like you've been eating much of anything."

"Yeah, well. The food here isn't really all that."

"Oh, really? I thought this joint had a slew of first-rate chefs?"

Stevie rolled her eyes. "Mom, it's a boarding school, not a cruise ship."

"What? No shuffleboard after dinner?"

"You're such a dork." Stevie bumped Evan's arm. "Dad called."

"He did?" Evan asked.

"Yeah. He said he was sorry he couldn't make it." She looked at Evan. "He told me you were working together again."

"We will be for a little while. I'm doing some research for him."

Stevie stopped to pick up an overstuffed blue backpack. "Looking for dirt on Senator Townsend?"

Evan gave her a surprised look. "Have you been watching Fox News again?"

Stevie rolled her eyes. "Gag. Not likely. Dad told me."

"What else did he tell you?"

"He told me that Senator Townsend might run for president in two years." They started walking toward the exit. Stevie waved at a group of girls standing near the door. They waved back. "My suite mates," she explained.

"Do you like it here?" Evan asked. She thought her voice sounded neutral enough.

"Yeah." Stevie turned to her. "A lot. Why?"

Evan felt embarrassed for asking. "I don't know. I wondered if you ever got lonely."

"You mean, do I ever miss being at home with you?"

Evan met Stevie's green eyes. God, the kid really did look like Dan. She nodded.

Stevie smiled. In that moment, Evan felt like the teenager in the relationship. "Yeah, Mom. I miss you, too."

Chapter 5

Evan's Monday morning "express" train back to New York City was running about forty-five minutes late, so she took advantage of the down time to grab a cup of coffee at Starbucks and check her email. She had two from Johnny Sloan. Johnny was a college pal who now worked as an under-secretary in the Virginia Public Records Office in Richmond. Evan had sent him the tag number from the black Saab that had been parked behind Townsend's house and asked him to do a quick records search on the owner.

Johnny usually bitched about helping her out, and insisted that one day she was going to get his ass fired, but he always came through. He owed her. She got him laid three years ago at a ViCAP seminar in San Diego, and he ended up marrying the woman. Evan figured that as long as their marital bliss endured, she'd continue to get prompt service from the Commonwealth PRO.

Johnny's first email was straightforward—containing only the name and address of the car's owner and the Saab's VIN number. The second email was a bit more intriguing. *Well, well.* Evan shot a quick email off to Liz at the State Department to see if anything pinged in her database. Then she logged into Yale's online alumni community, using Dan's password, and did a little poking around. *Bingo.* She thought that name had sounded familiar. Townsend had said he had nothing to hide, and given how easily she had found this, she guessed he might have been telling the truth.

She sat back, picked up her latte, and sniffed at it with disgust. *God*. Starbucks coffee sucked. It even smelled bad. Just like this job. What the hell was Dan thinking? He didn't need her for this textbook, petty-ante bullshit. She fished her phone out of her messenger bag and sent him a quick text message, asking to see him when he got back to D.C.

She smiled, thinking about her lunch date. But it wasn't like she wouldn't enjoy making Marcus choke on her expense report. She hoped this David Burke joint had a premier wine list.

Too bad she wouldn't have any more excuses to meet with the good-looking publisher after today.

Townsend's wife was intriguing. And forthcoming. That part was a surprise. Evan wondered what else she might be willing to reveal. Why she stayed enmeshed in a name-only marriage, for instance? Or what led her to hold Marcus in such disdain?

No. That one wasn't hard to figure out. Anyone with a triple-digit IQ could see through Marcus. And Julia Donne had plenty of smarts. Poise, looks, *and* smarts.

She looked at her watch. The train was now over an hour late. *Christ. "Express," my ass.* She tapped her cell phone against her knee and wondered if she should call Julia and give her a heads-up? No. She still had four hours—plenty of time to get there. And calling her this early was unnecessary. She sighed. And flimsy. She looked at her watch again. Who was she kidding? She just didn't want to look pathetic.

Even though she was.

Evan walked into David Burke Townhouse a hair before one-thirty. The host looked up from behind his white lacquered podium and smiled at her.

"Ms. Reed? Your party has already arrived." Before she had a chance to wonder how he knew who she was, he snapped up a menu and indicated that she should follow him.

Evan tried not to gape as she walked between the rows of tables and padded booths. The place had an abundance of mirrors, whimsical artwork, and couches upholstered in fabric that would make an ocelot wince. *Christ. It looks like a gay man exploded in here.* The décor was a collision of red, black, and white. She recalled that Julia had said the prices were high. She never said *anything* about the quality of the food. Evan began to have doubts about the wisdom of meeting there. Any of the dozen hot dog vendors she'd passed on East 61st Street were looking like better choices.

The host led her into a smaller dining room at the back of the establishment, and she saw Julia, calmly regarding her from a corner table near an open fireplace. She was wearing a black suit with a tailored white shirt. Evan wondered if she had planned her ensemble in advance. Suddenly, the décor didn't seem quite so offensive.

The host held her chair while she sat down, then handed her the menu and departed.

Julia smiled at her. "I saw you looking around as you walked back here. It's kind of overwhelming, isn't it?"

Evan picked up her napkin. It was nearly the size of a bed sheet. "I have to confess that I was beginning to doubt the wisdom of eating here. It's certainly . . . *eclectic.*"

Julia laughed out loud. "It does exude a certain Holiday Inn quality."

Evan leaned toward her and lowered her voice. "Is the food any good?"

Julia nodded. "Oh, yes. Thankfully, Mr. Burke's culinary gifts dwarf his uneven attempts at interior design."

"Thank god."

"How was Parents' Weekend?"

Evan smiled. "Parents' Weekend was about what you'd expect—a shameless sales pitch, engineered to make us all feel good about the ridiculous sums of money we're shelling out to teach our daughters how to stand up straight."

Julia looked amused. "And how is your daughter's posture coming along?"

"I'm happy to say that she still slouches with the best of them."

"She must take after you, then."

27

"Are you saying that I slouch?" Evan sat up straighter in her chair.

Julia seemed to notice and smiled. "No. I'm saying that she must share your streak of nonconformity."

Evan sat back and regarded her. "I thought I was here to dissect you?"

"I'm not very complicated. I fear you'll lose interest pretty quickly."

Evan met her blue eyes. "I don't think there's much danger of that."

Their waiter approached to ask if they'd had a chance to consider their beverage options. He told them he was featuring a very nice Spragia Gamble Ranch Chardonnay. He described it as dry, light, crisp—and one hundred and twenty-five dollars a bottle. Evan nodded enthusiastically. He smiled and departed.

Julia raised an eyebrow. "You weren't kidding about that expense report, were you?"

"Oh? Does that mean you're not picking up the tab? Damn."

Julia shook her head. "I'm afraid that my efforts to make Marcus suffer tend more toward the visceral."

"Meaning?"

"I'd be more inclined to bite his ankles than spend his money."

"Well, then, let's agree to pool our efforts. You can bite his ankles—an appalling image, by the way—and *I'll* spend his money."

Julia raised her water glass. "Deal."

They clinked rims.

"So. Since we're technically still on your nickel, what else did you want to ask me about?"

Evan deliberated. About a thousand responses to that question occurred to her—most of them unrelated to Andy Townsend. But until she met with Dan on Tuesday, she was still on the job. Anything else would have to wait. She sighed and looked at Julia, whose expression was unreadable. It wasn't fair. But not much in life ever was. She took another sip from her water glass. Might as well fill in a few blanks while she had the chance.

"You met Andy at Yale? Is that right?"

Julia lifted her chin slightly. For a second, Evan thought she looked disappointed.

"Yes. We met during my sophomore year at a Yale Democrats rally. Bill Clinton was speaking, and Andy and I were on the steering committee."

"And you started dating right away?"

"Not right away. Andy already had a serious girlfriend ... and I thought he was an arrogant prick."

Evan was startled by her directness. "Really?"

Julia raised an eyebrow. "Does that surprise you?"

"Well, no. But your use of the word 'prick' does."

Julia laughed. "It's a perfectly good Saxon word. Don't assume that I can't curse like a sailor just because I publish books by Hawthorne and Melville."

"I beg your pardon," Evan apologized. "You must be a hoot during fleet week."

Julia smiled, but made no response.

"I guess you already know that Andy met Dan during their junior year abroad?"

"Yes. They went to Jordan to study the Lost City at Petra."

"You were involved with Andy by then, correct?"

"That's right."

"But you didn't go abroad?"

"Yes, I did—just not to Jordan. I spent a year at Oxford."

"Learning the family business?"

Julia looked amused. "You might say that."

Their waiter arrived with the wine. After serving them, he reviewed the lunch specials. They made selections from the three-course *prix fixe* menu. Evan took another sip of the cold wine. She wasn't usually partial to chardonnays, but the waiter hadn't misled them. It was very good.

Julia set her wineglass down. "If you don't mind my asking, how did you meet Dan?"

Evan met her eyes. Against the backdrop of so much black and white, they looked almost neon. "It's not that dissimilar from your own fabled love story. We were both in grad school at Penn." She chuckled. "We met at a Bill Clinton rally, too."

Julia laughed. "It appears that our 42nd president has a lot to account for."

"No kidding." Evan sighed. "But in my case, it was more a function of too many tequila shooters, followed by a massive infusion of bad judgment."

"Really?" Julia crossed her arms on the table and leaned forward.

"Yeah. Let's just say that an unintentional one-night stand culminated in a gift that keeps on giving."

"Oh?"

"Oh, yeah." Evan sighed. "Are you Catholic, Julia?"

Julia shook her head. "Congregationalist."

"Of *course*." Evan rolled her eyes. "Well. Let me put it this way. Growing up Catholic is like going through life with a big piece of cosmic toilet paper stuck to the bottom of your shoe. You do your best to ignore it, but when push comes to shove, you just can't shake it off. And then you find yourself tripping over it at the most inopportune times. Like when you find out you're pregnant at the ripe old age of twenty-four."

"Good god."

"Precisely." Evan shook her head. "I knew it was a complete mistake. I knew that I had no business going through with it. I knew that I was probably the least likely person on the planet to *ever* have a kid." She leaned forward. "I was and am adamantly pro-choice, but, somehow, I just couldn't do it. It was an incredible, *surreal* predicament for me. Suddenly, I was in a place I never thought I'd be—facing choices I never thought I'd have to make." She shook her head. "There was no pat, political platitude I could fall back on. Not a single one. And there was Dan—begging me to get *married*."

"Did you love him?"

Evan looked at her like she had just sprouted a second head. "Love him? Hell, no. I fucked him, Julia. *Once*. Just to see what it would be like." She laughed. "It was ridiculous. I knew I was gay." Julia stared back at her, revealing nothing.

Damn, the woman must be one hell of a card player. "But I did it anyway."

"You didn't marry him." It was a statement, not a question.

"No. But Dan adopted Stevie, and in his offhand and clumsy fashion, he's actually a pretty decent father. He won't win any awards for attentiveness, but he hasn't screwed up too badly yet, either."

They sat in silence for a few moments. Evan realized that she had been doing entirely too much of the talking. And that was unlike her. Very unlike her. She took a healthy sip from her wineglass. She hadn't eaten any breakfast, and the stuff was really making her head feel fuzzy.

"Hey?" She waved her glass at Julia. "This is supposed to be your inquisition, not mine." She chuckled. "Maybe I *should* let you pick up the tab."

Julia smiled at her. "How about I pick it up next time?"

Evan couldn't hide her smile. Yeah. Fuzzy. Right now, fuzzy was feeling just fine.

Back in Chadds Ford that night, Evan had time to sit on her back porch with a mug of hot tea and try to figure out how far she was willing to go with the Townsend job. The senator himself, although not squeaky clean, was at least enough of a Ward Cleaver clone to make any serial gossipmonger lose interest after a few days of salacious headlines. He could weather that—especially if Dan got ahead of it and leaked it selectively. Evan picked up the yellow notepad from the table next to her rocker. His "hobby," however—now *she* was another story.

Evan sighed. *Christ.* It *would* get interesting, just when she had made up her mind to walk away.

Liz had emailed her back from State. The owner of the black Saab had a profile about two miles long. And most of the intel was classified. Liz couldn't offer it up. Not even to her.

Evan and Liz had engaged in an on-again/off-again thing ever since they had met two years ago, over the raw bar at a K Street shindig, and for the last six months, it had been mostly off-again. Liz was probably pissed at her. This email exchange was the first contact Evan had initiated with her since they spent the night together after a drunken encounter last Easter.

Shit. She really needed to clean up her act. She thought for the hundredth time about her lunch date. *Give it up. There's no way.* And even if there were, did she really want to go pissing in Townsend's pond? That was hardly professional. She finished her tea and sat staring into the empty mug. She wanted a drink. But she was only starting to shake off the buzz that had hovered around her all afternoon after downing most of that bottle of wine. Julia had drank only one glass. What the hell kind of restraint was that?

Restraint. Yeah. That summarized her to a T. Evan wondered what size clawhammer it would take to break through restraint like that.

When they parted, Julia told her that she'd be in Philadelphia next week for a bookseller's conference. She said she'd call Evan if she could shake free. They could do dinner on *her* expense account, she said, and Evan could order the most expensive wine on the menu. Evan recalled Julia's facial expression when she suggested that. She thought she had caught a glimpse of something lurking behind her reserve. But she had no idea what it was.

Evan was startled when a nighthawk landed on the porch railing, just a few feet away from her. It wasn't completely dark yet, and the moon was full, so she could see its telltale wing markings clearly. It stared back at her. She wondered which one of them was more amazed at the anomaly of seeing the other. She was confused because these particular birds generally made tracks for the southern border states sometime in late August. The rest of the year, they liked to hang out in the woods at the back of her property and make quick trips in after nightfall to pick at the lichen that covered the fieldstone on the north side of her house. Seeing one this late in the year was very unusual.

The nighthawk continued to stare at her. *You're a misfit like me,* his gaze seemed to say. *And you're stuck here, too.*

She found it hard to argue with logic like that.

32

◊ ◊ ◊

Evan bit the bullet and made arrangements to reconnect with Liz Burke. She took the train down to D.C. and met Liz for a drink at the State Plaza bar on E Street.

Evan didn't insult Liz by pretending that she was there to renew old acquaintance. They both knew what the meeting was about. After the waiter had deposited their first round of margaritas, Liz sat back and looked her over.

"I would never have pegged you as the Mata Hari type." Her voice was husky—like she'd had too many cigarettes. Evan knew she had been trying to quit. The way she kept fidgeting with her straw led Evan to assume that she wasn't enjoying much success.

"You think I came here to fuck you for information?" With Liz, it was a waste of time to be anything but direct.

"Let's see. I don't hear from you for six months, and then I get three emails and a phone call within a week? Yeah. The thought occurred to me." Liz was wearing too much mascara. It made her look almost cartoon-like. Her other attributes looked real enough. Evan wondered what Madam Secretary thought about necklines like that. Maybe one day, someone would pay her to find out.

"But you agreed to meet me anyway?" Evan sipped at her drink and winced. *Tequila. Bad choice.*

Liz laughed. It sounded hollow. "Why not? We can each get something we want."

"I have something you want?" It came out sounding coyer than she had intended.

Liz nodded. "Against my better judgment." She leaned over the table. Her styled blonde hair smelled like cloves. "I've never made a secret of that."

"Jesus, Liz. Don't you have any self-respect?"

"I work for the State Department. What do you think?"

Against her will, Evan laughed. It was true. Buying and selling information was Job One at State. And the commodity got traded for all kinds of currency. She shook her head.

33

Liz watched her in silence for a moment. "What's wrong, *Evangeline?* You suddenly have that Catholic schoolgirl look. Getting cold feet?"

Evan met her eyes. "No. Maybe I just realized that I like you more than you seem to like yourself."

"Oh, please. I already have a shrink. I came here to get laid, not to listen to a lecture on self-actualization." Liz finished her drink and started looking around for their waiter.

"Christ. When did you get so hard?"

Liz brought her eyes back to bear on her like the crosshairs of a shotgun. "When did you get so scrupulous? You sure weren't worried about propriety when you shoved your hand down the front of my pants in that bathroom stall at Wolf Trap last Easter."

Evan sighed. There was no winning this one. Liz was right, and she knew it. She glanced at her watch. She could catch the ten o'clock Metroliner back to Philly, and have two hours to sit in the dark and regret what she was about to do.

She finished her drink and tossed a twenty-dollar bill on the table. "Let's get a room. These shoes are killing me."

Liz snorted as she grabbed her purse. "Not as much as your conscience will."

Liz knew her well, and that jacked the suck factor of this whole interaction up into the stratosphere.

She really needed to clean up her act.

Evan sat at a small table in the corner of their hotel room. She transcribed the notes Liz had jotted down from Margo Sheridan's "file" at the State Department. This information alone was worth the trip to D.C. She knew better than to ask to keep the notes. Liz would destroy the sheets of paper as soon as their tryst was over.

Liz was fidgeting. Evan could tell that she needed a cigarette.

"Are you finished yet?" she asked for at least the third time.

Evan sighed and looked up at her. "Does it look like I'm finished?"

"Well, hurry the hell up, will you?"

"What are you so jumpy about?"

Liz shrugged. "Something about this one makes me nervous."

Evan was intrigued. Liz wasn't normally bothered by much of anything. She held up the stack of notes.

"What does this code mean?" She pointed to the top of the page, where Liz had written "1.4(c)" next to the names "Maya Jindal/Margo Sheridan."

Liz looked at it. "That's a security classification that prohibits complete access to her records."

"So, what does it mean?"

Liz exhaled. "What the hell do you think it means?"

Evan smiled sweetly at her. "Enlighten me."

Liz sighed. "It means that she must be up to something very naughty."

"You mean, something naughtier than her dalliance with a U.S. senator?"

"Puh-lease." Liz rolled her eyes. "They don't even bother with a classification for that one. No. This must be something grittier. A 4(c) relates to intelligence activities."

Evan was really intrigued now. "Can you find out what kind of activities?"

Liz looked at her with amazement. "You're kidding, right?"

"No."

"Sorry, babe. That one is above my pay grade."

Evan sat back and regarded her.

"Well, then—speculate. You've been at State long enough to make an educated guess."

Liz shrugged.

"Come on." Evan held up the sheets of paper again. "It says here that two of her uncles have ties to some very bad men back home. Is that it? Is that enough to get her coded like this?"

Liz shook her head.

"Then what is it?"

Liz shrugged again. "A 4(c) usually means that the *individual* is engaged in intelligence work."

35

Enlightenment was starting to dawn.

Jesus Christ.

"You mean, Margo is some kind of fucking spy?"

"I don't know what I mean. You asked. I'm just speculating."

"Is she Inter-Services Intelligence?"

"Christ, Evan. I have *no* idea." Liz was plainly finished with this conversation. "Hurry up and give me the fucking papers."

Evan handed them over. She already had what she needed. It was obvious she wouldn't be getting anything else out of Liz. Not tonight, anyway.

Liz took the sheets of notepaper and stuffed them into her purse.

"Don't ask me to do this again." She picked up her coat and walked toward the door of the room.

"I'll call you next week," Evan said to her retreating back.

"Fuck you." Liz opened the door and walked out without a backward glance.

The sound of the door slamming made her teeth rattle.

That went well.

Evan felt like she needed another shower.

Chapter 6

Dan stared at the red file folder that Evan had just tossed down on his desk.

"Here," she said. "I picked red because it seemed to fit so well with Hester Prynne's profile."

He wasn't in the mood to play word games with her. Not today. He was running about two hours behind, and he'd been fighting a migraine all morning.

"Are you going to tell me what the fuck you're talking about?"

"Come on, Dan. Even *you* managed to make it through freshman English."

"Yeah," he said, opening the folder. "I get the reference, but what's your *point?*"

She sat down in a sagging office chair that had seen better days and propped her feet up on the edge of his desk.

"Who do you have to screw to get a cup of coffee in this joint?"

He waved his hand toward the open door. "There's a coffeepot out there next to the photocopier. Drink it at your own risk. It's probably been cooking since last night."

"Wonderful. I think I'll wait. This shouldn't take long."

He looked up at her. She was dressed almost normally today. Gray slacks. A blue- and white-striped blouse. *Girl* shoes. He wondered what prompted the change. "You got a job interview or something?"

She met his gaze. "Maybe."

He shut the folder and rubbed a hand across his eyes. "Do me a favor and just tell me what's in here. I'm getting a migraine, and I really don't have the stamina to play 20 Questions."

"Okay." Evan said. "But, frankly, I'm more interested in what *isn't* in there."

"Meaning?"

"Meaning that your boy Townsend has been taking out more than the trash. And don't tell me you didn't already know about his extracurricular activities."

Dan sat back and sighed. "It didn't take you long to find out."

"Oh, give me a break. A gnat with a lobotomy could have found this. Her fucking car was parked behind his house the day I went down there to meet with him."

Dan rubbed his eyes again. "Christ."

"Was this some kind of audition? A way to show Marcus that I was worth the money?"

He shrugged. "Maybe."

Evan shook her head. "You didn't need me for this sophomoric crap."

"No." He flipped through the contents of the folder. "But I *do* need you for this." He held up a copy of the State Department summary Evan had compiled from Liz Burke's notes.

Evan plucked a piece of lint off her slacks and flicked it away. "That's classified."

"So? I thought you and Liz were *close*." He made air quotes with his fingers.

She sat back and crossed her arms. "Should I be surprised that you still take such a prurient interest in my personal life?"

"You're hardly discreet."

"Unlike your boy, Townsend, I don't have any need to be discreet."

He sighed. Nobody could get him from zero to pissed off as fast as she could. "Whatever." He decided to try a different approach. "How did your meeting with the ice princess go?"

She appeared unfazed. "Who do you mean?"

He sighed. He was really starting to lose his patience. "Ms.

38

Been There, *Donne* That. You come away with anything besides frostbite?"

"Maybe. It's too early to tell."

He narrowed his eyes. "Too early to tell? What the hell does that mean?"

"It means that it's too early to tell."

He sat back and rubbed his temples. "Marcus needs to know if she'll be on board for the campaign."

"Marcus can kiss my ass."

Dan snorted. "Don't tempt him—he's always had a thing for blondes."

Evan rolled her eyes. "I wouldn't be counting on Ms. Donne to belt out an encore of 'Stand By Your Man' at the next convention. I think that train has left the station."

"Shit."

"You can hardly be surprised. She was pretty forthcoming with her position. I gather that her estrangement from the senator is not a news flash."

He held up the red folder. "Does she know about this?"

Evan shrugged. "You tell me. How long has Townsend had a tandoor?"

"A what?" The fluorescent light overhead was buzzing, and the noise was like fingernails on a chalkboard. His headache had finally decided to leave the wings and take center stage.

"A tandoor, Dan. Townsend has a tandoor in his New Castle house. A *big* one."

"How the hell should I know how long he's had it?" He looked over at her. "What difference does it make?"

"His wife hates Indian food."

"Jesus."

Evan tugged a photograph out of the stack of papers inside the red folder.

"But I bet *she* loves it."

Dan stared down at the portrait of a striking, dark-haired woman. The caption identified her as Margo Sheridan, a lobbyist for the Tata Steel Group. She looked vaguely familiar, but he couldn't place her.

39

He could sense that Evan was watching him for a reaction. He looked at her. Her expression gave nothing away.

"What?"

"Don't you recognize her?"

"Should I?"

"I'll admit that she's got a bit more of the *Women's Wear Daily* thing going on than she had during your years at Yale, but it's not like you to forget a pretty face." She pulled another image out of the stack. This one he recognized right away. It was a photo of him, taken in Jordan during his year abroad. He was posing in front of the Nabataean temple in Petra with Andy and Maya Jindal. He flipped back and forth between the two images. *Jesus Christ.* He looked up at Evan.

"Maya is Margo Sheridan?"

"Cleans up pretty well, doesn't she?"

He sat back. "What the fuck?"

"Judging by the size of her file over at State, I'd say that Margo's day job hawking carbon credits for Indian steel producers isn't the only window dressing she's sporting these days."

"You don't know that."

She rolled her eyes. "Call it a hunch."

He sat back. "I need more than that if I'm going to approach Marcus with any of this. Right now, Andy's not guilty of anything more than roasting chicken in a clay oven with a college pal."

"I'm not sure his wife would agree with your assessment."

"There's only one way to find out."

Evan sighed. "You don't seriously expect me to be the one to ask her if she knows about this?"

"Why not? You're being well paid."

"I'm not some sleazy divorce P.I. with a grudge and a camera, Dan. You can do your own goddamn dirty work."

He gestured toward the folder. "I don't have to, now."

"Fuck you."

"Oh, come on. Don't try to tell me that you aren't the teeniest bit interested in finding out how much the *femme de glace* knows about Tata's golden girl." He leaned forward. "She knew her at Yale, too."

"What's that supposed to mean?"

"Let's just say that Maya was known to play *both* sides of the field. Julia hasn't always basked in the sainted reputation she enjoys today." He pointed a finger at Evan. "You and the former first lady might have more in common than you realize."

Evan sat staring across the office with an unreadable expression. He could see her drumming her fingers against the undersides of her chair. He knew she was waiting for her blood pressure to return to normal. She was agitated. Pissed off. He was glad she didn't have any coffee. He was pretty sure he'd be wearing it by now.

All in all, this was shaping up to be a fairly normal interaction for the two of them.

What felt like a full minute passed. Then Evan looked back at him. "So, what do you want?" Her voice was flat.

He fought hard not to smile. He knew he'd snagged her, and she knew it, too. "I want to know what's in that file at State. And I want to find out how much Julia knows about Andy and Margo, and whether or not she'll work with us to manage it if it leaks."

"*If* it leaks?" Evan sounded incredulous.

"Okay. When *we* leak it. I need to know if she'll be on board—regardless of her long-term plans."

She sighed. "If I'm going to move ahead with this, I need something else from you, too."

He was immediately suspicious. "What's that?"

"Julia mentioned that Andy was already involved with someone when she first met him at Yale. I need a name."

"Why?"

"Because I'm thinking about starting a fucking book club." She rolled her eyes. "Why do you *think*?"

"Whatever." He was in no mood for banter. "I'll get it for you."

"Soon, Dan."

"Tell you what. When you get me what I need, I'll give you a name."

41

Evan dropped her feet to the floor. "This stinks, Dan. And it's a familiar stench—the same one that hovers around you whenever you get involved with Marcus."

He rubbed his eyes again. This headache was shaping up to be one for the record books. "Well, thankfully, you're just the woman to clear the air."

"Go fuck yourself." She stood up and walked toward the open door.

"I want a summary report by the end of next week," he said to her retreating back. "Marcus is meeting with the DNC chairman on Friday, and I need time to review it first."

She looked back at him. "It's going to cost you."

"I'm aware of that."

"I really don't think you are." She turned and walked away.

He sat for a moment, listening to the overhead roar of the fluorescent light. His pulse was pounding in his temples like a jackhammer. *Christ.* He hated it when she was right.

Chapter 7

When the call came from Julia on Wednesday morning, Evan realized that she'd been waiting for it with dread and anticipation. Until she heard Julia's voice on the phone, she wasn't sure which emotion was likely to win her mental tug of war. She would have offered even money on either outcome.

Julia's meetings were wrapping up at four-thirty that afternoon, and she wasn't booked for her return flight to New York until Thursday morning. She was staying downtown at the Four Seasons in Logan Square, and asked if Evan would consider meeting her for an early dinner in the hotel's Fountain Restaurant.

Evan had a better idea.

"Do you have access to a car and driver?" she asked.

"Of course. Why? Is there a place you'd rather meet?" Julia sounded characteristically noncommittal.

"You might say that. How about you come out to Chadds Ford and let me cook for you?" The other end of the line was silent. "I know it's a bit of a haul, and I understand if you'd rather stay in the city."

"On the contrary," Julia's tone seemed genuine enough, "I was just trying to figure out if I could shake free any earlier and get a jump on the five o'clock traffic."

Evan's tug of war continued. Right now, *Team Anticipation* was pulling ahead. But she knew herself—*Team Dread* wouldn't give up without a fight.

"Great," she said with more calm than she felt. "Call me when you're on your way. I'll text directions for you to share with your driver. It should only take about thirty minutes to get here."

"Do I need to be concerned about what you might try to lure me into eating?"

Evan bit her tongue. It was too early in their—whatever the hell this was—for that kind of *repartee*. "With me, concern should always be your default response."

"I'll be sure to remember that."

"You won't regret it."

Julia laughed. "Red or white?"

Evan thought about that. "One of each?"

"That can happen. I'll call you later with an ETA." Julia hung up.

Evan glanced at the duplicate photos of Maya/Margo on top of her desk and the sheet of handwritten notes from her intel file at the State Department. Something lurched inside her, and she sat down on a wooden stool, still holding the phone.

Dread. It felt like dread.

Chapter 8

Evan was chopping vegetables for a salad when she heard the big Town Car drive up a few minutes before five. She walked out front to meet Julia, and they stood a little awkwardly in the front yard, watching the car as it backed out in a hail of gravel, then roared over a hill and disappeared from sight.

"Well, I feel like kissing the ground," Julia said. "That trip was a little too much like one of those theme-park rides at Disney World."

Evan thought Julia looked like a theme-park ride—one Evan wasn't quite tall enough for. Julia was casually dressed in black jeans and a dark blue silk blouse. In natural light, her hair had chestnut highlights. Once again, it was loose around her shoulders.

She knew she was staring. She needed to say something. Julia was standing there, looking back at her with that textbook poker expression of hers that revealed nothing.

"You really don't seem like the thrill-seeker type." That was genuine enough.

Julia held out a canvas bag that contained two bottles. "You'd be surprised."

Evan took the bag from her. "Not very likely. I'm pretty hard to surprise." She looked into the bag. One white. One red. "What do we have here?"

Julia shrugged. "Frankly, I have no idea. I asked the sommelier to pick out two wines that would go with anything. He seemed offended at first, but he got over it pretty quickly when I told him to make certain they were expensive."

Evan laughed. "Maybe we should open one and test how impressive your credit limit is?"

"Only after you've given me a tour of this amazing place." Julia gestured toward the eighteenth-century farmhouse that had been in Evan's family for generations.

It was a typical Brandywine River Valley fieldstone house—two stories, with pairs of black and white shutters on the front windows. It was small, but now seemed huge without Stevie. Evan was amazed at how her daughter's chatter and clutter filled up the empty spaces in her life.

"Sure. Let's go inside, and I'll give you the nickel tour."

Julia followed her across the lawn toward the front door. "Have you lived here long?"

Evan nodded. "About twelve years now—ever since my grandfather died. But I spent most of my childhood here—weekends, summers. Anytime my mother could dump me off and flee with one of her boyfriends."

"What about your father?"

They walked inside. Evan shut the big front door, and they stood facing each other in the small, dark foyer. "He was never much of a factor—not in my mother's life, and certainly not in mine. I don't even know where he is now."

"I'm sorry." Julia sounded like she meant it.

Evan could just make out the blue of her eyes. "Don't be. He was an asshole. But he did accomplish one thing."

"What's that?"

"He made me a lot more inclined to let Dan play an active role in Stevie's life."

"It sounds like you made a good decision there."

Evan nodded. "I think so. But what matters more to me is that Stevie thinks so. In this case, her opinion is really the only one that matters."

She spread her arms out to encompass the tiny space they stood in. "So, this, clearly, is the foyer. These stairs lead up to what's really a half story—two bedrooms and a small bathroom. Just behind you is the living room, and beyond that is the small room I use as my office."

Julia turned and walked into the medium-sized room with wide-plank floors and a raised-hearth stone fireplace. She didn't look at all out of place. But Evan supposed that Julia Donne would look like she belonged wherever her feet were planted.

"This is charming. I love the antiques." Julia traced the star pattern in the punched tin door of an oak pie safe. "Are they all family pieces?"

Evan followed her into the room. "Many of them are. I've added a few things over the years." The room had a low ceiling, and it made Julia appear even taller than she was.

"You have great taste. I love the colors."

"Pottery Barn deserves most of the credit for that."

Julia smiled as she picked up a framed photograph of Stevie. "Is this your daughter?"

Evan nodded and walked over to stand beside her. "Yeah. That was taken in August at Cape May. It was our last weekend together before she left for Emma."

Julia studied the photo. "She's beautiful."

Evan felt irrationally pleased. "Thanks. She looks like Dan."

Julia met her eyes. "She looks like you."

They stared at each other. Evan thought with disgust that she probably was blushing. It was a curse—one of many that came with having a fair complexion.

"Well," she hefted the canvas bag, "let's go on back to the kitchen and open one of these. We've got about an hour before dinner will be ready."

Julia set the framed photo back down and crossed her arms. "So, what are you feeding me?"

"You worried?"

"Should I be worried?"

Evan looked at her. "I thought we covered that."

47

Julia's gaze was unrevealing. "Okay, then. Yes. I confess to being a tad worried."

"You do?" Evan was intrigued. "I'm tempted to wonder what else you might confess to."

"I don't know. Maybe you should ask me something and find out."

Evan's head was starting to reel from this game of 3-D chess. She felt out of practice. "I think I need a glass of courage first."

Julia laughed and pushed past her to head for the kitchen. "Now who's worried?"

Khoresh Fesenjan—the chicken stew, with its combination of walnuts, cinnamon, and pomegranate juice—seemed like the perfect dish for this evening. Not really tart. Not really sweet. Not really spicy. But interesting enough to make you want to take just one more bite, so you could try and puzzle it out. To Evan, the dish was a lot like Julia, so it seemed like the natural choice.

And Julia, who claimed to dislike Indian food, seemed to be doing just fine with this everyday Persian fare. The weather was warm enough to allow them to eat outside at a small table on Evan's back porch overlooking a lawn that was mostly pasture. It sloped down toward a branch that divided her property from a neighboring farm. Cows grazed in the distance or lumbered down to drink from the slow-moving stream that eventually became part of the Brandywine River. The scene was so bucolic and serene that Evan felt the need to apologize, and she didn't quite know why.

"I guess this seems like an odd place for me to live."

Julia had been gazing out across the field, and brought her eyes back to Evan. She looked puzzled. "Why would you think that?"

Evan shrugged. "I'm not sure that I do, really. But I thought it might seem like a contradiction to you."

Julia seemed amused. "Not at all. I think it makes perfect sense."

"You do? Why's that?"

48

"Given what you do for a living, I can imagine that retreating to a place like this—a place that's so free from artifice—is a welcome change."

Evan laughed. "I guess that's true. It worked the same way for me when I was growing up."

"How so?"

"My mother lived in a less-than-desirable part of South Philly, and coming here was like being teleported to another solar system. It was impossible to believe that my other world—the one with junkies, hockey games at the Spectrum, and bars on every street corner—existed only a few miles up Route 1."

"I know what you mean."

Evan was dubious. "Haven't you spent most of your life in New York City?"

Julia nodded. "Except for boarding school at Exeter—my retreat." She shook her head. "I keep forgetting that you probably already know as much about my personal history as I do."

Evan blushed. "I apologize for that. I guess it seems pretty off-putting."

"No. When you marry a career politician, you pretty much check your right to privacy at the voting booth."

Evan let that one slide. She knew they'd get back to it in time. For now, she wanted to ignore the fact that Julia was an appendage of Andy Townsend. After tonight, she doubted that she'd get another chance to talk with her on such friendly terms. "Why do you characterize Exeter as a retreat?" She had her own reasons for asking. She wondered if Stevie felt that way about Emma.

Julia sipped her wine. They were drinking the second bottle—a nice Domaine Paul Pernot. "My home life wasn't exactly sustaining. I was an only child, and my parents engineered my future in the same way they engineered the expansion of the publishing house. In fact, there was very little difference in method. Their idea of 'parenting' had more in common with a crash course on mergers and acquisitions than anything put forward by Dr. Spock. The four years I spent at Exeter gave me some breathing space and allowed me the chance to at least *imagine* another life . . . before I stepped up to embrace my fate."

"Which was?"

Julia looked back at her with those incredible blue eyes that gave nothing away. "Go to Yale. Marry well. Take over the family business."

Evan was unprepared for such a direct response. "Well, I suppose there are worse fates."

"Really? I can't think of many that would have turned out worse for me."

They were silent for a moment. Evan twisted the stem of her wineglass between her fingers. "I confess that I really have no idea how to respond to that."

"Don't you?" For once, Julia's voice seemed to hold a trace of emotion. "Am I supposed to infer from this that you don't already know about Andy and Maya Jindal?"

Evan was every bit as shocked as she would have been if Julia had suddenly whipped out an accordion and started playing top hits from *The Lawrence Welk Show*.

"Jesus. You don't mess around, do you?"

"No. I generally leave that pastime to my husband."

She didn't laugh because the outside light was starting to fade, and the small oil lamp on the table wasn't bright enough to reveal whether or not Julia had intended her remark to be humorous. Evan couldn't tell by her tone. But then, that was nothing new.

"You don't give much away, you know that?"

Julia seemed unfazed. "I didn't think I had to with you."

For some reason, that response irritated Evan. "No. I guess you don't. Yes, I know about Andy and Maya. I wasn't certain that *you* did, however."

"And were you going to tell me?"

"I honestly don't know."

Julia sighed. She held out her glass. "May I have some more wine, please?"

"Of course." Evan pulled the bottle out of a bucket and refilled both of their glasses. When she finished, she shoved the now empty bottle back into its nest of melting ice with more force than she intended. Some of the liquid sloshed out onto the table.

"Are you annoyed?" Julia asked, after a moment.

"Yeah."

"May I ask why?"

"Because last week, my instinct was to walk away from this job. Now I regret that I didn't."

"Because of me?"

Evan nodded. "And me." She rubbed her forehead. "I don't like myself very much right now. I don't like who I have to be to do this work."

"That sounds pretty ominous. Is there more to Andy's infidelity than I realize?"

"I wasn't talking about *his* infidelity. I was talking about mine."

They sat, staring into the growing darkness.

"Now I'm the one who doesn't know what to say," Julia said in a quiet voice.

Evan sighed. "I'm sorry. I'm being a shitty hostess." She gestured toward their empty dinner plates. "Would you like something more to eat?"

"No. I'm very satisfied. It was wonderful. You're quite a good cook."

"I generally do okay with anything that ends up sitting on a bed of rice."

"It was delicious." Julia smiled. "I really thought you'd try to trick me into eating something curried."

Evan laughed. "Not on the first date." The words were out of her mouth before she could reel them back in. *Christ. What an idiot.* Panic raced up and down her frame. She was grateful the dim light hid her face. She knew she was turning fifteen shades of red.

"Is that what this is?" Julia sounded almost amused.

"You tell me." Evan had nothing to lose now.

It took Julia a moment to reply. "Did you really think I would've risked the ride out here with Evel Knievel if I had thought otherwise?"

Evan fought an impulse to pump the air with her fist. "I didn't know what you thought."

"Well, now that you know, maybe you can relax a little and ask me about Maya." Julia paused. "I'd rather you hear it from me than from Andy . . . or from her."

Evan shook her head. "I don't know that I want to." She met her eyes. "I'm . . . confused."

"About?"

"Pretty much everything." She leaned toward Julia. "Believe me. I never saw this coming."

"I didn't either."

Evan still didn't trust her instincts. "Are we talking about the same thing?"

Julia shifted in her chair and sat forward. Their faces were inches apart. "I think so."

Evan's pulse raced. This was a development she didn't need. It would complicate everything, and it didn't have a snowball's chance in hell of going anyplace good. She needed to slow it down while she still had the chance.

She had run a marathon once—all twenty-six point two miles of it. And the stamina it took for her to remain on her feet after running for five and a half hours was *nothing* compared to the effort it now took for her to move ten inches away from Julia.

She sat back against her chair.

"I don't want to fuck this up." The words sounded foreign to her. She thought about the night before with Liz. Her stomach turned over. For a moment, she thought she might lose her dinner.

"Do you think you might?" Julia didn't sound pissed. That was a first for Evan.

"Hell, yes. Count on it."

"I'd rather not." Julia sat back, too. "Okay, then. Let's define the rules of engagement."

Evan looked at her with amazement. "You're pretty calm about all of this."

"I try to be when it's important."

"Think you can teach me how to do that?"

"I really don't think I can teach you anything, Evan."

Goddamn. Evan realized that she was gripping the edge of the table. Her knuckles were starting to cramp. Distance. She needed distance. And fast.

"Okay. Rule one: we do *nothing* while I'm investigating Andy."

Julia folded her arms. "No more dates?"

"I didn't say that."

"Oh. My mistake. I guess you have a more narrow definition of 'nothing' than I do."

"It's an evolving concept."

Julia smiled.

"Rule two: you tell me everything you think I need to know about you and Andy—about Andy and Maya—and about *you* and Maya. As much as I hate to admit it, I don't have the stomach to comb through your past the way I have to root around in his."

"Agreed."

"Rule three." Evan thought about it for a minute. She couldn't come up with anything. "I guess there isn't a rule three."

"That's it?" Julia asked, surprised.

Evan nodded. "I think so."

Julia raised an eyebrow. "Remind me never to hire you to run a board meeting."

Evan laughed out loud. "You'd save a fortune on catering."

"And lose my shirt in the process."

That was an image Evan vowed to return to later, when she was alone and could really think about it.

"How about I lay out a few conditions of my own?" Julia said.

"Okay."

"I'd like to know anything you find out about Andy that concerns me *before* you tell Marcus."

That didn't seem unreasonable. And she wasn't asking Evan for censorship rights. "All right."

"And I'd like your promise that you won't collude with any efforts to coerce me into helping Andy or the party—unless it's something I freely offer to do."

"Of course."

Julia fell silent.

"Is that it?" Evan thought she'd have a few more demands.

Julia met her eyes. "There is one other thing that I'm somewhat reluctant to mention."

"What is it?"

"I'm not exactly 'out,' and there are some compelling reasons for that, which I'll happily share with you later on. But I don't want you to misinterpret my public demeanor as a sign of ambivalence. Until my situation with Andy is resolved, I need to be circumspect about my behavior. It's part of the bargain we hammered out when our marriage fell apart." She seemed to hesitate. "And there are a few, longer-term family complications that factor into it as well."

"All right." Evan didn't feel too optimistic about this one. It didn't sound simple, or like it was going to be wrapped up anytime soon.

Julia finished her wine. "So. Where do we go from here?"

Evan had about a hundred ideas, but most of them would have to wait. And by the look of things, it was probably going to be a *long* wait. She sighed. Cleaning up her act could really suck.

She pushed back her chair and stood up. "How about we go inside, and I make us some coffee? Then we can sit down in the light, and you can tell me all about Maya Jindal."

Julia smiled wryly. "Now, there's a mood-killer."

She stood up, too. Once again, Evan was struck by Julia's height advantage. Tonight, it seemed like all the advantages were on Julia's side. They picked up their plates and silverware.

"You know," Julia said. "There is one other thing I'd like."

Evan was afraid to ask, but knew she had to. She leaned over and blew out the oil lamp. "What's that?"

"I'd like to meet your daughter."

Evan smiled. Maybe she did have something on her side.

"It only happened once." Julia sat with her feet tucked beneath her on an overstuffed leather club chair. Her shoes were tossed on the floor next to the ottoman. Evan stared at them while she talked.

They were odd, almost comical. Yellow and black creations that looked like cast-off bowling shoes, but probably cost more than Evan made in a week. Well, until this job came along. Marcus was going to pay through the nose for this one.

Evan sat on the end of the sofa at a right angle to Julia. She knew it would be risky to sit next to her, so she had been relieved when they entered the living room with their coffee, and Julia dropped into the big armchair.

"And I knew it was a mistake." Julia looked up at Evan.

"A mistake?" Evan prompted, because Julia looked like she was expecting her to—not because she was anxious to hear the rest of her story. She didn't really want to listen to any of this. She was feeling sick. Sick from too much wine and too little sleep. Sick from jagged flashes of the night before with Liz. Sick from the revelations at dinner that hinted at what was possible, and what was impossible with the woman seated before her. Everything was piling up behind the façade of calm she was trying so hard to project.

"It all started a lot earlier—back when I first became engaged to Andy. He was a year ahead of me at Yale, and had gone on to law school at Columbia. Maya was at Columbia too, working on her MBA. The three of us were together a lot in those days. Whenever I went down to New York, Maya was there. She was like a staple in Andy's life." Julia shook her head. "I didn't really worry about it. It just seemed *normal*." She looked at Evan. "And Maya was already dating Tom Sheridan. They seemed pretty serious—were talking about moving to northern Virginia when she finished her program. He was getting ready for his first congressional bid."

"From Maryland?" Evan had actually met Tom Sheridan once at a K Street event hosted by Royal Dutch Shell. That was only a few months before his untimely death in Aspen. The three-term congressman, holidaying with some Yale frat brothers, decided to drink an entire bottle of Wild Turkey, and then try his luck navigating the steeps at Loge Peak. It had taken rescuers two days to find what was left of him.

"That's right. Tom was the one who got Andy interested in alternative energy issues. They actually coauthored a white paper for the U.N. Climate Change Council. It was that paper that launched Andy into the national spotlight."

"How did Maya factor into all of this?"

Julia leaned her head back against the chair and regarded Evan. "After Tom's death, Maya—or *Margo*, as she then preferred to be called—became a fixture in our lives. Andy felt terrible about Tom's accident—felt responsible."

That piqued Evan's interest. She'd read news accounts of the accident. "Why did he feel responsible?"

"He'd been on the Aspen trip, and had spent most of that afternoon in the lodge with Tom, drinking. Tom was an indifferent skier, but he was boasting about how he was going to tackle the expert slopes, and most of the other guys on the trip were teasing him and egging him on."

"Including Andy?"

Julia nodded. "But no one expected he would strap on his skis and try it alone. It was *insane*. He shouldn't even have been allowed to get up there. His blood alcohol level was off the charts when they found him. Andy was devastated."

Evan let out a slow breath. "I can see why." She watched Julia in silence for a minute.

Julia set her coffee cup down and crossed her arms over her abdomen. She looked completely closed off. Evan guessed it was a reflexive posture.

"So, what about you and Margo?"

Julia looked at her. For once, her gaze seemed to open up. It transformed her. Took years off her face. Evan thought she wore vulnerability well. Hell. She wore *everything* well.

"After the accident, Margo got a job working for Corus America in Wilmington. That put her in Andy's orbit a lot. And mine. I saw her frequently when I attended various state functions in Delaware with Andy. She always seemed to be underfoot."

There was a flash of white light, and off in the distance, a roll of thunder. No rain had been forecast, but these days, it rarely was. The storms rolled in unannounced, like unwelcome family members. Julia shivered.

"Are you cold?" Evan asked, reaching for a red fleece throw that was a favorite of Stevie's.

Julia smiled at her and took the blanket. "Thanks. I think it's the subject matter more than the climate." She draped the throw around her shoulders. "I'm not usually such a wuss."

"I don't think you're a wuss at all."

Julia met her eyes. "You don't? Well, brace yourself, then, because you're about to be disappointed."

Evan felt a twinge of panic. White light flashed again. The roll of thunder was closer this time. She gave Julia a look that she hoped expressed more confidence than she felt.

Julia was still looking back at her. "What was it you said about Dan? That you fucked him once, just to see what it would be like?"

Evan felt a prick of discomfort. She nodded. "That sounds about right." It still seemed wrong to hear a word like "fuck" roll off Julia's tongue. It didn't fit with her idealized portrait of the woman. It was as jarring as those goddamn yellow shoes. She realized that her fantasy was about to get blown to hell, and she didn't want that to happen. She wanted to turn back the clock. Rescind her invitation to cook dinner. Meet Julia in town, as they had planned initially. Meet in some public place where a conversation like this one could never happen.

Julia sighed. "One night, when Andy was in Dover, Margo showed up at our New York apartment. She was in town for an interview with *Corporate Knights*, and called to see if I wanted to grab a late supper. I didn't think anything about it. It wasn't uncommon for us to do things alone together. I'd gotten to know her quite well over the years, even though it was clear that she was primarily Andy's friend." She gave a bitter-sounding laugh. "All of that changed in a hurry."

Outside, Evan heard the rain start to fall. More thunder rolled. The lamp on the table behind the sofa flickered. She hoped the power would stay on.

Julia didn't appear to notice.

"After dinner, we went back to the apartment and had a couple of drinks. I'd had a particularly hard week at work. The board was opposing some staffing initiatives that were really important to me. I was in a fractious mood, and I was emotionally exhausted." She looked at Evan. "I'm not making excuses. I knew what I was doing. I just think that, under normal circumstances, I might have made a different decision."

Evan looked back at her without speaking.

"Maya—Margo—had always been attentive to me. I noticed it from time to time, but always ignored it. I knew that she'd had relationships with women in college, but that wasn't really uncommon at Yale in those days. I guess I chose not to see it, since I was trying so hard to avoid the whole issue myself." She took a deep breath. "You see, I always knew that I had a predisposition toward women. I just never had the courage or the wherewithal to explore it. It would have been impossible for me. Even during my years at Yale, when I could have done something about it, I didn't. It just wasn't part of the business plan. It would never have fit with the life my parents had mapped out for me— a life I bought into almost from childhood. There was never any question about what I would do—about what choices I would make. I was a Donne. And Donnes did only *one* thing." She fell silent again. "Until that night."

Evan tapped her fingers on the edge of the sofa cushion. *Stop!* She didn't need to know this. Marcus didn't need to know this. It wasn't part of the job.

"You don't have to tell me this." Evan extended a hand toward her. To her surprise, Julia took hold of it. She gripped Evan's fingers like a vice. Her hand felt soft and hot.

"I do. I want you to know." She released Evan's hand. "I had gone into the kitchen to mix us another round of drinks, and Margo followed me. All evening, she had been flirting with me—sitting too close to me in the cab, touching me, and rubbing up against me in our booth at dinner. It all went to my head. I was tired of fighting it—of fighting her. Andy and I had been arguing. He wanted me to spend more time with him in Delaware, and I was resisting. It was clear to me that it was all starting to unravel. He was already talking about a senate bid after his gubernatorial term ended. I knew I didn't have the stamina for that. I think, on some level, he knew it, too. And, of course, there was Margo—willing to pick up the pieces from *either* of us."

The rain fell harder now. The lightning was coming in rapid flashes—almost too many to count.

"When she touched me in the kitchen, I knew I was going to do it. She knew it, too." Julia shook her head like she was trying to clear it. "It was horrible and incredible, all at the same time. I hated her. I hated her because it felt so right. Finally, *something* in my life felt right." She looked at Evan. Her eyes were glassy. "Leave it to me to finally do something right for all the wrong reasons."

Evan didn't know what to say, so she said nothing. They sat in silence, listening to the storm.

"I told Andy, of course," Julia said, finally. "I was mortified. Guilty. And I wanted him to know about Margo."

"How did he respond?"

"He didn't. He shrugged and said, 'Shit happens.' I was stunned. It didn't change anything for him, but it changed *everything* for me. Of course," she looked at Evan, "I didn't realize by that time, he was fucking Margo, too."

"Jesus."

"In a nutshell."

A loud boom shook the house. The lights in the room flickered again, and then went out.

Evan groaned. "Christ. Hang on. Let me check the fuse box."

"Fuse box?" Julia sounded incredulous.

"Yeah. Welcome to life in the country." Evan got up and carefully made her way to the sideboard where she kept a flashlight. She turned it on and flashed its blue beam back toward the living room where Julia sat, still wrapped up in Stevie's red blanket. It looked purple in the halogen light. Julia sat there without moving, like an ice sculpture—a composition in blue, black, and purple. Evan was reminded of Dan's comment—*femme de glace*. Then, in the narrow beam of light, Julia smiled at her.

Dan was full of shit.

Evan turned toward the stairs that led to her dirt-floored basement. "I'll be back in a flash."

"No pun intended." The words floated back to her, disconnected. Everything felt disconnected. She was glad the lights had gone out. It gave her an excuse to get up and try to compose herself. It gave them both a chance to breathe.

Evan descended the wooden steps. The basement smelled musty. Water must be seeping in someplace. Probably around those cold frames her grandfather had built along the south side of the house. She made her way to the ancient fuse box. Yep. One of the fuses had blown. She checked the shelf next to the metal box for a replacement and uttered a silent prayer of thanks when she found a 5-amp bulb—the last one. She'd have to make a trip into Hills Hardware and buy some more—especially if these freakish storms were going to continue. *Jesus*. It was really pissing down out there. As she screwed in the new fuse, she thought about Andy's work on climate change. Maybe she should read some of his damn papers.

As soon as she flipped the circuit switch, the lights came back on. She stood there for a moment with her forehead pressed against the cold metal door of the fuse box. Then she turned around and started back up the steps. *Showtime.*

Evan walked back into the living room. Julia was on her feet, rummaging through her bag. She looked up and held up her cell phone.

"I didn't realize how late it is. I'm thinking that, with this weather, I should give Evel some extra notice about coming to get me."

Evan had been dreading a return to their conversation about Julia's horizontal two-step with Margo. Now she found herself regretting that they wouldn't be talking about it—or about anything. She was conflicted. Part of her wanted Julia to leave, so she could sit down in the dark with a big drink and sulk about how the universe continued to dangle things in front of her—things she'd always want, but could never have. Another part of her wanted Julia to stay, so she could try to convince herself that maybe they could find a way to work something out. It was hopeless. She was hopeless—a classic loser. She felt irrationally compelled to confess it.

"Probably not a bad idea," she said, instead. "The rain doesn't appear to be slacking off."

Julia looked toward the darkened windows that overlooked the front yard. They revealed nothing. "It ought to be a thrilling ride back into town."

"I should've picked you up. I'm sorry about that."

"Don't be. It was a wonderful evening. And if you'd been driving, we wouldn't have been able to pad my expense report in such grand fashion."

Evan smiled. "That's true."

Julia took a moment to text her driver before sitting down on the sofa. Evan sat down at the extreme opposite end. Not that that would offer much of a buffer. It was a small couch.

"So." She didn't really know what to say.

"So." Julia seemed to have the same problem.

"I'm so glad we had this time together." *Christ.* Where in the hell did that come from? She sounded like fucking Carol Burnett.

Julia laughed—a big laugh. She caught the reference, too.

Evan dropped her head back against the sofa cushion. "I'm such a loser."

Julia laid a hand on Evan's thigh. "No, you're not. You're adorable."

Evan looked down at her hand. It felt like a branding iron. "I am?"

"You are."

They stared at each other. "How long did you say it would take Evel to get here?"

Julia smiled. "I didn't say." She returned her hand to safer territory. "But I believe *he* said about ten minutes."

Evan chewed the inside of her cheek. Ten minutes? She could do a lot of damage in ten minutes. She looked down at the spot on her leg where Julia's hand had been. It still felt hot.

"Bummer."

Julia laughed again. "Next time?"

Evan met her eyes. "Next time." She remembered their earlier conversation about rules. "But only if we're free and clear of this business."

"Are you always so scrupulous?"

That reminded her of Liz's comment last night. *Shit.* Maybe she did need to see if her plaid jumper still fit. She really was acting like some bucktoothed goody two-shoes. One of those annoying suck-ups who stayed after school to clap Sister's erasers. She looked Julia up and down. Yeah. She could cover a *lot* of ground in ten minutes.

"No. I'm not normally scrupulous at all."

"Then why now?" Julia seemed more curious than anything.

"What was it you said a while ago? You try to be when it's important?"

Julia regarded her in silence for a moment. Then she nodded. "That's right."

"Well, I'm not sure about very many things right now, but I do think that maybe we can salvage something decent out of this mess. If we don't fuck it up before we get the chance to try."

"I hope you're right." Julia's tone gave no indication of what she thought their odds were likely to be. She jumped when the phone in her hand buzzed. She glanced down at it.

"It's Evel. He says he'll be pulling up out front in about two minutes."

Evan's insides felt like lead. "Okay. Let's get you an umbrella."

"Afraid I'll melt?" Julia's blue eyes looked teasing.

"No. That's not really the *Wizard of Oz* reference that occurs to me right now."

"It isn't?"

"No. I feel more inclined to hover over you and chant, 'Surrender, Dorothy.'"

Julia leaned toward her. She was suddenly so close that Evan had trouble focusing on her features. It wasn't a bad sensation at all. Julia smelled like lavender.

"I surrender."

Evan could feel her breath—faint puffs of air after each consonant. *Rules.* There was something about rules. She couldn't remember what it was. Julia's mouth hovered there, separated from hers by centimeters. Then it wasn't separated from hers at all. And neither was the rest of her. She had no idea which one of them had closed the distance. It didn't matter. *Christ. Two minutes?* They had two minutes. Judging by the surge of adrenalin that was about to short-circuit every synapse in her brain, she realized that ten minutes might just have killed her.

A flash of white from car headlights cut across the room. They broke apart and looked at each other guiltily, like teenagers who had been caught in the snare of a porch light by an unseen parent.

Evan released her. How in the hell had her hands gotten inside Julia's shirt that fast? Julia appeared equally stunned. For once, her legendary composure seemed to desert her.

"I'm sorry," Evan said. Even though she wasn't.

"I'm not." Julia wiped some lipstick off Evan's mouth. Her hand was shaky. "You aren't, either."

Evan resisted the impulse to bite her fingertips. *God.* She wanted to ingest the woman. "No. I guess I'm not."

They heard two short blasts from a car horn.

"Walk me out?"

Evan nodded. She stood up, uncertain that her legs would support her weight. They did. Apparently, her brain was still able to establish communication with areas south of her navel. She had no idea how that was possible.

"Let me get that umbrella." She started to head for the basement, but Julia stopped her.

"Don't bother." She gave Evan a look that was a heady mix of shyness and bravado. "I'm already wet."

Jesus. Evan closed her eyes. She felt like the floor was shifting beneath her feet. "Are you trying to kill me?"

"No." Julia remained silent until Evan opened her eyes and looked back at her. Then she smiled. "Not yet, anyway."

"All good things to those who wait?" *Great.* Now she was quoting Hannibal Lecter.

"Something like that." Julia reached for her hand.

They left the house and walked toward the waiting Town Car, ignoring the rain that soaked them both to the skin.

Chapter 9

After Julia left, Evan went back inside and stood still for a few minutes, dripping onto the rug in her dark foyer. She was full of nervous energy, and she needed something to do. She knew she was too keyed up to sleep, so that idea was out. That left her with only two options. She could go upstairs, whack off, and *then* try to sleep—unlikely—or she could dry herself off and try to work for a few hours. She lifted her arm and watched as rain water dripped from her sleeve to join the expanding pool at her feet. She remembered the days when she wouldn't have had to choose. She would've just whacked off, then worked. End of story. Growing old sucked.

Right now, just about everything sucked. Especially the mess she was making on this damn rug. Sighing, she pulled her shoes off and ran up the short flight of stairs to get some dry clothes.

As she changed into sweat pants and a faded t-shirt with *Penn* stenciled across the front in chipped letters, she wondered how Julia was faring on the ride back to town with Evel.

God. What the hell was she thinking? This woman was so out of her league. She needed to stick with the Liz Burkes of the world—women who gave as good as they got, and never looked much beyond the landscape of their own libidos. *They* were her ilk. Not Julia. Julia was something else. Julia was like a stray truffle, stuck in a steaming pile of shit beneath one of those Kennett Square mushroom tents. She didn't fit.

But Evan couldn't do anything about that right now. So she forced herself to think about the other parts of this story that didn't fit. Like that accident of Tom Sheridan's. Something about that narrative left a bad taste in her mouth.

She went downstairs and walked into her office. The photos of Margo Sheridan looked up at her from her desktop. She was tempted to take a Sharpie and add a big moustache to her perfect features. *Yeah. That would be a mature response.* Instead, she turned the photos face down and dropped into her grandfather's old Bank of England chair. The storm was still raging outside, but she supposed it would be safe to run her laptop off its battery pack.

She started by reading archived news reports of Sheridan's accident in the *Aspen Daily News* and the *Denver Post*. Details there were sketchy. The Pitkin County coroner said that Sheridan died from blunt trauma to the head and neck and ruled the death accidental. There was no mention of Sheridan's blood alcohol level in the published news reports, but that wasn't unusual. *The Washington Post* and *New York Times* articles were more detailed, but focused primarily on the aftermath of Sheridan's death, and questions related to who the governor of Maryland would appoint to complete his congressional term. There was also some lively discussion that reignited the ongoing debate about the use of helmets in downhill skiing, and several articles linked Sheridan's accident to the earlier celebrity deaths of Michael Kennedy and Sonny Bono. In general, the published news reports made little mention of Sheridan's grieving widow. She hadn't accompanied him on the skiing holiday. She had been in London at the time, interviewing with Corus Steel. Evan knew from Julia that Andy Townsend had been there, and she was curious to discover who else had participated in the Aspen reunion.

On impulse, she logged back into Yale's online alumni community and did some looking around. She lucked into a stray class note and photo posted by Gil Freemont, a classmate of Dan's. He had been in Aspen that weekend. The reunion photo showed a sweater-clad Freemont, seated at a table in a Snowmass pub, with Sheridan, Andy Townsend, and another man she did not recognize. He was identified as Adam Greenhill, another Yale frat brother. The table was covered with empty beer steins. According to Freemont's caption, the photo had been taken the day before Sheridan's accident. Evan stared at it. The men all looked laid-back and relaxed—preppy and successful in their designer ski clothes. She sat back, sighed, and reached for her mouse to close the window. Then she saw him.

Marcus.

He was standing at the bar in the background of the photograph—in a *suit*. Asshole. Only Marcus would wear a fucking suit to a ski resort. What the hell was he doing there? He wasn't a Yalie, and he certainly didn't look like he was there to enjoy a ski weekend.

She tapped the top of her mouse. Sheridan's accident had happened over two years ago, when Townsend was still a little-known governor from Delaware. It was only after Sheridan's death that Townsend had been catapulted into the national spotlight as the newest mouthpiece of the green energy coalition. Was it possible that Marcus had been sniffing around Andy over two years ago? Or had Marcus been working with Tom Sheridan?

Probably not. Sheridan had made no secret about his lack of political ambition.

Evan clicked back to the text of an interview he had given *The Baltimore Sun* about three months before the Aspen trip. The interviewer asked him to respond to rumors that he was thinking about resigning his congressional seat and signing on with Greenpeace USA. Sheridan's reply was predictably vague. He said he fully intended to complete his term, and he had made no decisions about his future beyond that. He would neither confirm nor deny the Greenpeace rumors.

There was really nothing unusual about any of this. Still. It bugged her. And she knew enough to pay attention to things that bugged her. Paying attention made her good at her job.

The easiest and most sensible thing for her to do would be to take the train down to D.C. and talk with Marcus. She toyed with that idea for a minute.

Screw it.

Any time she spent more than two seconds with that man, it took the metaphorical equivalent of a *Silkwood* shower to get over it. Besides, her grandfather always said there were more ways to kill a cat than by choking it with cream.

She opened a new browser window, pulled up the Southwest Airlines site, and looked for a nonstop flight from Philly to Denver. She smiled and selected the most expensive travel package. *You can pay for this, too, motherfucker.* Then she sent a quick email to Dan to let him know that she was heading out to Colorado tomorrow to look into Andy's ill-fated Aspen skiing holiday. She'd let him draw his own conclusions from that, but she made certain he had her overnight contact information in case anything concerning their daughter cropped up during her absence.

Her cell phone vibrated from its nest atop a stack of folders. She picked it up. It was a text message. She clicked on the view icon and smiled when the message displayed. It was from Julia.

> Survived the return trip and am safely back in my room. Not even raining here. Neglected to tell you that I leave on Sunday for two weeks in Europe. Any chance you'll be in New York before then? Dinner was lovely. Julia

Evan felt almost giddy. It was ridiculous. She knew she was flirting with disaster. She sat back and closed her eyes, remembering how it felt when Julia touched her. Against her better judgment, she lifted the phone, hit the reply button, and began to type.

> The spirit is willing, but the flesh is weak. How about Friday night? I can take the train and be there by dinnertime. Evan

68

She hit send, then turned off her computer and desk lamp and sat in the dark, holding her phone. It was absurd and surreal. The two of them made no sense. They had to be the worst combination since some moron mixed Grey Goose with Spam and called it an Atkins martini.

Her phone vibrated again. It felt hot against her palm.

> We'll consider it a (non) date. Call me Friday to work out logistics. Julia

She smiled. Maybe she was still young enough to work *and* whack off.

Chapter 10

On Thursday afternoon, Evan sat at a small table in Aspen's famed Woody Creek Tavern. She was working on a pint of Doggie Style Amber and wondering what you had to do to get a job naming beers. She thought she'd probably be pretty good at it. She was aware that people were staring at her. Correction: They were staring at her companion. She looked up at his handsome face.

Steve Kilgore was a five-year veteran of the Highlands Ski Patrol, and he had been the one who found Tom Sheridan's body behind a stand of trees near the Steeplechase run at Loge Peak. Kilgore looked like he had been ripped from the cover of a glossy vacation brochure—sandy-haired, bronzed, and fit. Evan thought his name should be Dirk, Brick, or Rock. Something else. Something butcher than Steve. She wondered what the average tenure was for one of these guys, and if their insurance policies paid for the gallons of bleach they must all use on their teeth.

He had been flirting with her ever since they sat down. *Christ.* She felt old enough to be his mother. Judging by the looks he kept getting from the plasticized dowagers at other tables, she didn't suppose he viewed their age difference as much of an obstacle. These guys were like Olympian gods out here, and they knew it. But Evan had an agenda, and it sure didn't involve letting Steve plant a ski anywhere near her bunny slope.

"So." She met his eyes. They were almost teal in color. She

thought about Julia. *God.* Did all genetically perfect human beings have blue eyes? "You said you were the first person to see Mr. Sheridan after his accident?"

"That's right." He popped a tortilla chip loaded with guacamole into his mouth.

"Did you notice anything unusual?"

He chewed. "You mean, other than the fact that he was dead?"

Evan sighed. This was going to be a long conversation. "Yeah. Other than that."

He thought about it. "No. Not really." He reached for another chip. "Well, maybe one thing."

"What?"

"He had G-wax on his skis." Steve shrugged. "I thought that was odd, considering where we found him."

"G-wax?"

"Yeah. It's a green-colored wax that you use when you're skiing the G-Zone—or the north-facing slopes."

"And this was odd?"

"Yeah. Sheridan was skiing on the edge of the Y-Zone. The snow is nowhere near as cold there. He wouldn't have needed green wax."

Evan thought about that. Julia had said that Sheridan had been an indifferent skier. "Did you tell anyone about this observation?"

"No. I didn't think it really mattered." He shrugged and reached for another chip. "He was plainly an amateur. The skis didn't even release when he fell."

"What do you mean?"

"He still had one ski attached when I found him. In fact, that's *how* I found him—the end of the ski was sticking up out of the snow that had fallen overnight."

"What kind of skis was he using?"

He raised an eyebrow. "K2 Apaches."

That didn't really mean much to Evan, but then, she wasn't much of a skier. "And that was odd? I mean, since he was plainly such an amateur?"

He drained his beer. "I'd say so. You generally don't strap on

71

high-dollar skis with the wrong bindings." He saw their server across the room and held up his empty glass. "But I heard he was pretty toasted on the ride up there, so probably he was just drunk and careless." He looked at her. "It happens a lot more than you realize. Only the high-profile accidents make the evening news."

"Where did you hear that he was drunk? That wasn't in any of the news reports I read."

He shrugged. "I heard it from the guy who took him up on the snowcat. Sheridan and some other dude were pretty obnoxious on the ride." He leaned toward her. "It's a pretty exhilarating view. If you're up for it, I'd be happy to take you there."

Yeah. I just bet you would. She ignored his offer. "There was another guy with Sheridan? Nobody mentioned that in any of the coverage."

Steve sighed and sat back against his chair. "That's what Gene said."

"Does this Gene still work here?"

He nodded. "Yeah. I suppose you wanna talk to him?" He smiled at her. "I can make that happen."

Evan was surprised by his offer. "You can?"

"Sure." He gestured toward the bar. "He's standing right over there."

She turned in her seat and looked across the crowded room to a tall, skinny man in a bright red Columbia jacket. He was leaning up against the bar, paying for what looked like a take-out order. This was shaping up to be her lucky day.

Gene looked like a modern-day caricature of Ichabod Crane. Clearly, the ski resorts didn't apply the same runway-ready standards to their heavy equipment operators. She turned back to Steve, whose eyes were fixed on her chest. She stifled an expletive.

"Would you do the honors?" She hesitated and forced herself to soften her tone. "I'd really be grateful."

He raised a sandy eyebrow before climbing to his feet. "Sure."

Gene Simmons—Evan couldn't get over *that* irony—was more than helpful. Not only did he rescue her from the amorous clutches of Steve, he offered to ferry her up to Loge Peak so she could look around. He was working the afternoon shift anyway, and he insisted that it was no trouble to let her ride along. The mountain didn't actually open for skiing until November, but she decided it couldn't hurt to make the trek to the ridge and see firsthand where Tom Sheridan took his fatal nosedive. Her appointment with the Pitkin County coroner's assistant wasn't until three, so she had plenty of time to scope out the site.

Gene was mostly silent on the ride up. He responded to the majority of her questions in monosyllables. He stood silently next to her as she looked over the stand of pine trees where the ski patrol had found Sheridan's body. It was a desolate spot, far beyond the in-bounds runs. The air was thinner. She shivered as she thought about Sheridan lying there for two days.

"Steve said that some of the other passengers you carried up to the summit that day complained about how obnoxious Mr. Sheridan was."

Her companion nodded.

"Was he drunk?"

Gene shrugged. "I can't say. I didn't really see him." He jerked his head to indicate the snowcat. "The skiers ride in a car that's towed behind me."

"But you heard people talking about it when you dropped them off at the summit?"

"That's right."

"What did they say?"

He looked at her. "That they were loud and rude."

"They?"

"Yeah."

Evan bit back her impatience. "Who was with him?"

Gene shrugged again.

"Was it another man? A woman?" She paused. "A St. Bernard?"

He looked at her again. This time with amusement. "A man."

"Did you see him? Do you remember anything about him?"

"Not really. He was garbed up, carrying his skis. Didn't see his face."

"Tall? Short?"

Gene thought about it. "Tall. Looked fit, from what I recall."

"Anything else?"

"Not really. He had nice skis."

"Skis?" Evan sighed. Simmons remembered *nothing* about the man with Sheridan, but remembered what kind of equipment he was carrying.

"Yeah. Apaches."

"Apaches?" Steve had said that Sheridan was wearing Apache skis when Steve found his body. Correction: He was wearing *one* Apache ski.

"Are you sure it was the *other* man carrying the Apache skis?"

"Yeah. I noticed them because my son had just bought a pair." He shook his head. "They cost like a thousand bucks. Crazy, if you ask me."

Evan kicked at a clod of snow with the toe of her boot. *What the fuck?* How the hell did Aspen law enforcement miss that piece of data?

"Did you notice what kind of skis Mr. Sheridan was carrying?"

Simmons shrugged. "Nope."

"But he was carrying skis?"

"Yeah. Everybody who rode up on that trip was."

"You mean that sometimes, people make the trek up here and don't ski back down?"

"Sure. Sometimes, people just want to hike from here to the summit. Then they ride back down later."

Evan looked at the stand of scrubby pines again. She felt like something was poking her in the gut. The same thing that had poked at her last night, as she sat in the dark after reading all the news accounts of Sheridan's accident. *Marcus.* Somehow, it all came back to Marcus. *That motherfucker.* She couldn't avoid talking with him now. She glanced at her watch. Then she looked up at Gene.

"Got time to run me back down?"

He looked surprised. "That's it? You done already?"

She nodded. "Yeah. I'm done."

He turned and headed back toward the snowcat. As Evan trudged along behind him, she hoped her words wouldn't end up being prophetic.

The Pitkin County coroner's assistant wasn't a lot of help. She was a cranky forty-something with a bad dye job, an attitude, and a pronounced case of post-nasal drip. She made it clear that it was a burden for her to even discuss the Sheridan case. Fortunately for Evan, the records had not been sealed.

Sheridan's autopsy revealed that the congressman died from blunt head trauma, not exposure. His BAC levels were extremely high, but the coroner's office was quick to say that these results were inconclusive since the samples had been collected two days postmortem. Sheridan's chief of staff had arrived on the scene the same day his body was discovered and taken custody of the remains. Margo arrived a day later. In accordance with Indian tradition, Margo had Sheridan's corpse cremated in Colorado and returned to Maryland with his ashes.

"Anything more you can tell me about his injuries?" Evan asked.

The assistant sniffed and flipped through a stack of pages in a manila folder. "He sustained fractures to his skull and cervical vertebrae, and a lacerated spinal cord."

God. "Does the file say *where* he sustained the skull fracture?"

The assistant sighed and reopened the folder. "Yes. Sheridan sustained a linear fracture of the posterior left parietal region."

Evan smiled at her. "Translation?"

She stared back for a moment. Then she pointed to the area above the back of her own left ear. "Right along here."

"So he got hit on the *back* of the head?"

"That's right." She sniffed again.

"Does that seem at all odd?"

"Odd?" The assistant closed the folder. She seemed exasperated. "In what way?"

Evan shrugged. "Well, I'm not a practitioner of this particular sport, but it seems that an out-of-bounds skier would be likelier to hit a pine tree head on."

75

"Not necessarily. He had a broken tibia, too. He could have lost control when his binding didn't release, and then contacted the tree while he was tumbling."

"I guess that's possible."

The assistant looked at her watch. "Is there anything else you need?" She pulled a gnarled-looking Kleenex out of her coat pocket and swabbed at her nose.

Evan toyed with the idea of hanging around and asking inane questions for another twenty minutes, just to piss the bitch off. "No. Thank you. You've been *very* helpful."

The woman nodded and walked off, leaving Evan standing alone in the small, dingy sitting room off the main foyer of the building. *Jesus. Must be her time of the month.* She left the building and headed toward her rental car and the two-hour drive back to Denver.

Chapter 11

Evan was beginning to wonder if Tom Sheridan's death was really an accident. But what she couldn't come up with was any kind of motive. At least, none that held water. It appeared pretty clear to her that at the time of his death, Sheridan was poised to give up his congressional career and join ranks with other like-minded environmental zealots. And who would bother knocking off a Greenpeace activist? They were about as threatening as a fart in a stiff wind. None of it made any sense. And she didn't want to end up looking like one of those pathetic conspiracy theorists who clogged up chatrooms on the Internet.

She knew she had to talk with Marcus—find out what he was doing in Aspen that weekend. And she needed to talk with Andy Townsend again. If for no other reason than he might be useful to parse whatever line of bullshit she was certain Marcus would feed her.

Thinking about Andy made her think about Julia. But that wasn't saying much. Ever since their unsettling encounter on Wednesday night, her thoughts hadn't strayed very far from the tall beauty.

She looked at her watch. She'd be at Penn Station soon. Then she was meeting Julia at her Upper East Side apartment. They were going to dinner. And on Sunday, Julia would leave for London. She'd be gone for two weeks. *Two weeks.* That should give Evan enough time to get her head out of her ass and think straight. And she needed to think straight. She was losing focus—and losing focus made her miss things. She couldn't afford that. Not now.

Just like she couldn't afford to get any more involved with Townsend's wife. It was insane.

Yeah. Insane. She shook her head. And that's precisely why she was riding this goddamn train right into the middle of her worst nightmare. *Shit.* She might as well be swinging a lariat and yelling "yee-ha!" She knew she was headed toward disaster, but she could no more stop herself than Sheridan could stop his last, wild ride into that stand of pine trees on top of Aspen Mountain.

Evan thought about Julia. She thought about what it felt like to touch her. She closed her eyes and tried to ignore the way her heart was beginning to race. *Christ.* She was like a horny adolescent in the throes of her first crush. For once, she was glad that Stevie wasn't around to witness her agitation. She'd bust her in about two seconds. Stevie was quick that way. She was like Dan.

She understood now that Dan was playing her—that he knew Julia would be too tempting a morsel for her to resist. Julia was the bait Dan dangled in front of her to keep her moving forward on this case. As pissed off as that made her, she had to hand it to him. So far, his little scheme was working like a charm.

A crackly loudspeaker roared to life, and Evan jumped. A garbled voice with a thick New Jersey accent announced that they'd be pulling into Penn Station in five minutes. She sighed and flexed her fingers a few times to try and get her hands to stop shaking.

She pulled the slip of paper with Julia's address written on it out of her jacket pocket and stared at it again, hoping that somehow, what it said might have changed in the ten minutes since she'd last looked at it. Nope. It still read 71 East 71st St.—right smack in the middle of New York's Gold Coast. She shook her head as she shoved the scrap of paper back into her pocket. It was like Julia, she thought, to give her the 71st St. address—ignoring the more celebrated main entrance on Park Avenue. So many things about Julia didn't fit—especially, her interest in Evan.

The car lurched and groaned as the train pulled to a stop at its platform. All around her people stood up and collected their newspapers and laptops.

Toast, she thought, as she continued to sit and look out the grimy window at the beehive cluster of activity that was Penn Station on a Friday night. *I'm fucking toast.*

Julia opened the door to her luxury twelfth-floor apartment and stood there, framed in the back-lighted opening like one of Botticelli's models. Except Julia had darker hair . . . and, regrettably, she wasn't standing on a clamshell in the nude. Instead, her feet were planted on polished marble tiles that probably had been imported from Carrara, back when this building had been constructed, in the early 1930s. Evan stood there without speaking, holding the small slip of paper with Julia's address written on it out in front of her like a placard.

"You have *got* to be kidding me with this," she said.

Julia looked amused. She shifted her weight and leaned against the massive door.

"With what?"

Evan dropped her arm. "Seriously. *This* is where you live?"

Julia cast a quick look over her shoulder at the interior of the apartment. "Apparently. But, in fact, I spend more time in my office than I do here."

Evan made no effort to enter the residence. Julia seemed to accept the curious standoff without question. Another minute passed while they stared at each other. Julia was casually dressed in faded jeans and a striped boat-neck sweater. She looked like a J. Crew ad.

"Do I need to take my shoes off?" Evan finally asked.

Julia rolled her eyes and glanced down at her feet. "Not unless you're wearing cleats."

"No. I generally reserve those for game days."

"That's right," Julia said, smiling and meeting Evan's eyes. "And we agreed not to play games, didn't we?"

Evan thought about that. Right now, their agreement

seemed like a bad idea. A *very* bad idea. Julia looked amazing in the subdued light of the hallway. But then, Julia would look amazing in any light—or in no light. That last thought made Evan feel even more awkward and flustered, and she didn't think that was possible.

"Yes, we did. And right now, I'm thinking that arrangement wasn't one of my better ideas."

Julia leaned her head against the doorframe. "Well, why don't you come inside, and we'll discuss the pros and cons of renegotiating?"

Evan sighed. "Before I do, there is one thing I have to ask you."

Julia looked slightly wary. "Okay."

Evan smiled at her. "What's it like to run into Vera Wang at the trash compactor?"

Julia threw her head back and laughed out loud. Then she grabbed Evan by the arm and yanked her through the doorway. "Get in here, you idiot."

Julia's apartment was small, by Park Avenue standards, but it was elegant and tastefully furnished. She explained that her grandparents had purchased the single-level, three-bedroom residence when they moved the firm's offices from Boston to New York in 1935. Through the years, the Donne family had retained the coveted piece of real estate, which now sat right in the center of the nation's most expensive zip code. Julia had lived here with Andy, before he became governor of Delaware. And it was here that she'd had her ill-fated one-night stand with Margo Sheridan.

Evan tried not to think about that as she stood in Julia's living room, admiring the tall windows and beautiful pieces of framed artwork.

"Are these all originals?" she asked, indicating a long wall lined with paintings.

Julia nodded. "I can't take credit for them. My grandmother was the collector. She had quite a good eye, as it turns out."

Evan walked over to the paintings and peered at a block-letter signature in the lower left corner of a large canvas. *Corot. Jesus.* She turned to Julia. "You think?"

Julia seemed embarrassed. "Like I said, I can't take any credit for these. Gramma was great friends with Electra Havemeyer. They bought many things together during their travels in Europe. Eventually, this collection will go to the Met, where it belongs."

"Eventually?" Evan asked.

Julia shrugged. "It doesn't belong to me. My parents still own it, *and* everything else in here." She met Evan's eyes. "So you see, I'm really just a tenant."

"A squatter?"

Julia smiled. "More or less."

Evan raised an eyebrow. "Pretty high-class squatting."

"Believe me when I tell you that these trappings don't take much of the sting out of the job description."

"So why do you keep doing it?"

Julia looked at her. "I've been asking myself that same question."

"And?"

She slowly shook her head and looked away. "I don't know. There's just so much noise surrounding it all."

"Noise?"

She nodded. "Noise. Like voices—all shouting different things at the same time. Andy. My parents. Marcus. The firm." She met Evan's eyes. "You."

Evan hesitated. "What does your own voice say?"

"Ah, that's the million-dollar question, isn't it?" She shrugged. "I don't know. I can't hear it over the noise."

Evan wasn't sure how to respond. "Maybe I need to stop talking, then."

Julia stepped toward her. Her blue eyes filled up Evan's plane of vision. "Maybe." The single word hung in the small space between them.

Evan knew the next move was hers to make. She made it.

When they separated, they were both breathing unevenly. Julia rested her forehead against Evan's. "This isn't in our rule book." Her voice sounded shaky.

Evan closed her eyes and pretended for a moment that this wasn't a titanic mistake. Julia's long body felt warm and strong. Her skin smelled like lavender. It was all making her feel dizzy. "I suck at rules."

Julia laughed and tugged her closer. "I guess I do, too."

Evan moved in to provide another example of her disregard for rules when, someplace inside the apartment, a clock began to strike. The succession of notes rang out like blows from a hammer. *Stop*, they said. *This isn't right. The two of you aren't right.*

She dropped her arms and stepped back.

Julia looked confused. "What is it?"

Evan shook her head. "I can't. We shouldn't."

After a moment, Julia laid a hand against the side of Evan's face.

"Not now . . . or not *ever*?" she asked.

Evan closed her eyes and leaned into Julia's hand. "I don't know." She turned her head and kissed Julia's warm palm. "You know I'm right."

Julia didn't respond. After a moment, she withdrew her hand and straightened her sweater. "How about we have some dinner, then? And you can fill me in on your trip to Aspen."

Evan felt like a colossal fool—a *horny*, colossal fool. "Great," she said, trying to sound upbeat. "What do you feel like?"

Julia chewed the inside of her cheek and didn't respond.

Christ. Evan knew she was blushing. "I guess I walked right into that one."

"It's okay." Julia smiled. "I'm actually way ahead of you. I already have dinner here for us."

"You cooked?" Evan asked, amazed.

Julia turned and headed toward her kitchen. "Nope. I don't cook—remember? I got take-out. *Great* take-out."

Evan followed her. "Really?"

Julia nodded. "Like dim sum?"

Things were looking up. "I *love* dim sum."

"I had a feeling you might." Julia opened the door to a tall, stainless-steel wine fridge and withdrew a bottle. "Café Evergreen's are the *best*. I got us a grand assortment."

Evan perched on a high stool. "Well slap my ass and call me Sally. Maybe we have a few things in common, after all."

Julia smiled as she handed her the bottle and a corkscrew. "Here's something else we have in common."

Evan examined the wine—a Seghesio. *Nice.* She looked up. Julia was watching her. Evan wasn't used to seeing her expression so unveiled. "What?"

Julia shook her head. "It's nothing. Open the wine, and we'll eat. Then maybe later, when we've had a chance to relax, we can reconsider the parameters of our relationship."

Evan removed the foil from the top of the wine. "Okay. But I've gotta warn you. It's pretty hard to get me to change my mind."

"I hope so." Julia gave her a look that made her toes curl up inside her shoes. "I love a challenge."

Evan was glad she was already sitting down. It was going to be a long evening.

"Tell me what you'll be doing in London," Evan said.

They had finished their meal, and were relaxing in one of the apartment's smaller rooms, enjoying the last of the wine. This room was more modestly appointed. A wood fire burned in a limestone fireplace, and Evan wondered who got tasked with the job of hauling those perfectly cut logs up to the twelfth floor.

Julia sat back against the sofa cushions. Evan noticed that she was shoeless, and that she wasn't wearing any jewelry—not even a watch. But then, Evan noticed everything about her.

"We're thinking about acquiring a smaller firm there. One that specializes in nonfiction and literary monographs. They do a fair amount of business in e-books. I'll be meeting with their board and discussing possibilities. I'll also be spending a few days in France with my parents. They live there now."

"Has your father retired from the firm?" Evan asked.

Julia shrugged. "In fact, but not in deed. He still sits on the board, and is very quick to offer up bits of unsolicited, sage advice. Particularly when he thinks I'm about to do something that will royally fuck up the family business."

Evan laughed.

Julia eyed her with amusement. "You find that idea entertaining?"

"Not at all," Evan said. "I find your turn of phrase entertaining."

Julia rolled her eyes.

"No, really," Evan said. "It's like hearing Jackie O. say something like 'cocksucker.' There's just no way to prepare for it."

"You're nuts."

Evan looked around the elegant room with its twelve-foot ceiling. Then she looked back at the beautiful woman seated next to her on a sofa that had probably cost a king's ransom.

"I'd have to agree with that."

They stared at each other.

Julia waved a hand to take in their surroundings. "This doesn't define me, you know."

"It doesn't?"

"No, it doesn't. But I fear you'll never know that because you won't allow yourself the chance to see beyond it."

Evan wasn't sure how to respond to that—especially since it was the truth.

She stared across the room at a paneled wall lined with family portraits. Generations of Donnes peered back at her from their gilded frames. She thought about her own family history, and the few faded Polaroid images she had of her mother, snapshots taken on birthdays or the occasional Christmas holiday at her grandfather's house in Chadds Ford. Phantom images that had been captured before her mother stuffed her clothes and her CDs into a duffle bag and disappeared in the middle of the night, leaving a teenaged Evan to wake up alone in their southwest Philly row house.

Yeah. She had a little trouble seeing beyond that.

And right now, she had the more immediate problem of seeing beyond Julia, who had managed to shift closer to her on the sofa.

Evan turned and met her eyes. "This is a mistake." She didn't recognize her own voice. It sounded weak and unfamiliar.

Julia held Evan's face with warm hands. "Probably."

"We shouldn't."

Julia nodded and pulled her closer. "But we're going to, anyway."

They kissed, and Evan gave up her fight. She knew that they were going to go everywhere, and nowhere. It couldn't end any way but badly, but she knew that neither of them had the sense or inclination to stop it. She pushed Julia back onto the sofa cushions.

"I should go."

It was a little before five in the morning, and Evan knew that if she left now, she could make it to Penn Station in time to catch the six-ten back to Philly.

Beside her, Julia stretched and craned her head to look at the bedside clock. Then she dropped her head back onto the pillow and yawned. "It's barely five. Why not try to rest for a few hours?"

They hadn't done much sleeping.

"Don't you need to get packed for your trip?"

"Yes, I do. But I hadn't planned on starting before sunrise." Julia sounded amused—and sleepy.

Evan sighed.

"What's the matter?"

"Nothing." Evan looked at her. Even in the half-light of the bedroom, she could make out the blue of her eyes. "Everything."

Julia took a moment to reply. "You want to run." It wasn't a question.

"Don't you?"

"Not from you."

Evan was silent.

Julia sighed, half sat up, and leaned on an elbow. "I thought I would tell you this over breakfast, but I see now that I might not get the chance."

Evan looked at her. "Tell me what?"

85

"I talked with Andy yesterday. I told him that I was filing for divorce."

Evan was stunned. "You did?"

"Yes, I did. I don't see any reason to put it off any longer."

"How did he react?"

Julia shook her head. "He was angry—tried to talk me out of it. Said it was a mistake—that we just needed more time together." She met Evan's eyes. "Then I asked him if that meant he was planning to stop seeing Maya. Suddenly, he didn't have anything to say." She sighed. "I told him he could have the two weeks while I'm away to figure out how he wants to manage the news. I'll file when I get back. I'm going to tell my parents when I see them next week. That's partly why I'm taking this trip."

Evan didn't know what to say. She stared down at the tangle of bedclothes that covered their naked bodies. She knew she should be happy about this development, but she wasn't. All she felt was fear.

"Does this scare you?"

Evan looked at her. She had no reason to deny it. "Yes."

Julia rested a hand on Evan's forearm. "Why?"

Evan shrugged. "Because I'm a chickenshit who now has no place to hide."

Julia looked surprised. "I didn't expect you to be so honest."

"How did you think I'd react?"

"I wasn't sure. Part of me thought it might guarantee that I'd never see you again."

"Is that what you want?" Evan hoped she didn't sound as pathetic as she felt.

Julia smiled at her. "No. That's the *last* thing I want."

Evan released the breath she'd been holding. "What's the first?"

Julia moved closer. Her breath was hot against Evan's neck. "I was kind of hoping you'd help me figure that out."

Jesus. Julia's mouth slid down along her shoulder.

"I still think this is a bad idea," Evan whispered, as she dropped back on the bed and pulled Julia on top of her.

She felt Julia smile against her chest. "I'm sure you'll find ways to prove it."

They didn't talk much after that. There really wasn't anything more to say.

Chapter 12

Evan finally made it to Penn Station at two-twenty that afternoon. She was in line at the ticket window when her cell phone
vibrated. She smiled as she pulled it out of her jacket pocket,
thinking it was probably Julia. The readout surprised her. The text
was from Marcus.

> Got your message about meeting. Am now in New York,
> but will be back in DC on Tuesday. Can meet you then, if
> you don't mind coming down. Dan told me about Aspen
> trip. Eager to hear details. Marcus.

She tapped her phone against her thigh as the ticket line
inched forward. *Where was he?* Even if she told him she was in
New York, too, there was no guarantee he'd be free to meet with
her. She took a quick look down at her clothes. They weren't too
rumpled. She could pass. And she'd had a shower. She smiled.
Well. *They'd* had a shower. Sighing, she stepped out of line and
walked over to a metal bench. She sat down and texted him back.
Five minutes later, her phone vibrated again.

> Am free until 4:30. Can you meet me in 20 min. at The
> Houndstooth?

The Houndstooth was a gastropub about two blocks up 8th

Avenue. Anyone who was in and out of Penn Station a lot knew about it. She glanced up at the digital display over the ticket counter. She could walk there, meet with him, and be back in time to catch the four-thirty Keystone Express to Philadelphia. With luck, she'd be home by seven. She sighed. Might as well get it over with. And it would save her a trip to D.C. on Tuesday. She texted back that she'd be there. As she was zipping her phone back into the interior pocket of her jacket, it vibrated again. She pulled it out and looked at it in confusion. Another text message. And this time, from Julia. She smiled when she read it.

Got proof?

Shaking her head, she picked up her messenger bag and headed for the 8th Avenue exit.

Evan sat down in a booth at the restaurant, and less than five minutes later, Marcus walked in. She noticed him right away. He was remarkable because he was unremarkable. Not really tall, but not short. Not thin, but not paunchy. Not yet old, but not young either.

He stood inside the door for a moment, squinting into the bar area while his eyes adjusted to the lower light. If she took him out of his goddamn Ben Silver suit and tossed him into a crowd, he would completely disappear. He sure didn't look like a kingmaker. Yet he was. She'd need more than the fingers on half-a-dozen hands to count up the members of congress who owed their Capitol Hill addresses to him. But he had never shown any interest in running a presidential campaign—until now.

She hated guys like Marcus. They used anything to get their drones elected, and they never let a little thing like the truth get in the way. She had worked for him once before, about six years ago, on a senatorial campaign in Pennsylvania. It had been a dirty race in a mid-year election. One of the most contentious in recent history. Control of the U.S. Senate was up for grabs, and the stakes were high. The sitting president wanted a Republican in the seat, and, thanks to Dan, the party hired Evan to vet their candidate—a former steel worker turned state representative and one-time mayor of Johnstown. On the surface, the guy was a textbook candidate. Nice family. Wife and three kids. Lived in a modest house overlooking the Conemaugh River in Cambria County. Taught Sunday school at the local Methodist Church. Coached little league baseball. And, as Evan later found out, liked to stay up into the wee hours trolling Internet chat rooms for teenage boys.

Somehow, that last tidbit never made it into the candidate's bio sheet. Marcus made certain of that. His man got elected, of course. And by the time the sitting senator got busted for soliciting sex from a minor in the workout room of a Cincinnati hotel, Marcus had moved on to his next campaign. His job wasn't to pass judgment on the morality of his candidates—it was just to get them elected. And he was very good at his job.

Evan didn't speak to Dan for six months after that episode. And she swore she'd never work for Marcus again. Yet, here she was, meeting the scumbag to discuss his latest *cause célèbre*.

She really needed to clean up her act.

Marcus finally saw her and waved a bony hand in her direction. For some reason, his long fingers always unsettled her. She suppressed a mental shiver as he approached her table and slid into the booth opposite her.

"You must walk fast," he said, checking his watch. "I was only fifteen minutes away."

She shrugged. "I didn't want to waste any time. I've got a train to catch."

"Going back to Philadelphia?"

She nodded.

"What brought you to New York?"

She met his level gaze. "Research."

He chuckled. "Research?" He sat back and unbuttoned his jacket. "And how is Mrs. Townsend? Are you finding her a willing subject?"

"Fuck you."

"Now, now." He gestured toward their approaching server. "Let's at least place our order before we start slinging expletives around."

Evan ordered a club soda with lime. Marcus asked for a dirty martini. Evan found that strangely appropriate.

"It's not like you to mix business with pleasure," Marcus said, as the server walked off. "The senator might not take it well if he finds out you're fucking his wife."

Evan saw no reason to argue with him. "He'd have to roll off Margo Sheridan to notice."

Marcus was unfazed. "He wouldn't be the first one, now, would he?"

Evan leaned back. She felt her blood pressure rising, but she was determined not to let this motherfucker see it. "You're such a bright guy, Marcus. I wonder why you felt the need to hire me, if you already knew so much."

He spread his hands before lacing his fingers together. "You never know. Even the best of us miss things from time to time."

"Like who killed Tom Sheridan?"

He was silent for a moment. His dark eyes gave nothing away. "Tom Sheridan died in a skiing accident."

"That's right," Evan said. "You were there, weren't you? Funny how none of the news accounts mentioned that."

The waiter arrived and deposited their drinks.

Marcus stirred his martini with its long cocktail pick and ate one of the fat olives. "Is this what you wanted to talk with me about? My Aspen trip?"

"Why were you there? You don't seem much like the skiing type."

"I had business."

"With?"

He met her gaze, but didn't reply.

"Okay." Evan pulled a folder from her messenger bag. She took out a copy of the photo she'd found at the Yale alumni site and pushed it across the table toward him. "So your *business* just happened to take you to the same bar where Sheridan was carousing with a bunch of his frat brothers—including Andy Townsend?"

Marcus glanced at the photo, then sat back and smiled at her. "You've always been good at ferreting out the details. You're just a bit more challenged when it comes to connecting the dots."

Asshole. "Well, then, it's fortunate that I have you to illuminate me."

"I can assure you that there was nothing sinister in my presence there. The party approached me about Andy."

"Andy?"

He ate the second olive from his drink. "That's right. If you'll recall, this was the same weekend that Art Jacobsen announced his decision not to seek reelection to his senate seat in Delaware. The party had already been eyeing Andy as an up-and-comer. It seemed like a good opportunity to feel him out and see if he had any aspirations beyond the governor's mansion in Dover."

Evan was still unconvinced. "Dover is an hour away from your office on M Street. Why fly all the way to Aspen to have your little fireside chat?"

He shook his head. "You really need to do your homework, Evan. I'm from Denver. Ring any bells for you?"

Christ. She *had* forgotten that. Marcus studied at Colorado with Josef Korbel. He was in the same freaking class with Condi Rice. She closed her eyes. And that whole thing about Jacobsen. She'd missed that connection, too. This was exactly what she feared would happen if she allowed herself to get distracted.

"What's wrong?" Marcus asked without a trace of warmth. "Not enough sleep last night?"

Evan opened her eyes and glared at him. He'd made her look ridiculous, and he knew it. He was all but smirking at her.

"You really ought to just take the plunge and get yourself laid, Marcus. It's a whole lot better than fantasizing about what the rest of us do."

He laughed and drained his martini. "Classy comeback. Is that a bit of South Philly humor?"

"Fuck you."

92

He shook his head and looked her over. "Can't dress you up *or* take you out. I wonder how long it will take Ms. Donne to reach that same conclusion?"

Evan had two choices. She could retake control of this conversation, or she could toss the rest of her drink in his face and leave. As tempting as the second alternative was, she opted to try the first.

"Do any skiing in college?"

He narrowed his eyes. "What?"

"Something wrong with your hearing? You went to Denver. It's pretty famous for its Alpine ski teams. You ever participate in any of that?"

He didn't reply. She noticed that he was tapping his middle finger against the stem of his empty martini glass. He'd be a shitty card player.

"Come on, Marcus. It will take me all of two seconds to find out."

"I did a little skiing."

"Keep up with it?"

"Where are you going with this?"

"According to you, I'm not going anyplace. I'm just trying to make polite conversation."

He sighed. "Yes. I still ski from time to time."

"Do any skiing the weekend you were in Aspen with Andy and Tom Sheridan?"

He was stabbing random patterns into his napkin with the cocktail pick. "I wasn't in Aspen for recreational purposes."

"So, that's a no?"

He dropped the pick. "That's a no." He folded his arms. "Are you accusing me of something?"

"Not yet."

He exhaled. "Be careful, Evan."

"Is that a threat?"

"No, it's a warning." His voice was cold. "Stay on task. You were hired to investigate Andy—not me, and not Tom Sheridan."

She nodded. "I'll keep that in mind."

"See that you do." He pulled his wallet out of an interior pocket and extracted a twenty. Then he looked around the bar and waved their server over. "I'm not going to authorize reimbursement for any more of these random fact-finding junkets of yours, either. Leave the SVU crap alone and do your job." He met her eyes. "This isn't Pennsylvania."

Evan sat back against the padded booth. "That reminds me. How's your favorite pedophile doing? Should be out of the joint by now. He gonna run for national office again?"

Marcus refused to take the bait. "Just remember what I said."

She smiled sweetly at him. "I remember everything you say, Marcus."

He got up. "I trust you can find your way back to the station?"

She nodded.

"Great. I'll tell Dan about our conversation."

"You do that."

He turned and left the bar.

Evan continued to sit there. The waiter approached the table and asked if she wanted anything else.

"Yeah. Bring me a Goose gimlet." He nodded and turned back toward the bar. "Make it a double," Evan called after him.

Why the fuck not? She wasn't driving.

And she wasn't going anyplace, either.

Chapter 13

Waiting around wasn't one of Evan's strong suits.

Fortunately, it didn't look like a busy night, so she guessed she wouldn't have to cool her heels for very long. Stopping by here on her way home from the train station had been an impulse. She didn't usually give in to impulses, but lately, she'd been doing it a lot. Too much. She needed to get her focus back. And she needed to be honest about what she was up to.

She sat back on the hard bench and tried to enjoy the dim light and the quiet.

It always smelled like varnish in here. She thought it funny, how that was the thing that resonated the most for her about this place—the smell. She found it comforting. She associated it with calm and order. Maybe that was what made her such a compulsive housekeeper. Her mother would laugh at that. She had never been much for keeping things tidy. The carnage of her personal life was proof of that.

Evan hated chaos. She lived her life to avoid it, and she did her best to insulate her daughter from it. Yet now, she felt like she was drowning in it.

Next to her, a wooden door opened and closed.

Showtime.

She got up, entered the small booth, and closed the door behind her. After a moment, a slide in the wall moved back.

"May the Lord be in our hearts and minds."

Evan was silent. After a respectful interval, the voice on the other side of the screen continued. "How long has it been since your last confession?"

Evan sighed. "About fourteen years, give or take."

The man on the other side of the wall chuckled. "Hello, Evan."

"Hello, Tim."

"It *has* been a while. What brings you here tonight?"

She sighed again. "Beats me. I was passing by and saw that your lights were still on."

He laughed. "How is Stephanie faring at school?"

Evan smiled. "She's doing just fine. She seems to have made the adjustment better than I have."

The shadow on the other side of the screen shifted. "You know, we could always just meet for coffee, like normal people."

"No. I kinda like this arrangement. It's easier for me to talk when I don't have to stare at your uniform."

"So this is an official visit?"

"I don't know. You tell me."

"Okay. Confess to something, and I'll let you know if it qualifies."

Evan laughed. "If you weren't a priest, I'd have to marry you."

"If you weren't a lesbian, I'd be hard-pressed not to take you up on it."

She sighed. "I think I'm in trouble, Tim."

"How so?"

"I'm working on something for Dan. A job. And it's getting . . . complicated." She paused. "I think I'm fucking up, and I don't seem to be able to stop myself."

"Is this about you and Dan?"

"No."

"So it's about the work?"

"Yes and no."

"Another person?"

"Yeah."

Tim sighed. "Evan. I left my secret decoder ring in my other suit. Why not just tell me what you're concerned about?"

She stayed silent.

"Evangeline?"

"Yeah, okay." Tim could get away with calling her that. They'd been friends since they were kids.

She tapped her fingers against her knees. She had come here to tell him, so why was she dragging her feet? "So there's this woman. And she's married. To the guy I'm vetting."

"I see. And you're attracted to her?"

That was putting it mildly. "You might say that."

Tim was silent for a moment. "Is she gay?"

"Yes, but she's not out. Her situation is . . . complicated."

Tim sighed. "You mean, it's complicated by something *other* than the fact that she's married, she's gay, and you're getting paid to investigate her husband?"

"Yeah. I know that sounds ridiculous."

"No, Evan. It sounds *delusional*. You have better sense than this. What's going on?"

She shook her head. "I don't know. I can't make myself walk away from it."

"Are you in love with her?"

Evan felt like the walls of the tiny booth were closing in on her.

She was tempted to get up and leave. She had been crazy to come here. It was just another example of how out of control she was.

"Evan?" She could see Tim's shadow. He was leaning closer to the screen.

"I'm here." She thought about his question. "I don't know. Maybe." She waved a hand in frustration. "How in the hell would I know? I've never been 'in love' before."

She heard Tim exhale. "Describe to me how you feel when you think about her."

That was easy. "Sick. Pathetic. Like something is eating its way through my insides. Like I'm the world's biggest chump."

Tim laughed.

"I'm glad you find this so amusing." His calmness was bugging the piss out of her.

97

"I'm sorry, Evan. It's just that there's no act of contrition that's going to get you out of this one."

"What's that supposed to mean?" She was losing patience with this whole enterprise.

"I think you know what it means. The question is what you decide to do about it."

"How the hell do I figure that out?"

"The same way you figure everything else out. You get more information, and you try to make the best choices you can."

She sighed. "I don't think I *have* any choices."

"You're wrong. There are always choices. Sometimes, we just refuse to see them because we fear them—or because they're masquerading as something else."

"Great. That's just what I wanted to hear."

"Sorry, girlfriend. That's the best I've got."

She sighed. "Life had to be simpler in the days when all you had to do was buy a few indulgences."

He laughed. "Well, if it makes you feel better, you can always make a generous donation to our building fund."

"I'm sure. What kind of scam are you running now?"

"We need a new gym floor in the community center."

"Right." She stood up. "I'll see what I can do." She hesitated, and then laid the palm of her hand flat against the screen. "Thanks, Tim."

"You've got good instincts. Use them. Listen to your heart. Don't confuse it with the noise coming from any other . . . extremities."

Evan was startled by his use of the word "noise." She had the freakish sense that coming here had been the right thing to do, after all.

"I'll say a prayer for you after you've gone," Tim said.

"I know you will." She opened the small paneled door and walked out without looking back.

No matter how many times Evan tried to puzzle it out, she couldn't understand why someone like Julia Donne would allow herself to be taken in by a transparent social climber like

Andrew Townsend. After Julia's admission that she thought Andy was an arrogant prick when she first met him at Yale, Evan was even more curious about what had shaped up to be a name-only marriage.

Dan finally relented and coughed up the name of Andy's pre-Julia inamorata: Tessa Bronfman.

Now *she* had been quite a catch—one of several distant heirs to the Seagrams fortune, back in the days before Edgar Jr. squandered most of the family money on ill-fated Hollywood ventures.

After some digging, Evan was able to locate Bronfman—now Tessa Kaplan, Esq.—in Jacksonville, Florida, where she worked for a nonprofit focused on Jewish advocacy issues. It took a little persuading, but she finally was able to convince Ms. Kaplan to meet with her to discuss her former relationship with Townsend.

Evan didn't hesitate to pull out the big guns when she had to, and Kaplan reluctantly consented to the meeting when Evan suggested that the party would be *very* grateful for her cooperation. Evan had done her homework—the Jewish Advocacy Center was staring down its nose at hefty cuts in federal funding. Hinting that Kaplan's project might find a coveted spot in the party's pork barrel went a long way toward lowering roadblocks to conversation.

Thank god the dictates of *noblesse oblige* were still alive and well—at least among the privileged alumni of the nation's Ivies.

The day after returning from New York, Evan hopped a Southwest flight bound for Jacksonville. Kaplan agreed to meet her for a late lunch at Bistro AIX, an upscale restaurant located in the city's historic San Marco district.

Evan really hated Florida, but right now, she welcomed its blue skies and warmer temperatures. Philadelphia had been cold and spitting snow when she left. As she walked from the airport terminal to the rental car lot, she found herself regretting her decision to fly back to Pennsylvania that same evening. A nice stroll along the beach might go a long way toward lifting her spirits.

She left the airport campus and attempted to merge onto I-95 toward Daytona Beach. A shirtless asshole in one of those topless

Barbie Jeeps cut her off. Evan could hear strains of ABBA's "Dancing Queen" trailing in his wake as he blew past her.

Fucking Florida.

No. Going back tonight was the right decision.

The self-styled historic district of San Marco was comprised of several blocks of refurbished storefronts that housed quirky retail shops and designer eateries. She eventually found a place to park her rental car and walked two blocks to the restaurant.

Since she was a few minutes early, she had time to relax and look over the menu offerings at Bistro AIX while she waited on her lunch date.

Nice. Marcus should choke on this one. The least expensive lunch entrée clocked in at thirty-five dollars. Maybe she should order a couple of appetizers, too.

She looked up as she sensed someone approaching her table. Tessa Kaplan. Evan recognized her from her Facebook profile and the photos posted on her firm's website.

The tall blonde was predictably great-looking, but that was hardly a surprise. Andy was nothing if not consistent. Tessa. Julia. Margo. All beautiful. All powerful. All women with unquestionable pedigrees.

Tessa stopped at Evan's table.

"Excuse me. Are you Evan Reed?"

Evan stood up to shake her hand. "Yes. You must be Tessa Kaplan."

She smiled. "I am. I hope you haven't been waiting too long. I got stuck in a traffic jam on the Acosta Bridge."

Evan noticed that she had traces of a unique accent—probably tied to her childhood in Toronto.

"No problem." Evan gestured to the other chair. "I've only been here a few minutes."

Tessa pulled out the chair and sat down. She pushed her long hair back from her face and stole a quick glance at her watch.

"In a hurry?" Evan asked.

Tessa met her eyes. She looked embarrassed. "I'm sorry. That was rude of me."

Evan didn't say anything.

"I guess you can tell that this makes me a bit uncomfortable. I haven't had any kind of contact with Andy since college. More than fifteen years ago now."

"I understand. But I appreciate your willingness to talk with me."

Tessa lowered her eyes. "I wouldn't exactly classify it as willingness."

Evan was intrigued. "No. I understand that. And I'm sorry that this is uncomfortable for you."

Tessa ran her fingertips back and forth across a crease in the tablecloth. "Uncomfortable doesn't even begin to characterize it."

Evan was about to invite her to elaborate when their server approached to take their beverage orders and offer painstaking detail about the lunch specials. He droned on for so long that Evan's annoyance dissolved into incredulity. How the fuck could someone memorize that much minutiae about so many different dishes? And what person in their right mind would *ever* order Carp in Fennel Sauce?

After they gave him their drink orders and he drifted off, Evan and Tessa looked at each other with blank expressions. Then they started laughing.

"Eat here often?" Evan prompted.

Tessa shook her head. "No, and I don't think I'll make a habit of it."

"Well . . . I passed a rib joint about two miles back that way," she jerked her thumb in the general direction of the St. Johns River, "if you want to make a break for it."

Tessa seemed more relaxed. "No, we're here. Let's just man up and make the best of it."

"Man up?"

Tessa shrugged and smiled. "Too many years living in the shadow of Daytona."

Evan nodded. "Well, if we're going to stay here and brave the menu, why not go ahead and dispatch the difficult part of our conversation, too?"

Tessa stared at her for a moment. "Okay. What would you like to know?"

"For starters, how long did you date Andrew Townsend?"

"Nearly two years—most of my freshman and sophomore years."

"How did you meet?"

She sighed. Evan noticed that she was again trying to smooth the crease in the tablecloth. "I ran indoor track and field, and Andy introduced himself to me one day after I ran some heats at Coxe Cage. He was sitting in the stands with some frat brothers who were dating other girls on the team."

"And you liked him?"

She laughed. "What wasn't to like? He was funny, smart, and handsome. After I showered, we went out to a bar on Audubon Street." She shrugged. "We were pretty much inseparable after that."

"Was it serious?"

She met Evan's eyes. "He thought so. He was always talking about what we'd do after graduation—where we'd live. Even then, he was interested in politics—not a life that had much appeal for me."

"No? What did have appeal for you?"

"Nonprofit work, mostly. I knew I wanted to go to law school, and I had no desire to stay in the Northeast. But Andy was determined to go to Columbia and work in New York."

"Why?"

"Because he had contacts there. He already had feelers out for post-graduate employment with DuPont. I think his father had connections in their capital investments division. I, on the other hand, was determined to get as far away from New York as possible."

"May I ask why?"

She sighed. "I didn't have the best relationship with my father in those days, and I certainly didn't want to park myself under his thumb in Manhattan." She laughed. It sounded bitter to Evan. "Andy, on the other hand, got along *great* with Daddy. The two of them were like co-conspirators, trying to arrange everything for me—from where I'd spend my junior year abroad, to where I'd go to law school."

"Did you talk with him about this?"

"Of course I did. We had countless arguments about it. Some of them publicly. I broke up with him half-a-dozen times, but he always convinced me to give him another chance."

"How did he manage that?"

She laughed again. "Do you *know* him, Ms. Reed?"

Evan nodded. "I've met him."

"Well, believe me when I tell you that he can be very compelling when he's going after something he wants."

"And he wanted you?"

She thought about that. "At first, I thought he did."

Evan waited.

"Then it became clear to me that what he really wanted was unobstructed access to Daddy's money."

The server arrived and deposited their drinks—two tall glasses of iced tea, garnished with sprigs of mint that were the size of magnolia leaves. Evan tried to sip from her glass without poking out an eye.

"So, how did you finally break it off?"

"I told him it was over—for about the twentieth time—and for about a week, I thought he'd finally given it up. Then, one Saturday night, he showed up at a club in New Haven when I was out with someone new, and he made a terrible scene. He'd been drinking, and he started shouting at me—telling me I could never leave him. When I told him to back off and stay away from me, he snapped. Called me a whore and said I'd be sorry for leading him on. The guy I was out with tried to intervene, but Andy punched him and made a grab for me. It took two bouncers to subdue him and get him out of there." She stopped and raised a hand to her forehead. "It was horrible—surreal. He was like someone I didn't know. I thought about pressing charges, but I knew my father would never forgive me. So I did the next best thing."

"Which was?"

She shrugged. "I transferred to Princeton."

"Jesus."

Tessa met Evan's eyes. "I'm sorry. I'm sure this isn't what you wanted to hear."

"No," Evan agreed. "It isn't. But we need to know about it just the same."

"Well, in any case," Tessa pulled the tree-sized sprig of mint from her glass of tea and dropped it onto the table, "I don't expect you'd have to worry about that kind of behavior from him now."

Evan raised an eyebrow. "What makes you say that?"

Tessa waved a hand. "He married some publishing heiress, didn't he?" She smiled. "So he doesn't have any reason to resort to such desperate behavior now." She leaned forward and lowered her voice. "You don't have to worry about me disclosing any of this and ruining his chances at getting the nomination. I have my own life now, and I have *no* desire to reenter the family limelight. No one in Jacksonville knows who I am, and I'd really like to keep it that way."

Evan nodded sadly. "I was pretty certain you'd say precisely that."

Tessa looked confused for a moment. "Isn't that what you wanted to hear? Isn't that why you came down here to meet with me?"

"Yes," Evan said with resignation. "That's *exactly* why I'm here."

Chapter 14

Margo Sheridan worked out of a small suite of offices located in a massive, multiuse complex in Reston, Virginia—one of the nation's first planned communities. Evan thought that Reston was a lot like the fictional town of Stepford: suspiciously glossy and perfect.

Just like Margo.

On paper, she was one of the chief liaisons between India's Tata Group and the various Clean Development Mechanism brokers that had sprung up in the wake of the 1997 Kyoto Protocol. Her primary job was to oversee the buying and selling of Certified Emission Reductions, or carbon credits, for various Tata subsidiaries. This was the practice that allowed Tata and its tentacled companies to build international goodwill by investing in green energy initiatives in emerging markets. In exchange for their good deeds, they were permitted to skirt compliance with emission caps in their own business ventures, making millions of dollars in the process.

Vocal critics of this Kyoto loophole, led by Greenpeace, suggested that conglomerates like Tata used the CDM swaps as a smoke and mirrors routine to avoid cutting back the whopping CO_2 emissions that were being belched into the atmosphere at their own primary manufacturing centers. With enough green window dressing, they argued, no one would really care that Tata was rapidly turning India into the new China—especially when it came to breathable air. Other people argued that CO_2 levels were CO_2 levels, regardless of where on the planet you lived, and that multinational organizations like Tata were helping the planet more than they were hurting it.

Whichever side of the debate you came down on, one thing was certain: Trading carbon credits was now big business, and *lots* of people were cashing in on the profits.

It wasn't clear how much of a stumbling block Tom Sheridan had become to Margo's meteoric rise within the Tata Steel Group's multifaceted organization, but Evan guessed that her marriage to a Greenpeace apologist didn't play too well with the boys in Mumbai.

Like Tom Sheridan, Andy Townsend had become a mouthpiece for the green energy movement, but, unlike Sheridan, Townsend owed more of his political success to his financial backers in the private sector. More than one purveyor of nuclear power showed up on his campaign finance reports. Although she couldn't prove it yet, Evan would've bet her grandfather's farm on the likelihood that Tata, in the guise of some one or other of its subsidiaries, had helped to swell Townsend's campaign war chest.

On a personal level, she had to admit to being more than mildly interested in meeting Margo. She was Andy's longtime lover—and Julia's ex-lover. That second fact resonated for her almost more than the first. If she told herself the truth, she'd admit to being consumed by curiosity about the woman who had finally coaxed Julia into cracking the door of her high-class closet.

"Get more information," Tim had told her.

Well. Here she was, headed for the Reston Town Center, about to do just that.

She needed to talk with Margo, anyway, so why not kill two birds with one stone? Maybe some pieces of this puzzle would fall into place if she met the woman who Andy and Julia both found too enticing to resist.

Who was she kidding? She really just needed to see what kind of woman Julia found attractive. Correction: What *other* kind of woman, because she knew that, apart from their gender, she and the former Maya Jindal had next to nothing in common.

Dan had brought her up to speed on the few details he knew about Maya's background, and Evan's buddy, Ben Rush, a P.I. with fingers in every government pie, had helped her fill in the rest of the blanks. Ben was a wiretap specialist who frequently did "off the books" freelance work for the justice department.

According to Ben, Maya had been raised in a small town in the Punjab Province of British India, near the Pakistan border. Her family owned several lucrative pine oil and sugar processing plants, and were able to send each of their five daughters abroad for their educations. Three of Maya's sisters studied at Oxford. Maya and her youngest sibling, Chandra, attended Yale, their father's alma mater.

Maya's father was a distant relative of the Jindal Steel Jindals, but he fell out of favor with the family when he married a Sunni Muslim from Lahore. To make matters worse, his bride was the daughter of a Pakistan Steel executive—Jindal Steel's lead competitor in the expanding global market.

Maya spent most summers during her college years working for her maternal grandfather at his corporate office in Karachi. Her duties there were unclear. Evan didn't find much of a paper trail. Ben told Evan the only way to get a beat on the details of *that* piece of missing history would be to travel to Pakistan—not something the U.S. Department of State would be likely to sanction, and not something Evan could expect Marcus to pay for.

Maya met Andy and Dan during their junior year abroad in Jordan.

After graduating from Yale with a degree in economics, Maya got her MBA at Columbia. She started working as a lobbyist for Corus America right before the Dutch conglomerate got snapped up by the Tata Group in 2007. Since then, she had gravitated toward managing the firm's international CER programs. She spent lots of time traveling, dividing her time between her home office in Reston and the firm's corporate offices in London and Mumbai.

She also appeared to spend a fair amount of time with Andy at his house in Old New Castle.

She was a person of interest at the State Department because of her business and family connections with Pakistan. Two of her uncles were on the government's watch list because of their suspected involvement with Lashkar-e-Taiba—the Pakistani terrorist group implicated in the 2008 Mumbai bombings. Maya's own murky connections to Pakistan Steel made her file folder at the State Department a bit thicker, too. According to Liz Burke, her involvement with a sitting U.S. senator raised more than a few eyebrows in the administration.

The more Evan learned about Maya/Margo, the more persuaded she became that Andy Townsend's back-door dalliance with her would prove to be the Achilles' heel Dan had hoped to avoid. Julia's decision to file for divorce would quickly peel back the veneer of respectability and stability that Andy wore like a mantle. Once the media got hold of it, America's Eagle Scout would soon be stripped of a few merit badges. Could he survive? Would exposure of his longtime sexual relationship with a Muslim who had questionable ties to militant political factions within Pakistan lead to his political undoing?

Not her problem.

She hopped off the bus at Reston Town Center Station, and made the short walk to Margo's office complex at One Freedom Square.

Margo was running behind.

She rounded the corner of the long hallway that led to her office too quickly and snagged the sleeve of her blouse on a broken branch projecting from an overgrown ficus tree. She tugged her sleeve free and looked at it in disdain. *That's the same, sodded limb I tagged yesterday. They need to prune this damn thing—or move it.* She glanced at her watch. Ten minutes late. She was sure the woman would be waiting for her. Andy said she was a stickler for being on time.

She felt agitated. Anxious. And that wasn't normal for her. She didn't like being dominated by her emotions. It clouded her judgment. It was too easy to make mistakes. And she couldn't afford any more sophomoric mistakes. Not now. She'd already exhausted her quotient.

All last night, she had tried to parse possible explanations for Evan Reed's reticence about this encounter. Explanations apart from the obvious ones that accounted for why the woman wanted to meet with her in the first place.

Evan Reed. Her reputation certainly preceded her. She was a legend on Capitol Hill. Anyone inside the beltway who was even tangentially involved in national politics knew about her. Many had endured her scrutiny, few had survived unscathed.

Margo had known that today's meeting would happen. She had known it the moment Andy told her that Dan had hired Evan Reed to do his background check. The only question in her mind had been how long it would take the tenacious little dust-buster to follow the breadcrumbs that led straight to her doorstep. Margo had guessed not long.

As usual, she had been right.

Andy had said that his meeting with the mother of Dan's daughter that day in Old New Castle had been a surprise. She was younger than he expected. And better looking. A *lot* better looking. He was unprepared for that. He knew that Evan Reed was gay, so he assumed she would conform to the usual stereotypes.

He had shared his impressions with Margo later that night, as they lay in bed together. "She's not really mannish at all—kind of hot, actually."

Margo was incredulous. "What did you expect? That she'd show up dressed in flannel and hip waders?"

He shrugged.

She rolled her eyes at him. Men were so predictable. They were reliably dense and literal. "Just like me, and your sainted wife, I suppose?" she asked him with a raised eyebrow.

She saw a stunned expression on his face. "Julia isn't gay," he said.

"Really?" she replied. "Could've fooled me."

Andy colored. "That was an aberration."

"Right. You keep telling yourself that."

He ran a hand up the inside of her thigh. "And you're not gay either."

She didn't reply. It was easier to let him believe what he chose. What was and wasn't true about her didn't really matter—it wouldn't change anything.

The door to her private office was open and, inside, she could see a woman standing near the windows that overlooked the plaza below. Margo entered the room, and the woman turned around.

Andy was right. She *was* attractive—in a Jodie Foster, girl-next-door kind of way. She still had a leather messenger bag slung over her shoulder. So, Margo hoped that meant that she hadn't been waiting too long. She looked harmless, but Margo knew she was anything but.

"Ms. Reed?" Margo approached her and held out her hand. "I'm Margo Sheridan. I hope you haven't been waiting long."

Evan Reed smiled as they shook hands. It made her look even more girlish. Margo guessed she was somewhere in her late thirties. She knew from Andy that her daughter was a teenager. "About ten minutes. Not long." Her voice was low. Sexy. "Please call me Evan. And thank you for agreeing to meet with me."

"My pleasure." Margo gestured toward a sitting area. "Would you like to sit down?"

"Thanks." Evan walked over to a pair of matching leather wing chairs, sat in one, and crossed her legs. She straightened the crease in her gray trouser leg with the fingers of her right hand. Margo noticed that her nails were short, but well cared for. "I can appreciate that this meeting might be awkward for you, so I'm thinking it might be useful just to acknowledge that, before we begin our conversation."

Margo sat down opposite her. "On the contrary. I've been looking forward to meeting you. You have quite a reputation in Washington."

Evan gave her an amused look. "Really? That statement covers a lot of ground."

"In this case, I was talking about your *professional* reputation."
Margo paused. "But it is true that your other . . . interests . . . are
somewhat legendary."

Evan laughed. "Legendary? Damn. I need to raise my rates."

Margo smiled. "You don't seem surprised."

Evan's gray eyes met hers. "Hell no. Nothing about this town
surprises me."

"It seems you're in the right line of work, then."

Evan rested both hands on the arms of her chair. She looked
perfectly composed, but Margo suspected that she wasn't. "It's a
job."

Margo was intrigued. "Are you saying that you don't really
enjoy getting paid to pick through the flotsam of other people's
lives? I would find it fascinating."

Evan stared at her a moment. "It has its compensations."

"So I've heard."

Evan shifted in her seat and re-crossed her legs. "Is there
something you'd like to share with the rest of the class, Ms.
Sheridan? I'm not sure I'm following your train of thought."

"Aren't you? I thought I was being rather unsubtle."

Evan narrowed her eyes. "How about we reboot this conversation? I can promise you that any lingering curiosity you might
have about *my* private life is misplaced, and not worth your
time."

Margo smiled. "Don't be so modest."

Evan ran a hand through her short, blonde hair. Her agitation
was starting to show. She stared out the window for a moment.
Then she sighed and met Margo's eyes. "It's clear that we're talking
on several levels. Why not just cut to the chase?"

"Meaning?" Margo asked, surprised.

"Meaning, let's play trade."

"Trade?"

"Yeah. *Trade.* It's a game kids play. I put something out
there—something you want. And *you* put something out there.
Then, we trade."

Margo was intrigued. "You mean we swap information?"

Evan gave her a slow smile. "For starters."

Margo sensed that she was losing control of their interview. "How do we play?"

"You seem inclined to want to ask *me* questions. Here's your chance."

Margo sat back. "All right."

Why not? She was positive that Evan already knew what she needed to know about *her*. Why not satisfy a little of her own curiosity? She gave her an appraising look and didn't attempt to conceal her appreciation. "So, tell me, is Julia still great in the sack?"

She thought she saw a nerve twitch in Evan's cheek, but, otherwise, she had no visible response to the question. "News certainly travels fast. I'm amazed at how well-informed you are."

Margo noticed that Evan made no attempt to deny her inference. She chuckled. "Andy's not as oblivious as you might think." She leaned forward and touched Evan on the knee. "He'll never agree to the divorce. He won't let her go."

Evan stared at the spot where Margo's hand still rested on her leg. Margo withdrew it, and Evan looked up and met her eyes. "He will, or he won't. That's between Andy and Julia. I have no part in it."

"Don't you?"

"What do you mean?"

Margo laughed. "You're either lying, or charmingly obtuse. I don't think it's a happy coincidence that dear Julia suddenly wants her freedom. Do you?"

Evan chewed the inside of her cheek. "While we're on the subject of happy coincidences—your husband's untimely death certainly made things simpler for you and the aspiring senator."

Margo felt her cheeks warm. "Are you suggesting that Tom's death wasn't an accident?"

Evan raised an eyebrow. "Oh my. Is that what I did? I thought I was just making an observation."

Shit. That was stupid. She needed to calm down.

Evan leaned forward. "There's only one way you could be privy to so much information, *Maya*. Tell me about your relationship with Marcus."

"What are you talking about?" Margo asked, stunned.

"You. Andy. Marcus. Your perverse little troika. You're up to your shapely eyebrows in something. Just what kind of twisted angle are you working? And why drag me into the middle of it all if Marcus already knew about you and Andy, and about Tom's *accident?*"

They stared at each other in silence. The seconds ticked by.

"Marcus underestimates you."

Evan smiled. "But you won't, will you?"

Margo stood up. "I think we're finished here."

Evan sighed. "Too bad. We didn't even get to the good stuff."

"That's all right. It turns out you don't really have anything I want to trade for."

Evan stood up too. "I'll take that as a compliment."

Margo turned and walked toward the door. "Enjoy your romp with Julia. It won't last long."

Evan gave her a thin smile and extended her hand. Margo shook it briefly. Then Evan left the office and disappeared down the hallway. Margo shut the door and leaned her back against it. She closed her eyes. *Bollocks.*

Everything had just got a lot more complicated.

She walked over to her desk and unlocked a drawer, then pulled her cell phone out of her bag and punched in a code. She sat down when the connection went through, and the phone on the other end started to ring. It was going to be a difficult conversation.

Evan was trembling with rage when she stopped in the plaza outside Margo's office building.

Jesus H. fucking *Christ.* She made herself sit down on a low wall overlooking a fountain. She needed to compose herself. *What the hell was that about?* It sure hadn't gone the way she had thought it would. And *this* was the woman Julia slept with? God.

She made Liz Burke look like Little Bo Peep. No wonder Julia was horrified.

Margo Sheridan. She certainly was . . . *exotic*. Sexy. Alluring. And dangerous—like a cobra. It was clear that she knew how to use her charms.

Evan was more persuaded than ever that Andy was a dupe— a rube. A pawn of some kind.

But what was the connection between Margo and Marcus? There *had* to be one. How else would she have known about Evan's relationship with Julia?

Relationship. *Christ*. She shook her head to try and clear it.

Yeah. That's what it was, all right. She'd taken care of that. She was in it with both feet, now. What was it that Margo had said to her when she was leaving? *It won't last long?* Just a parting shot—she knew that. But it had found its mark—hitting her dead-on, right where she was most vulnerable.

Back in Chadds Ford that evening, Evan sat in her grandfather's Bank of England chair and tried to work. She was making lists, sorting through everything she knew, and most of what she suspected, about the players in this bizarre little costume drama. She had filled half a legal pad with names—each with neat rows of facts, observations, and caveats listed beneath them. She was trying to make sense of it. Look for connections. Isolate things that didn't fit.

So far, she was being a hell of a lot more productive draining a large tumbler of Belvedere. She couldn't concentrate. Her thoughts kept wandering. She glanced again at her watch. *Five hours ahead.* Julia was probably in bed by now. It would be ridiculous to call. She'd only been gone two days. *Christ.* She was pathetic.

She forced herself to look at her lists again and tapped her pen in agitation.

"It won't last long." Margo's parting salvo bounced around inside her head like somber chords from a requiem.

Maybe it was over already.

She took another swig from her glass. The ice was nearly gone.

All that remained was an opaque little wedge that rocked and fought to remain afloat. *Give it up*, she wanted to tell it. Embrace your fate. There are worse ways to wind up than becoming one with a glass of Belvedere. She should know.

She had no one but herself to blame. She knew better. She knew better, and she did it anyway. Just like Julia said she would.

Maybe she was like her mother after all. Always putting the cart of pleasure before the tired old horse that would somehow have to haul all the leftover debris back to the barn.

Clean up your mess. That was her mantra for Stevie. Her best parental advice. The accumulated wisdom of her entire, shopworn life, rolled up into one, four-word platitude.

Well, she had one hell of a mess now. And no fucking clue about how to clean it up.

Her phone rang. She stared at it for a moment like it was an unfamiliar object that had just dropped from the sky. It rang again. She picked it up.

"Reed."

"Evan? It's Dan."

She sighed. He knew about her meeting with Margo earlier. He was probably calling to fire her ass.

"Hello, Dan. I bet I can guess why you're calling."

"No." He sounded distressed. "Listen . . . I need to let you know that . . . Evan, there's been an accident."

She sat up too quickly, and vodka sloshed out of her glass. It ran down her forearm and dripped onto her notepad, blurring the lines between her tidy, printed rows.

"What happened? Is it Stevie?" Her heart was hammering.

"No. Not Stevie." He paused. "It's Julia. In London. A car accident. She was on her way back to her apartment after a late meeting."

Evan's head started to tingle. White spots flashed before her eyes, and she thought for a moment that she might faint. She grabbed the edge of the desk with her free hand. "Is she—?"

"No." Dan cut her off. "No. She's in a hospital. Injured, but alive. Her driver was killed, though." He paused. "I'm sorry. I knew you'd want to know."

Jesus. Alive? She's alive. "How badly was she hurt?"

"I don't know any more details."

"Andy?"

"Andy is in L.A. He's the one who called me."

Evan's head was still reeling. She needed to think. She needed to plan.

"Is he going to London?" Of course he would go. She was his fucking *wife*.

"I don't know. I think things are . . . strained between the two of them right now." He paused again. "He asked me to tell you."

"Why?" Who was she kidding? She knew the answer to that.

"I don't think he wanted her to be there alone. He does still care about her, whatever their other issues are."

"Her parents? They're in France . . ."

"I don't know any other details."

She waved a hand in frustration. "I've been drinking. I can't—"

"There's a flight to Heathrow that leaves at seven-fifty," Dan said. "I'll send a car for you. Just get your shit packed."

"I owe you for this."

He laughed. "Yeah. I'm a prince, all right."

"Sometimes you are."

"I'll be sure to remind you of that."

"I know you will."

"Think an eight-hour plane ride will give you enough time to sober up?"

Eight hours? Jesus. She smiled through her anxiety. "Barely."

"I'll have the driver call you, and I'll text you the name of the hospital. Now get your ass in gear."

He hung up.

She looked down at the blurry mess the vodka was making as it slowly seeped into the legal pad.

Fuck it.

She pushed back her chair and ran for the stairs.

Chapter 15

Heathrow Airport at nine in the morning on a weekday was choked with bored and weary-looking business travelers.

Evan walked toward a beefy customs agent with a handlebar moustache, who stood, akimbo, next to a row of blaze-orange stanchions. He met her eyes as she approached, then briefly lowered his gaze to take in her black messenger bag. She had been counting as she drew closer to the screening area. Customs agents appeared to be tagging every seventh passenger. By her count, she was number six. The portly man in tweed behind her, who had wheezed his way across the Atlantic, was going to have to wait just a tad longer for his next cigarette.

She took twenty minutes to reach the baggage claim, and another twenty to retrieve her suitcase and make her way to ground transportation. The air outside the terminal was heavy and dense. The sky was gunmetal gray. It wasn't raining, but it had been. Every exposed surface was wet. It was cold, too. She pulled the open edges of her jacket together and took a deep breath.

Diesel fumes.

Yeah. She was back in England.

Evan hadn't been to London for nearly two years, but she knew the city well. She'd spent a year living there as an undergraduate, studying research methods at the University of London and doing an internship at the British Museum. She had returned several years later, during a hiatus from graduate school, for a six-week stay with her former host family. She was pregnant by that time, and her accompanying feelings of confusion and desperation led her to seek out the only place besides her grandfather's farm where she ever felt grounded.

Her host parents, Michael and Susan Shore, were a steady and practical couple who ran an upscale hostel that overlooked the Thames, near Hampton Court. Evan had been one of four international university students who billeted with them for a year, during college, and she was the only one who hailed from the U.S.

The Shore family lived modestly. Their two teenaged children were vivacious and irreverent, but happy and devoted to their parents. Evan recalled watching their familial interactions with fascination. During the first few months of her stay, she felt like a visitor from another planet, observing the curious behaviors of an alien species. Members of the Shore family *talked* with one another. They expressed interest and curiosity about each other's lives. They took their meals together. They even ate sitting down—*on chairs*.

Evan found the typical, teenaged antics of the Shore children captivating. She was mesmerized by the easy camaraderie and trust they shared with their parents. Observing them, she began to understand that there were other paradigms for how families could function. Motherhood, as Susan Shore practiced it, began to look less like a lifetime prison sentence with no promise of parole.

Evan had already decided to *have* the baby when she traveled to London to recover from the shock of discovering that she was pregnant. Her conservative Catholic values had already reared their biased heads and strong-armed her into *that* decision. The quiet and constant example set by Susan Shore convinced her, ultimately, to *keep* the baby.

So keep her, she did.

She had since been back twice, with Stevie, to visit the hostel that now loomed so large on the landscape of her emotional horizon. Stevie loved the Shore family nearly as much as Evan did and found their home to be an easy and unaffected oasis of calm in an otherwise chaotic world.

Evan was returning to London in trouble once again. She was tempted to smile at the irony. But this time, she doubted that even the wise and steady counsel of the Shore family would be enough to rescue her.

Her grandfather would have said that she was up to her ass in alligators. A colossal mess.

She didn't know any more details about Julia's condition. She didn't know if her injuries were minor or life-threatening. She didn't know if Andy or Julia's parents planned on traveling to London to be with her. She didn't know if Julia was even in a position to *want* anyone with her. And she certainly didn't know how Julia would react to her showing up uninvited, like some kind of heartsick puppy.

She only knew that it didn't make sense for her to continue to stand outside the terminal at Heathrow Airport in the cold while she deliberated. She needed to keep moving—even if it was in the wrong direction.

Normally, she would take a bus into central London and navigate her way from there. But she was in no mood to waste any more time waiting, so she hailed one of the omnipresent black cabs and gave the driver the address of the Royal Marsden Hospital in Chelsea. He raised an eyebrow, but said nothing as he switched off his "for hire" light and hopped out to stash her suitcase in the boot of the cab. Evan noticed that he was of Indian or Pakistani descent, and that reminded her again of her fractious interaction with the former Maya Jindal.

She wondered what Maya would think about her behavior now—flying off, literally, on some ill-fated fool's errand.

She was a sap, and she knew it. But she couldn't deny her need to be there. The chips would fall where they would fall, but she needed to see Julia. She needed to see her, and she needed to touch her—just one more time, before she walked away from her for good.

The cab exited the airport and turned onto the M4. Evan

noticed that it was raining again. Fat drops hit the cab and rolled across the windows like dollops of paint.

Who was she kidding? She needed to see Julia once more—be certain that she was alive and well—before Julia could walk away from *her*. That's really what this trip was all about.

"You want to run," Julia had said the morning after they spent the night together.

Well. Here she was—traveling halfway around the globe to do just that.

The whole thing was crazy and counterintuitive, beyond sense and reason . . . vintage Evan.

The cab continued to eat up the miles as it rolled past fields and hedgerows. The rain was falling harder now. Evan stared out the window at a watery blur of green and gray, until the landscape morphed into the red brick and white-painted patchwork of towns. The driver exited the M4 and drove along narrow streets lined with houses that had mullioned windows and gauzy curtains. Lorries, buses, and cabs began to outnumber cars as they drew closer to London.

Evan's stomach growled, and she realized she hadn't eaten anything since lunchtime the day before. She'd had no appetite on the long plane ride. The vodka she'd drunk at home the night before had long since fled her system, but left her insides feeling flat and sour.

She pulled her cell phone out of her messenger bag and scrolled through her backlog of text messages until she found the last one she'd received from Julia—the one she'd sent on Monday night, after her first full day in England.

> Long, but uneventful trip. Merger talks with Waverly going well. Weather is lousy. English landscape reminds me of the cows in Chadds Ford, and one other thing I find myself missing.

Evan ran her fingers over the smooth screen of her phone, wishing she could feel the sentiment behind the letters. Wishing she could feel anything besides the fear and hopelessness that seemed to have taken up permanent residence in the pit of her stomach.

They were inside the city limits now. The hospital wasn't far away. Evan glanced at her watch and realized she needed to reset it to GMT. She pulled it off her wrist and advanced the hands five hours. Nearly eleven-thirty. Jesus. Ten hours to cross five time zones.

The driver turned onto a wide avenue lined with what looked like identical white office buildings. He slowed as they reached the center of the block and turned right into the main entrance of the imposing red brick Royal Marsden Hospital. He pulled to a stop in front of a stone entryway and half turned in his seat to face her.

"Marsden Hospital. Okay?"

Evan nodded. "Thank you."

He gestured toward the meter. £68. *Christ.*

Evan dug her credit card and a £10 note out of her bag and passed them both up to him. "I appreciate the ride. I know it was a long distance to travel."

He took the cash and the card and smiled at her. "No problem."

After he swiped the card, he hopped out of the cab and unloaded her single suitcase from the boot. Then he nodded at her, climbed back into the car, and drove off.

Evan stood there for a moment, staring up the steps at the large glass doors that led into the lobby of the hospital. She took a few deep breaths before grasping the handle of her bag and walking the final few yards of her three thousand, five hundred-mile journey.

Chapter 16

Evan's inquiry about patient Julia Donne met with blank looks and no information. She was handed off to the head sister in short order, and she fought to stifle her panic as she approached the nurse's station that was just down the hall from the reception area. The middle-aged woman who met her there looked Evan up and down, taking in the black roller bag she was pulling along behind her.

"Are you a family member?" she asked. It was more like an accusation than a question.

"Yes," Evan lied.

The sister glanced again at Evan's suitcase.

"I only just arrived from the U.S.," Evan explained. "I came straight here from the airport."

The sister looked dubious, but sighed as she rifled through a stack of charts piled on top of the counter.

"Miss Donne was discharged over an hour ago." She looked up at Evan over the rim of her wire-framed glasses. "Since you're a family member, you'll already have her home address."

Bitch. "Yes, thank you."

The sister started to turn away, but Evan stopped her. "Can you tell me anything about her condition?"

The sister looked at her without emotion. "Only that she was well enough to be discharged. Now, if you'll excuse me, I have patients to attend to."

Jesus, Evan thought. *Let's hear it for the National Health. Or maybe she just doesn't like Americans.*

"Thank you for your time." Evan turned away and walked slowly back toward the main entrance. *Great. Now I have to find her London address.*

On the other hand, she had a lot to feel good about. If Julia had been discharged, then she must not have been seriously hurt. She felt some of her anxiety subside. Exhaustion stepped forward to take up the slack.

She walked to a bench near the lobby doors, sat down, and took her cell phone out of her bag. She pulled up Julia's last text message again. Bingo. *Waverly.* She connected to the hospital's WiFi network and did a quick Internet search for publishers named Waverly in London. Only one came up: Waverly Monographs on New Oxford Street. Then she looked up the names of several florists in the vicinity.

She punched in the phone number for the publisher and waited until a sotto-voiced receptionist answered.

"Hallo," Evan said, using her best British accent. "I'm calling from Jamie Aston Flowers on Great Portland Street. We have a slew of bouquets for a Miss Julia Donne, and only just received word from Royal Marsden that she's no longer in hospital. The sister there told us we could get a delivery address from you."

"Of course," the voice on the phone said. "One moment please, and I'll get that for you straightaway." She put Evan on hold.

Score, Evan thought.

After a minute, the woman came back on the line. "Ms. Donne's residence is at Number 12 Brook Street, Mayfair."

Evan rolled her eyes. *Of course it is.*

"Thanks so much, luv," she said. "We'll get this lot straight out to her." She hung up.

Christ. Brook Street. Right in the middle of Grosvenor Square. How rich is this fucking family?

She sat there, weighing her options. She could find a hotel first, and then call Julia. She could just show up at her doorstep and hope for the best. Or she could call another cab and hightail it back to Heathrow.

The last option was sounding like the best one to her. She felt ridiculous. And exhausted. Her stomach growled again. She needed food, and she needed sleep. And then, she needed to have her head examined. She closed her eyes.

Her cell phone vibrated, and she nearly dropped it in surprise. She looked down at the display. She had an incoming text message—from Julia.

> Hello, you. Odd tidings. I was involved in a horrible hit and run accident last night. I'm shaken, but okay. Give me a call? I'm at the flat today, so don't worry about when. Don't worry about anything. Just call when you can. Love, Julia

Love, Julia?

She held the phone against her forehead. Grosvenor Square. She could take the tube and get off at Bond Street.

She stood up and walked toward the exit. When she got outside, she noticed that it had stopped raining.

As it happened, Julia's flat at Number 12 Brook Street was just a block away from the homes of Jimi Hendrix and Georg Frideric Handel. In typical fashion, the Donne family had chosen well, and Evan thought the odds were pretty good that this quirk of geography would make the market value of their small piece of real estate soar beyond all comprehension. She thought it odd that compositions as unlike as *Messiah* and "Purple Haze" had been composed in back-to-back townhouses that were separated by a measly six inches of plaster.

But that was London—a city of contradictions.

She'd opted for another cab, after all. She was too tired to drag her suitcase through the throngs of pedestrian traffic on the streets, and didn't have the stamina to wrestle it up and down the endless banks of escalators that led to and from the trains in the Underground stations.

The cab deposited her in front of Number 12, and she took the stairs from the street that led to the upstairs apartment units. Julia's family occupied Flat A, the front unit that overlooked the street. Evan saw the name *Donne* etched into a brass plate on the upstairs directory. It looked like it had been there for some time. She wondered which member of the publisher's family had originally purchased the residence.

She stopped in front of an unassuming wooden door and tried to compose herself. After standing there for a full minute, she realized that nothing in her demeanor seemed likely to improve, so she gave up and pushed the buzzer.

She heard the sound of footsteps, then the door opened, and Julia filled the narrow space.

They stood there staring at each other—like statues in some bizarre tableaux. Julia's eyes grew wide, and her jaw dropped. She looked confused. Then stunned. Evan noticed that she had a large bruise on the right side of her face, but she appeared to be all right otherwise. At least, she didn't seem to be sporting any obvious bandages or casts. She was wearing what looked like yoga pants and a loose-fitting tunic top. Even with the purple bruise covering part of her face, she looked gorgeous. Evan stole a quick glance at her feet. Barefoot. What was it about Julia and shoes?

She didn't have much time to ponder that before Julia grabbed her by the lapels of her jacket. The next thing she knew, her face was full of lavender-scented shoulder, and Julia's arms were wrapped around her and holding her tightly.

"I can't believe it. I can't believe you're *here*. Oh, my god."

Evan raised her arms and hugged her gently. She didn't want to hurt her, and she worried that Julia might have other injuries that didn't show.

"Dan called me. He said that Andy asked him to." Evan started to draw back, but Julia still held her fast. "I had to come. I would've gone crazy worrying." She turned her face into Julia's neck and inhaled. *It's her. She's alive. She's fine.*

And I feel like an idiot.

"I'm sorry to just show up like this," she said. "I should've tried to call you first—got more information about your condition."

Julia just hugged her tighter. She felt a kiss on the side of her head. "Don't be ridiculous. I was terrified. I wanted *you*. I just didn't know how to ask." She finally drew back so she could meet Evan's eyes. Her own looked glassy. "The hospital called Andy. It was an automatic, next-of-kin thing. I was unconscious when they admitted me."

Evan carefully touched the side of Julia's face. "I went there, first."

"The hospital?"

"Yeah. They told me you had just been discharged."

Julia took hold of her hand as she lowered it. "Come inside."

Evan grabbed the handle of her suitcase and pulled it behind her into the flat. Julia closed the door behind them. This place was far less spacious than the New York apartment—still elegant, but less formal. Maybe it was the scale? Or the intimacy of the smaller rooms? Evan decided that she liked it.

She smelled fresh coffee. She was tempted to keep moving and follow her nose toward the tantalizing smell. She'd now been up for twenty-one hours. She turned around to say as much, but ran right into a soft and warm wall of Julia, who pulled her close.

"Thank you. Thank you for being here."

Evan just nodded. She didn't really trust herself to speak. She figured the odds were pretty good that she'd say something stupid. So she just stood there, with her face pressed into Julia's sternum. God. Even barefoot, the woman was half a foot taller.

Evan felt Julia's mouth moving across her hair, then along the side of her face. When Julia's lips reached hers, she gave up on her clumsy attempts at caution. Julia didn't seem to mind.

They spent a couple of minutes getting reacquainted.

Evan's emotions were on overload from anxiety and exhaustion. She suspected that Julia's were about the same. They began to sway as they stood there, hanging on to each other.

Evan drew her face away. "We need to sit down." She was out of breath, and her voice sounded husky.

126

Julia pulled her close again. "I don't want to let go of you."

"You don't have to let go of me. But if we don't sit down someplace, you'll have to carry me."

She felt Julia smile. "I could do that."

"I don't doubt it."

Julia released her and stepped back. "Come on, then. I just made some coffee. Would you like some?"

Evan nodded. "That's probably a good idea. I need to stay conscious for a while longer. I still have to find a hotel."

Julia walked into the small kitchen that opened into the main living area. She turned around and looked at Evan. "Don't be ridiculous. You can stay here with me."

"Julia—" she began.

"Evan. You flew halfway around the world to be with me. So why not actually *be* with me?" Julia paused. "I want you here. Please. Stay with me."

Evan sighed. So much for best-laid plans. "All right."

Julia smiled and poured their coffee.

Evan grew suspicious. "Do you always get your way?"

"*Get* my way, or *have* my way?"

Evan rolled her eyes. "Oh, I already know the answer to *that* one." She took off her jacket and hung it on the handle of her suitcase. Then, she walked to the sofa and flopped down. Big mistake. The thing was too comfortable. She didn't see herself getting back up anytime soon. She followed suit with her hostess and kicked off her shoes.

Julia joined her and set their coffee cups down on a glass-topped coffee table.

Evan turned to Julia. The light pouring in from the front windows of the flat illuminated her blue eyes and made the purple bruise on her face look even more pronounced. She touched it gently. "Tell me what happened."

Julia leaned into Evan's hand. "It was horrible. James, my driver, was killed." She shook her head. "He has a wife—two children." She raised a hand to her mouth. "*God.*"

Evan pulled Julia into her arms. "I'm so sorry."

127

Julia relaxed against her and took a moment to compose herself. Evan was amazed at how natural it felt to hold her—almost like they'd done this hundreds of times before. She stroked Julia's long hair. It felt soft and thick, like Stevie's.

"We were on our way here from a late meeting on the South Bank," Julia said in a quiet voice. "It was a van. It came out of *nowhere* and hit our car. We skidded across the opposing lane and went over a low wall near the London Eye. The car rolled over and stopped against a tree. I was wearing my seatbelt . . . I don't know why. I think that saved me. James wasn't moving. I remember calling out to him before I lost consciousness, but the car was on its side, and I couldn't get out of my seatbelt. I guess I passed out after that. The next thing I knew, I woke up in the hospital at Chelsea. They told me James was dead—that he'd been killed instantly." She shook her head. "I was bruised, and had a concussion, but I was okay. They kept me overnight for observation. Then Marshall Waverly was kind enough to escort me back here, after I was discharged. He only just left a few minutes before you arrived."

Jesus. "What about the lorry?"

Julia shook her head. "I don't know. The driver didn't stop."

"Did the police come and talk with you?"

Julia nodded. "Yes. But I couldn't remember anything useful. It all happened so fast."

"Did you notice what color the van was? Whether or not it had any writing on it?"

"Blue? It was blue, maybe—or some other light color. I don't remember it having any writing on it, but it might have. I only saw a flash of it before it hit us."

"That's okay. Maybe there were eyewitnesses who saw something."

She felt Julia shrug. "Maybe. But it was so late in the evening—well past dark. I don't think there would have been much pedestrian traffic at that hour."

Julia sighed and shifted even closer to Evan.

Evan ran a hand gently up and down her back. "It doesn't matter. All that matters is that you're okay."

"And that you're here with me."

They sat in silence for a while, listening to the traffic on the street below the front windows. A clock ticked someplace inside the flat. The heater cut on and off. Evan knew that if she stayed in this position much longer, she'd fall asleep. Against her chest, Julia's breathing deepened. She was drifting off, too. Evan supposed that she hadn't slept much last night, either.

Their untouched cups of coffee sat cooling on the table in front of them. Evan sank further back against the fat pillows on the sofa. It felt wonderful. Julia stretched out, too—half on top of her. She was taking slow, even breaths now. Evan thought for the hundredth time about the question Tim had asked her in the confessional after she'd spent the night with Julia in New York. It pissed her off at the time, but that was because the enormity of her response shocked and scared her.

It *still* scared her. But lying to herself was a worse option than facing the truth. Even if the truth would eventually end up biting her on the ass.

She yawned and resettled her arms around Julia.

Facing the truth doesn't make you vulnerable—concealing *it does.* How many times had she told Stevie that? People got into trouble when they became too invested in keeping their secrets, secret. Maya was Andy's secret. And Marcus? God knew what he was hiding. And what about Julia? Was Evan now Julia's secret to keep?

She yawned again and closed her eyes. She couldn't really do anything about that. Not right now. All she could do was thank god that the woman now asleep on top of her was alive and safe. That's what this mixed-up trip was really all about.

Well. That and one other thing she needed to admit—at least to herself.

"I love you," she whispered into a maze of dark hair. Everything else could wait.

She was dropping off when she heard a sleepy voice beneath her mutter, "I love you, too."

Chapter 17

Evan woke up several hours later. The first thing she noticed was that the flat was nearly dark. Only a few narrow slashes of light were creeping in around the blinds on the front windows that overlooked Brook Street below. The second thing she noticed was how stiff her back was from sleeping so long in such a cramped position. The third thing she noticed was how strangely familiar it felt to have Julia draped across her like a human blanket.

Then her stomach growled. Loudly. After a few seconds, it growled again.

Julia stirred on top of her. "Is that you?"

"I'm afraid so. I'm sorry. I haven't really eaten since . . ." *When was it?* "Since sometime yesterday."

"Well, I think we need to fix that." Julia lifted her head from Evan's chest. "Don't you?"

Evan smiled. With her mussed-up hair and her sleepy blue eyes, Julia looked like a teenager.

"Are you offering to cook for me?"

"Do you really want me to?"

"I'm actually hungry enough to risk it."

Julia swatted her on the arm before sitting up. "Be careful what you wish for."

"I generally am." Evan sat up, too.

Julia yawned and ran her hands through her dark hair. "My god. How long did we sleep?"

"I don't know." Evan glanced at her watch. "About three hours?"

Julia shook her head. Then she looked at Evan and smiled again. "You make a great pillow."

"Thanks. I was just thinking the same nice thoughts about you."

Julia smiled and stood up. "Why don't we go raid the fridge and see if we can cobble together something edible?"

Evan stood up and followed her to the small, open kitchen. Julia switched on some lights along the way.

"That could work. I'm pretty good at making unlikely combinations work."

"Oh really?" Julia laughed and gave her a suggestive look. "Is this some kind of epiphany?"

Evan blushed. "That isn't really what I meant."

"I know." Julia stepped over to her and kissed her on the temple. God, the woman smelled great. "But I'll take comfort in your innocent boast, just the same."

Evan was still embarrassed. Her stomach lurched, and she suddenly remembered saying "I love you" to Julia before they fell asleep. *What a schmuck.* She wondered if Julia remembered it, too. She wondered if Julia remembered saying it back.

She was too uneasy to ask. Instead, she went to the fridge and pulled the door open. "So, whatcha got in this thing?"

Julia pulled a couple of plates out of an overhead cabinet. "I think it's your normal, Central London takeaway fare."

Evan found a bowl of Greek salad and a clear plastic box that contained flat slabs of what looked like Mediterranean pizza. Another container held some crusty, fried somethings. Evan pulled that one out and opened it. She looked up at Julia in surprise.

"This looks like pakora."

"It is. Eggplant, I think."

"But you said you hated Indian food."

Julia shrugged. "I do. *Did.*" She smiled at Evan again. "I'm trying to broaden my horizons."

Evan couldn't hide her smile. "If you develop too much of a taste for these, you'll soon be broadening more than your horizons. I have to threaten my daughter with death and dismemberment to get her to eat things that aren't batter-dipped and fried."

Julia laughed. "There's not much danger of that. I tend not to obsess about things."

"I've noticed." Evan pulled all three of the containers out of the fridge and placed them on the small bar that separated the kitchen from the sitting room. "How *do* you stay so composed?"

"Composed?"

"Well, yeah. I'd say you're pretty composed. Balanced. Moderate." Evan shrugged. "You seem so freakishly centered that I wonder sometimes why you're dabbling around with . . . *this*." She wagged a finger between them.

Julia gave her a confused look and imitated her gesture. "This?"

"Yeah. *This*. Us."

Julia rolled her eyes.

"No. Come on. Really. Why, Julia?"

"Why what? Why do I find you attractive, or why am I allowing myself to act on the fact that I find you attractive?"

"Yes."

Julia laughed, and Evan knew she probably was blushing again. It wasn't like her to be so fucking coy. She hauled up one of the padded stools and dropped down on it.

"Forgive me for being so pathetic. I blame sleep deprivation and the lingering effects of the bottle of Belvedere I killed thirty-six hours ago."

"You're not pathetic. You're adorable."

Evan covered her hot face with her hands. "Stop it. This isn't helping."

Julia went to the opposite side of the bar, leaned on it, and rested her weight on her forearms. Her face was inches away from Evan's.

"What *would* help?"

Evan dropped her hands and met Julia's eyes. Big mistake. *Jesus*. She really was in too deep. "I have no idea."

"How about we start with this?" Julia kissed her. It took a minute. When they finished, she drew back and rested her forehead against Evan's. "Then we eat something, and go to bed."

132

"Okay." She was too tired to argue—even with herself.

Julia smiled and stood up. "I'm going to heat up some of everything. Want to set the table?" She gestured to the small dining area behind them.

"Sure." Evan collected the plates and silverware and carried them to the table—mahogany, probably Regency, and probably authentic. It had four large chairs and a matching sideboard covered with framed photographs.

She picked one up and examined it. "Are these your parents?" The photo showed a very attractive elderly couple standing together in what looked like part of the Tuileries Garden in Paris.

From the kitchen, Julia craned her neck to see what Evan was looking at.

"Yes. In Paris. Where they live now."

Evan placed the photo back in its spot. "They certainly look . . . *impressive.*"

Julia chuckled. "That's a diplomatic way to describe them."

She said something else, but the sound of the microwave drowned it out.

Evan looked at the other photos—some of a much younger Julia with her parents, and some of Julia's father with other, sturdy-looking businessmen. An obvious wedding photo showed Julia and Andy looking young and happy, dressed to the nines, and posing with Julia's parents in front of City Hall in New York. One photo showed Julia and Andy on the polished wood deck of a sailboat in some exotic location. Another showed them in front of the Roman Coliseum, leaning against the back of an open sports car. A third photo had been taken on a skiing holiday. They posed with another couple, probably in Switzerland. That one caught her eye. She didn't realize that Julia was a skier, too.

"You like to ski?" she asked, picking up the photo.

Julia walked over to her, carrying a platter of steaming food and a bowl of salad. "Not so much. But Andy loves it." She set the food down. "These aren't my photos. My parents use this flat more than I do."

Evan looked at her. "You don't owe me any explanation. I know you're married, and I know that, at one time, it was a choice that worked for you."

Julia nodded and gave Evan a sad-looking smile. "I think you might be the only one who understands that."

"It only matters that you understand it." Evan started to set the photo back down when something in the picture caught her eye. *Jesus Christ.* She looked at Julia, and then she looked back at the photograph. Her hand started to shake.

This was *not* happening. It had to be some kind of perverse coincidence.

Andy was posing with one arm looped around Julia's shoulders. His other arm was wrapped around a pair of bright yellow skis. Bright yellow K2 skis with the word "Apache" stenciled across them.

Fuck. *Jesus H. fucking Christ.*

Now what?

Long after Julia had fallen asleep, Evan lay awake staring at murky patterns in the shadows on the pressed tin ceiling. It was raining again. She could hear water running along the eaves trough outside, over the bedroom windows. Brook Street was quiet. The traffic had all but subsided.

Julia slept with her head on Evan's shoulder. An arm and a leg were spread across her torso like tethers. She couldn't escape if she wanted to—and right now, she didn't want to—at least, not from Julia. The rest of this burgeoning mess? Hell. She'd lay a patch, putting all of that behind her.

She hadn't told Julia about the skis.

The truth was that she didn't know for certain if it even *meant* anything, other than underscoring the fact that Andy Townsend had expensive tastes. She took a deep breath. Julia's body rose and fell with it. *Shit.* The best example of Andy's expensive tastes now lay comatose on top of her. She didn't need any more proof of it.

But what about the goddamn skis? What if it had been *Andy* who had accompanied Tom Sheridan up to Loge Peak that day? What if it had been Andy who had swapped skis with the inebriated congressman? What if Andy's sexual relationship with Margo began *before* Tom's death? What if Tom found out about it and confronted him?

And what happened to the skis when Steve Kilgore found Tom's body? Did Margo claim them with Tom's other effects? Were they still sitting in some Pitkin County impound locker? Had they been sold at public auction?

And, more importantly, did Andy still have *his* pair of bright yellow K2s?

And what about Marcus? Why *had* he been in Aspen that weekend? Was it possible that the story he told Evan was the truth? Was he simply out there, in his home state, on a fishing expedition for the party—trying to flesh out Andy's level of interest in running for Art Jacobsen's senate seat?

Christ. It was all such a fucking quagmire, and she kept sinking deeper into it.

And there was one other thing. However it came about, Tom Sheridan's death cleared the way for Andy to launch his national political career. And Julia's recent decision to file for divorce threatened to expose his relationship with Margo—potentially derailing his presidential aspirations. That possibility shed a gruesome new light on Julia's accident. Already, the whole episode had too much of a Princess Diana ring to it to suit her. And she didn't believe in coincidences.

Jesus. Was she *really* poised to consider accusing a sitting U.S. senator of murder? It was *insane.* And if she ended up being right, what the hell would she do with the information, and how would she keep Julia safe?

She needed to talk with Dan—see if he could shed any light on the situation. Even though Dan was working for Andy, she trusted him, and she knew he'd never be involved in anything this sinister.

But what about Marcus?

She sighed.

Now, *he* was another matter. Marcus would've stepped up to

135

manage the career of fucking Ted Bundy, if the party told him he had a shot at winning.

She started when a hand slid up her arm and came to rest against her chest. She hadn't realized that Julia was awake.

"Go to sleep. Stop thrashing," Julia mumbled.

"I'm thrashing?"

"It's a preemptive request."

Julia yawned, and Evan felt warm breath against the side of her neck. She smiled. "Okay."

"Are you all right?" Julia's sleepy voice was nearly a whisper.

Evan tightened her arms around her and kissed the top of her head. "Yeah. Go back to sleep."

She closed her eyes and forced herself to concentrate on the sound of the rain until she dropped off, too.

Chapter 18

Julia was scheduled to spend three more days in London before leaving on Sunday to join her parents in Paris. She asked Evan to stay with her for the rest of her time there. Her meetings with the Waverly board were wrapping up on Friday, so that meant they could spend the evenings and all day Saturday together, sightseeing or relaxing in the flat.

Evan didn't need any arm-twisting to agree. She had already determined that she was going to do some poking around in the area where Julia's accident had taken place.

They had breakfast together in a patisserie near the flat, and then Julia took a cab to the Waverly offices on New Oxford Street. Evan walked to the Bond Street tube station and rode the Jubilee Line to Waterloo. The South Bank was bustling, but she knew that the area would have been much less congested late on a Tuesday night. Julia's dinner meeting had been at Chez Gerard, and the small French restaurant was only about a hundred yards from the Royal Festival Hall arts venue near Waterloo Bridge. It was also within spitting distance of the British Film Institute. She walked first to the BFI complex and picked up a circular to see what movies, if any, had been playing or letting out near the time of Julia's accident. The flyer indicated that two films let out at eleven, and one at eleven-twenty. Julia's accident happened a few minutes after eleven-thirty. Half-a-dozen pubs and twice as many restaurants peppered the area. Most London pubs now

137

closed at eleven, a number of late-night stragglers should have been making their way to their cars or the nearby tube station.

She walked the short distance from Chez Gerard, where the limo driver had picked Julia up, down Belvedere Road to the site of the accident, near the entrance to Jubilee Gardens. Little evidence of the fatal crash remained, except for some chalk-like scrapes on a low concrete wall, and, off the road, some ruts in the grass and deep scarring in the bark of an enormous elm tree. Evan stood there, feeling half sick as she thought about how differently this all could have come out. *Julia could have died here. Her driver did die here.*

She stepped over the wall, walked to the tree, kneeled and pressed her hand into the wide gash left by the car. This damage was all that remained to suggest that, in an instant, dozens of lives had changed forever.

"Did you know 'em?"

Evan was startled by the voice. She hadn't heard anyone approach. She stood up and turned around to see a skinny man holding a rake. *He must be a groundskeeper.*

"Yes," she said. "I do know one of them—the woman who survived."

The man shook his head. "Awful business, that." He nodded toward the tree. "Likely some sodded kids out on a bender."

"What do you mean?"

"The ones who ran 'em off the road. They didn't stop, see. Ran right out of the Shell Centre lot over there and t-boned 'em. Probably kids who had nicked a car and were out joyriding." He shook his head again. "Rammed 'em arse over tits, then high-tailed it out of here. Probably ditched the van on the other side of the river and run off on foot. They couldn't have got far."

Evan was intrigued. "Why do you think that? Did you see the accident?"

He jabbed at the loose turf with his rake. "No. Don't work down here after dark, see. But I heard that the lorry they was driving was all but done for."

"Really? Who told you that?"

138

He looked her up and down. "You sound like a Yank. Are you a copper?"

She smiled. "No. I'm just in town, visiting a friend. A good friend. The one who survived the accident." She held out a hand. "My name's Evan Reed."

He stared at her for a minute before shifting his rake to his left hand and reaching out to shake hers. "Reggie Pease."

"You work here every day, Reggie?"

He nodded. "Here, and at the London Eye." He gestured with his chin toward the huge Ferris wheel that was a landmark for tourists.

"So who told you about the lorry? Was it someone who saw what happened?"

He seemed to deliberate for a moment—like he was trying to decide how much to tell her.

"Reggie?"

He sighed. "Look. My pal Donny—he's a good sort. But his bird's a right dog's wife. Sometimes he steps out—just for a night off, see. No harm in that. Tells her he's out with his kids up in Hoxton. So he was at the pub that night, just for a little bait and switch. He was on his way back to the car park here when he saw the crash. He didn't talk to the Bizzies—couldn't let his bird know he was down here, see. So he tells me about it the next day at work."

Evan took a deep breath. "What pub, Reggie? Where was Donny that night?" She took a step closer and laid a hand on his arm. "Look, I don't want to get Donny into any trouble. But maybe somebody else saw what happened, too."

Reggie turned around and pointed back up Belvedere Road. "Ping Pong. On the Terrace."

Evan nodded. "Is Donny working today?"

Reggie shook his head. "He's off. Gone on holiday to Blackpool. Won't be back until Monday."

Fuck it. Evan dug into her messenger bag and pulled out a notepad and pen. She scribbled down her cell phone number. "If you remember anything else, or if you hear from Donny, would

139

you call me at this number? I'll be in London for two more days."

He took the slip of paper from her.

"Don't know much else," he said. But he shoved the paper into the front pocket of his shirt.

"Thanks, Reggie."

He nodded and walked back to an electric cart full of lawn implements. Evan watched him with a sinking feeling. She quickly jotted down Reggie's name and what she knew about Donny. Then she walked back up to Belvedere Road and made her way toward Waterloo Bridge and the Terrace area of Festival Hall.

Ping Pong was a bar and dim sum restaurant tucked into a corner of the Festival Terrace, near Queen Elizabeth Hall. It was on two levels, and had a large bar area that spilled out onto a concrete walkway. Evan guessed it would be jamming on nights when there was a concert in the great hall. At first glance, the place didn't seem like the sort that catered to a local clientele. She pulled open the large glass door and walked inside. It was early, but the bar area was dotted with a few lunch patrons. She sat down on a padded bench at a small table and looked around.

She knew the place was a franchise, but the decor had a pretty upscale feel—more like a teahouse than a pub. The ceiling was covered with Chinese characters. She picked up the spirits list printed on a tent card that sat on the tabletop and looked it over. Pretty limited. Four or five Asian beers—only two on draught— and a dozen or so designer cocktails. Most of those were curious, tea- or herb-infused concoctions made with indifferent liquors.

She set the card back down. Whatever Donny was coming here for, it sure wasn't the swill.

A chesty, redheaded server, wearing a tight black t-shirt with "ping pong" stenciled across the front in bright blue letters, approached her table.

She handed Evan a menu.

"Get you something to drink, luv?"

Evan took the menu and smiled at her. "Sure. My pal Donny

told me to come up here and grab a bite. He said you'd take care of me."

The server stood there tapping her pen against a leather-covered notepad.

"Donny?" She looked confused. Then she glanced out the window toward the embankment. "You mean the bloke who works at the London Eye?"

"That's right. *Donny.*"

"Oh. You'd want Lisa, then."

Sweet. "Lisa. That's right." Evan glanced at the bar. Several other black-shirted servers hung around—only one of them appeared to be doing anything. "Is she working today?"

The woman snorted. "We're *all* working today." She clicked the end of her pen. "Start of a long weekend. Look, luv, if you know what you want to drink, I'll give her your order and have her bring it over. She's not working the bar today, but we aren't that busy yet."

"Thanks. I'll have a Tiger."

"Pint?"

Evan shook her head. "Bottle." She smiled. "A bit early in the day for me."

The redhead looked her over. "I dunno. You seem like you could hold your own." She sighed and snapped her order pad closed. Evan thought she probably was pissed about losing the eighteen percent gratuity. "I'll get Lisa."

She walked off.

Evan watched her approach the bar and stop to talk with an equally chesty blonde. She began to see the appeal of the place and wondered if the food was any good. She chuckled, thinking about all the businessmen who claimed they *really* went to Hooters for the wings.

In another minute, Lisa approached her small table, carrying an open bottle of beer and a pilsner glass. She set both down in front of Evan and stood there quietly regarding her. She was a pretty girl—probably in her early twenties. She had multiple piercings in both ears. Part of a tattoo poked out above the neck-

141

line of her black t-shirt. She looked uncomfortable. She kept shifting her weight from one foot to the other.

"You must be Lisa?" Evan smiled. "I'm Evan." She poured some of the beer into her glass. "I was just talking to one of Donny's mates at the Gardens, and he told me to pop in here for a meal—said that Donny comes here a lot."

Lisa shrugged. "He comes in sometimes for a bite after his shift."

Evan nodded. "Does he ever stay until last call?"

Lisa glanced nervously toward the bar. "Look. I don't want any trouble, okay? I haven't done anything wrong—just a bit of snogging in his car. That's all. No harm in that."

Shit. She thinks his wife sent me. "Look, I'm not here about *that*. I'm here because I know Donny saw the crash that happened near the Gardens on Tuesday night. A friend of mine—a *good* friend—was in the car that got smashed up." She held Lisa's gaze. "Donny's on holiday, but I thought that maybe you were with him—that maybe you saw it, too?"

Lisa glanced again at the bar.

"Look. I've got other tables. Do you want anything to eat?"

Evan sighed. She wasn't the least bit hungry, but she needed an excuse to prolong their interview. "Sure." She handed Lisa the menu. "Pick something out for me." She smiled at her. "I trust you."

Lisa took the menu from her and stood there a moment longer. Then she gave Evan a short nod and walked off.

Evan sipped at the pale lager. For an Asian beer, it had a familiar, Western taste. She shook her head, marveling that products like this one had to sink to a level of complete blandness to succeed in the global market. She took another sip. Still, it didn't exactly *suck*. It just wasn't very unique or interesting.

She didn't know what she hoped to accomplish by trying to run down potential eyewitnesses to Julia's accident. What would she do with the information? She was certain that the London metro police were conducting their own investigation. Maybe they had contacted Donny already? Maybe they knew about Lisa, too?

Maybe Reggie was right, and the missing van belonged to some joyriding kids who were just out carousing past curfew?

Maybe she should stop pissing in other people's ponds?

But something nagged at her gut. And it wasn't this indifferent beer.

Julia.

Was it too much of a coincidence that Julia's near-fatal accident happened on the heels of her telling Andy that she was filing for divorce? It was a ridiculous proposition. A bizarre coincidence. In his twisted way, Andy loved Julia. Dan told her that, the night he called her about the accident. And Margo—she said the same thing.

Correction: Margo didn't say Andy *loved* Julia. She said Andy would never let her go.

Fuck. It still didn't make sense. She was on a fool's errand with all of this—seeing plots and conspiracies around every corner. This always happened whenever she allowed her brain to take a backseat to her emotions. She needed to quit thinking with her clit.

She shook her head and took another sip of the beer.

Hell, it wasn't her clit that was the problem—not this time. This time, it was her *heart.*

She was startled when she realized that someone had approached her table. She looked up to see Lisa standing there with a tray that held a steaming bamboo basket and some tiny bowls of sauces.

She set the assortment of items down in front of Evan. "I thought you could try this sampler—see if there's anything you like. It's got two meat and three veggie dumplings."

Evan lifted the top off the basket. Through a whirl of steam, she saw five fat dim sum in various-colored wrappers. They smelled delicious. Maybe she was a little hungry after all.

She smiled up at Lisa. "Thanks. This looks great. I'm sure it'll be plenty of food."

Lisa nodded, but continued to gaze at Evan. She was slowly rapping the empty serving tray against the outside of her leg.

"Look," she began in a quiet voice. "I *was* with him that night. We were walking to the car park—just to have a drink before heading out. Nothing wrong with that. I finished my shift, and he waited outside for me. He's a nice bloke. Comes here a lot. I don't do married men, but there's no harm in having a drink and a bit of a snog now and then, is there?"

Evan shook her head. "I told you, I'm not here about you and Donny." She hesitated. "Believe me, I know what it's like to fancy someone who's married. I'm only interested in finding out if anyone besides Donny saw the crash that night. I'm not from the police. I'm just a good friend of the woman who survived. I want to make sure someone wasn't trying to hurt her on purpose. You know what I mean?"

Lisa stared back at her for a moment before glancing over her shoulder at the bar area. The restaurant was still fairly quiet, and several of the servers were gathered around one of the wall-mounted televisions, watching replays of a soccer match. She looked back at Evan and sighed, then pulled out a bench and perched on it.

"Look. I did see it. We were right near the gardens when the car passed us. It was a silver Maybach. I remember 'cause Donny said he knew a bloke who worked on 'em, and they cost about a half-million quid. Then a lorry came out of the Shell Centre and smashed it— pushed it right across Belvedere and rolled it over the wall. We didn't go any closer. Donny said we had to get out of there. I felt *terrible* about not trying to help—especially when I heard that the man in the car died." She shook her head. "I'm glad your friend survived."

Evan nodded. "I am, too."

"That's it," Lisa continued. "That's all I know."

"Can you tell me anything about the lorry? The color? The make? Did it have any writing on it? Anything?"

"No writing. Blue. It was blue—a Caddy Van." She thought about it. "Had a Sixt sticker on the back."

"*Six?* You mean the number?"

"No—*Sixt.* S-I-X-T. A car-hire place. They have lots all over London."

"Are you sure about that?"

"Yeah. Donny and I both saw it. It happened right in front of us. After it hit the Maybach, it took a few seconds to right itself before it went on. Donny said it was done for—the engine on it was grinding."

"Did you see who was driving it? Was there more than one person in it?"

Lisa shook her head. "Didn't see anyone—no passenger, anyway. Not unless there was someone in the back."

Evan sighed.

"Lisa, you've really been a lot of help. I can't thank you enough for deciding to talk with me."

Lisa shrugged. "Tell your friend I'm sorry we didn't try to help. It was wrong. We should have."

Evan touched her on the forearm. "It's okay. The driver was killed instantly, so you couldn't have helped him, and my friend wasn't seriously hurt."

Lisa nodded. "Thanks for telling me that." She stood up. "Enjoy your lunch. I'll be back to check on you." She walked off toward the bar.

Evan picked up her chopsticks and stabbed one of the dim sum. A gooey mixture ran out around the holes and puddled on the bottom of the bamboo basket.

Fucking great. This mess just gets better and better.

She wondered how-in-the-hell many Sixt lots there were in London, and how long it would take to figure out which one of them had rented the blue van. She glanced at her watch. It was just after 6 a.m. in D.C. Ben Rush would bitch about her waking him up at this hour, but she'd make it worth his while. He had moles in every major city on the planet. Why not see what contacts he had in London?

In the meantime, she'd finish her lunch, and ask Lisa to point her in the direction of the nearest Internet café so she could do a little research of her own. She had about five hours to kill until Julia would be finished at Waverly. Why not burn up some shoe leather and see what she could find out?

145

She had a hunch, and if it panned out, she'd have a beat on where to start looking for leads.

Evan's research revealed that there were eleven Sixt locations in and around metro London. If she eliminated the two airports, that knocked it down to nine. Of the nine, only three kept vans and tipper trucks on their lots. Ben was able to tell her that two of the three locations had rented Caddy Vans that were not turned back in on Wednesday when they were due. One had been hired by a catering service when their own lorry had gone down for repairs. A private individual had rented the other van via the company's website.

Ben wasn't able to get any more information than that. She didn't know if the van in question was blue. She didn't have a name or a description of the person who picked it up. She didn't even know for sure if the van that caused the crash had been rented in London. *Hell.* She was finding out that Sixt lots were like nail salons, and there seemed to be two or three of them in every fucking hamlet in England.

But she had to start someplace, so she Googled the address and made her way across central London to the Sixt lot at Kings Cross. It was on a narrow street lined with warehouse-style buildings and a few innocuous storefronts. Most of the vehicles appeared to be stacked up inside the massive garage adjacent to the rental office, or stored at a fenced car park that was half a block away.

Evan entered the tiny reception area and tried to make a quick assessment of the two people working the counter. Which one would be likelier to dispense information she had no right to request?

It was a toss-up.

A middle-aged woman wearing a tight orange sweater looked tired and bored. She kept fussing with some stray strands of platinum hair that wouldn't stay behind her ear. She was chewing gum, and Evan could hear it cracking all the way across the small lobby. At a second window, a stocky East Asian man with a crew cut and a skinny orange tie was sorting through a stack of papers with a yellow highlighter. When he glanced up and noticed her staring at him, he stared right back, giving her a good once-over.

Bingo.

Smiling, she approached his window.

He pushed his stack of papers to the side and capped his highlighter.

"Do you have a reservation?" He looked Korean, but had no trace of an accent.

Evan was tempted to tell him that she had tons of reservations—about nearly everything. But that wasn't why she was there.

"No, actually. But I *do* have an unusual request, and I'm hoping you can help me out."

He looked intrigued. "What's that?"

Evan glanced over her shoulder. There were no other patrons in the office. She inclined her head toward a small, open office area just to the right of the service counter.

"Could we maybe talk over there? I promise not to take up too much of your time."

He followed her gaze and then shrugged. "Sure." He turned to address his gum-cracking colleague. "Judy, I'm going to pop over there for just a second. Will you mind the counter?"

Judy stared at Evan for a moment then tucked her hair behind her ear and nodded. "No problem, Han."

The phone rang, and Judy snatched it up. "Sixt, Kings Cross."

Han walked out from behind the counter and took a seat at the small metal desk. Evan followed him and sat down on a straight-backed chair that had a large, dried coffee or Coke stain on its burgundy-upholstered seat.

She leaned forward, rested her arms on the edge of the desk, and lowered her voice. "So, this is kind of embarrassing. But I think my brother's in a bit of a jam. He's fallen in with a bad lot, and he's got in over his head. He helped me move into a new flat on Tuesday, then hooked up with some of his mates and went clubbing." She paused. "I think he might have been involved in a smash-up with one of your lorries. I don't know for sure, and I

147

haven't heard from him. But I think they rented the van here, and I just want to find him. He's been in trouble before, and I want to get to him before the cops do. You know what I mean? He isn't twenty-one yet, so I wanted to find out if you maybe knew which one of his mates did the actual rental? Then I'd know where to look for him."

Han hesitated for a moment and glanced at Judy, who was still talking on the phone.

"What kind of van was it?"

Score. "A blue Caddy Van."

He sighed and pushed back his chair. Then he stood up and went to the stack of papers he had been sorting through when she first came in. He leafed through them and withdrew a form, then returned to his seat.

"We rented a blue VW Caddy Van on Tuesday afternoon to a Mr. Dakkar Nemo."

Dakkar Nemo? Evan was stunned and tried to conceal her reaction. *Are you fucking kidding me with this?* "Did he list an address?"

Han looked over the rental form. "152 Kemp House, City Road, EC1. Did the rental online. All we did was deliver the van. I wasn't working that day, so I didn't see who picked it up."

"He used a credit card, then?"

Han looked down again. "A prepaid Post Office Travel Card."

Fuck it. Of course. "Did the van get turned in on time?"

Han laughed and rolled his eyes. "Not really. Looks like your instincts were spot-on. It was smashed up and abandoned. Cops found it near St. Bride's and hauled it over to the Bidder Street car pound this morning."

Evan sighed.

"Any of that helpful?"

She nodded. "Yeah. It is. Thanks, Han. I *mean* it. You're a real mate to help me out."

He nodded. "I have four brothers—I know what you're about. Good luck, okay?" He stood up. "I have to get back to the window now."

Evan stood up and held out her hand. "I appreciate your help."

They shook hands.

Evan walked back outside and stood, fuming, on the sidewalk. *Dakkar* fucking *Nemo.*

Some asshole had a bizarre sense of humor. "Nemo" was the Indian antihero of the Jules Verne novels.

"Nemo" also was Latin for "no one."

Nice. And certainly not a coincidence.

She pulled out a notepad and jotted down the address Han had given her. She was pretty sure this would be a dead end, too, but she needed to check it out anyway.

Inside her coat pocket, her cell phone vibrated. She pulled it out. *Text message from Julia.* She punched the button, and the message displayed.

> Looks like we'll be finishing up early. I should be able to
> shake free by 4. Eat in or dine out? Julia

She thought about it for a moment before hitting the reply button.

> In. Don't want to miss the chance to torment you with
> alien spices. Meet you at the flat? I'll do the shopping.
> Evan
> P.S. How are you?

She hit send and waited for Julia's reply. It didn't take long.

> Sold. I'll see you there. J.

Her phone vibrated again as she was slipping it back into her pocket.

> P.S. I'm fine. Anxious to see you.

Smiling, she checked her watch. One forty-five. She should have enough time to check out the Kemp House address before heading back to Mayfair to do her shopping. She hefted her messenger bag up onto her shoulder and went back up Brewery Road toward Kings Cross. She had no idea where in the hell City Road was, and she needed to find a WiFi location to find out before heading for the tube station. She knew that wouldn't be too hard—London was shaping up to be like every other city on the planet, with a Starbucks café about every twenty feet.

She rounded the corner onto Kings Cross and stifled a laugh. One of the iconic green signs was about half a block away.

Yeah. A shitty cup of coffee would be the *perfect* complement to this little research venture. So far, things were going *great*, and she was enjoying exactly the kind of success she would've been happy to live without.

The Kemp House address turned out to be a boarded-up storefront. A tiny placard in the corner of a front window indicated that the building was owned and managed by London Virtual Office Services. *Nice.* Whoever rented the Caddy Van was a pro, and they knew how to cover their tracks.

Evan was now certain that Julia's accident had actually been a failed murder attempt. Correction: It hadn't failed at all—just claimed the wrong victim. Now she was faced with a real dilemma. What did she do with her suspicions? She had no proof of anything, and she could hardly tell Julia that she had a fantastic notion that someone—possibly her husband—might be trying to kill her. Julia would think she was a lunatic.

Maybe she was.

But she had to do *something*. If she were right, then whoever was behind this would certainly try again. And she needed to find a way to stop them before they got another chance.

She was mulling over all of these things as she walked down Brook Street with her bag of groceries a few minutes before four. She opened the street door that led to the flats above Number 12, trudged up the stairs, and fished the extra key Julia had given her that morning out of her pocket. She rounded the corner at the top of the steps and was surprised to see the door to Julia's flat ajar.

For a split second, panic shot through her, and she worried that someone had broken into the flat. She stopped, cold, in the hallway, deliberating about what to do.

"I saw you from the front window," Julia called out. "Come on in. I just got here, too."

Jesus. She relaxed and shook her head. *I need to get a fucking grip.*

She walked inside and closed the door behind her. Julia was in the kitchen, opening a bottle of wine. She had already changed out of her business suit, and was wearing black jeans and an oversized, man's pullover sweater. Evan guessed it probably belonged to her father. She looked fabulous. She smiled at Evan.

"Welcome home."

Julia pulled the cork from the bottle with a loud pop.

Things were definitely looking up.

Evan went to the kitchen and set her bag of groceries down on the countertop. She let her messenger bag slide off her shoulder onto one of the bar stools.

"That's the nicest thing I've heard all day."

"What? This?" Julia held up the wine cork.

"Nope." Evan walked over to Julia and stood just in front of her. "But that's a close second."

Julia leaned forward and kissed her.

They parted, and Julia continued to hold her face between warm hands. "What's the first?"

Evan closed her eyes. "Welcome home. It's been a long time since anyone's said that to me."

Julia tugged her closer. "We need to change that."

Evan wrapped her arms around Julia's waist.

They stood there quietly for a moment. The rest of Evan's twisted realities were still there, lurking just beyond the tree line of conscious thought, but she ignored them and let herself sink into this rare moment of calm.

Julia drew back and kissed her on the forehead.

"What are you feeding me?"

Evan smiled at her. "Hungry?"

Julia rolled her eyes. "You have *no* idea. I don't know who does Waverly's catering, but it's ghastly food. I barely ate anything—just enough to be civil."

Evan chuckled and started unloading her groceries. "Good thing you only have one more day to endure it."

Julia walked to a cabinet and withdrew two wineglasses. "Not anymore."

"What do you mean?" Evan asked.

"I think my accident must have softened the old boys up. We agreed on all terms today. It's pretty much 'done and dusted', as they say over here." Julia went to Evan and set down the wineglasses. "I'm a free woman for the next *two* days. So," she bumped Evan's arm, "got any plans for the weekend?"

Evan was shocked, but relieved that she had already run down all the leads she had managed to unearth related to Julia's accident. She couldn't accomplish much else here. What she needed now was to get back to D.C. and huddle with Ben. Then she had to talk with Dan—and Andy.

She gazed at Julia and feigned thoughtfulness. "Well . . . I don't know. Can I get back to you?"

Julia narrowed her eyes. "Really? Just what *were* you up to all day?"

Evan continued to unload her bag. "Oh, the usual. Cruising bars, picking up women . . ."

"Getting reacquainted with old friends?"

Evan gave her an enthusiastic nod. "And making a few new ones."

Julia sighed. "So many women, so little time." She shrugged. "Guess I'll just have to strike out on my own." She turned and started to walk off.

Evan grabbed her by the arm and yanked her back around. "Nuh uh."

Julia raised an eyebrow. "*Nuh uh?*"

"That's right. You go *any place*—you go with me. I'm sticking to you like white on rice."

Julia glanced at the assortment of food items that littered the countertop. "That sounds remarkably like whatever you're planning for dinner."

Evan looked down at the colorful assortment of fresh vegetables, spices, and Basmati rice.

"Um, well." She looked up and met Julia's blue eyes. *Fuck. Big mistake.* "Stick with what you know?"

Julia moved in closer. "My sentiments exactly."

They indulged in a few minutes of nonverbal communication. Eventually, Julia shifted, and moved her mouth against Evan's ear. "I was wrong," she whispered. Her voice was husky.

"What about?" Evan was out of breath, too. The scent of lavender was driving her crazy. Being this close to Julia was driving her crazy. The whole fucking situation was driving her crazy. She needed to sit down.

"I'm not really very hungry."

Jesus. Evan could barely stand. She moved her hands against the warm skin beneath Julia's sweater. "Got any ideas?" *God. She really needed to sit down before she fell down.*

Julia grasped her hand, then pulled her toward the hallway that led to the bedroom.

Evan followed her without speaking. Lying down would work, too.

Chapter 19

Verulamium, on the banks of the Veru River, was a Roman town situated just south of the cathedral city of St. Albans, in Hertfordshire. It was an easy train ride from London, and Julia suggested that it might be a nice place away from the city for them to spend their last two days together in England.

Evan had no problem with that idea. She was now nervous about how vulnerable Julia was in London, and she was trying, silently, to puzzle through how she could protect her from any more "accidents."

They checked into a room at the five-hundred-year-old St. Michael's Manor on Fishpool Street, in the heart of St. Albans. The hotel was just a stone's throw away from the cathedral and abbey, and not far from the historic Roman ruins at Verulamium. Evan had visited the cathedral at St. Albans many times during her year as a student at the University of London, and she loved it because it was so unlike many of the grander historic churches in England.

They made the short walk to the church after checking in and unpacking, and strolled through the massive structure that had been constructed during the time of the Normans but still remained an active center of worship.

In the north transept, they paused to admire a colorful, construction paper display about the Sermon on the Mount, created by "Mrs. Fowler's Sunday School Class." There was also a prayer board, weighted with petitions, and Evan fought off an impulse to grab a stub of pencil and a slip of paper out of a can at its base to add a request of her own to the mix. She looked up and realized that Julia had been watching her deliberate. She shrugged to cover her discomfort and embarrassment.

Julia smiled at her. "I think maybe your mother knew what she was doing when she named you Evangeline."

Evan rolled her eyes.

Julia touched her on the arm. "Don't do that."

"Don't do what?"

"Don't pretend that your faith doesn't matter to you."

Evan bit back a reflexive response. She really didn't want to tell Julia to go fuck herself. Not here—not in the middle of a tenth-century cathedral. And not really anyplace else, either.

"Okay, I won't," she said, instead.

Julia smiled. "I meant what I said the other night."

"What?" Evan asked, confused.

"I love you."

Evan was stunned. She hadn't really expected that. She thought Julia had just been exhausted and half asleep when she'd said it—that she probably didn't even remember it.

"Oh." She backed up a step and dropped down onto a small folding chair. "Okay."

"Is it?" Julia continued to stand in front of her, illuminated by a backdrop of Beatitudes.

Evan nodded. "Yeah." She cursed herself for her lack of eloquence. Her brain felt like mush. "Why are you telling me this now?"

"I don't know." Julia's blue eyes lifted up to take in the soaring arches over their heads. "It seemed like a good place to make this kind of admission."

Evan smiled. She took hold of Julia's hand and tugged her over to sit on a chair beside her. "I love you, too."

"I know." Julia looked smug. "You told me."

Evan knew she was blushing. Again. "I didn't think you heard that."

"Oh, I heard it all right. You can't take it back, now."

155

"I don't want to take it back."

Julia squeezed Evan's hand between hers, which were characteristically warm. "Good."

Evan just gazed at her. Julia looked so beautiful it almost hurt. She was filled with about a dozen ideas about what she'd like to *do*, but didn't really know what else to say.

Julia took care of that for her. "I'm hungry. Want to find someplace to eat?"

Evan just nodded. They stood up and walked across the smooth stone floor toward the entrance to the cloisters. The light outside was starting to fade, but if they hurried, they could make it back to their hotel before dark.

The next day, they followed the remains of a Roman wall that lined the walk from St. Albans to the ruins at Verulamium.

Sections of the wall and the crumbled remains of a bathhouse, a theatre, and the "London Gate" entrance to the city of St. Albans were all that survived to remind visitors of the epic struggle the ancient Britons once waged against the occupying Roman army.

Evan and Julia walked among the stones that made up the spectator area at the site of the Roman theatre. The temperature was hovering right around the fifty-degree mark, but it felt colder. Rain was forecast again for overnight. Already, the air was growing heavier as moisture rolled in from the Channel coast off to the south. There weren't many tourists on this late October day, so they took their time, stopping to share the bag lunch and thermos of coffee an obliging kitchen staffer had shoved into Evan's hands as they prepared to leave their hotel earlier that morning.

They sat on a low section of wall that afforded a spectacular view of the excavation. The afternoon sun was hitting the square tower of the Abbey, visible over the tree line in the distance. There were several small birds flitting around near the base of the single column that towered over what once was the stage area. The bright yellow coloring of the birds captivated Evan. They looked splendid against the backdrop of so much stone and dying grass.

"What are those?" Evan asked, nudging Julia and pointing toward the birds. "They're beautiful."

Julia squinted in the direction Evan indicated. "Yellowhammers, I think. It's not uncommon to see them in this part of the country in the late autumn."

Evan laughed. She hadn't really expected an answer. "I should know better than to ask a publisher a rhetorical question."

Julia looked amused. "I don't deserve any special credit for knowing that. My mother is quite the amateur ornithologist. I spent more Saturdays than I can count being dragged around from one depressing bog to another, while she crawled around on her tummy with her spyglasses and her notepad."

"Really?"

"Uh huh. She even tried to coerce Andy into accompanying her on some of her Twitcher runs. That didn't last long."

Evan was intrigued. "What the hell is a Twitcher?"

Julia laughed. "A Twitcher is a committed bird-watcher. True aficionados will travel great distances and spare next to no expense to add some new, rare species to their ongoing lifelist. My mother had the inclination and the financial wherewithal to indulge her voyeuristic passion for the sport, and she was an avid practitioner."

"But Andy didn't enjoy it?"

"Not so much. Oh, he *tried* at first—like the dutiful son-in-law he was determined to be. But eventually, he grew bored with it and cared more about pursuing his own interests than indulging hers." She gave a bitter-sounding laugh. "I remember the way he finally got her to quit inviting him along on her birding adventures."

"How was that?"

"He showed up impossibly late for an outing one morning in the Hamptons. We were staying with them at their house there for the Thanksgiving holiday. My mother was furious, and embarrassed."

"Why embarrassed?" Evan refilled their plastic cups with what was left of the coffee.

"Because mother was meeting up with some fellow Twitchers near Montauk that morning. There had been reports that a large flock of razorbills was making its way up from the Sound, and the area birders had staked out the site to watch their flight. But Andy laid waste to all their plans when he showed up impossibly late with his *dog* in tow."

"Oh, no."

"Oh, yes. The dog took off down the beach, barking and chasing anything that moved—including the razorbills. Needless to say, mother was incensed with him, and she never asked him to accompany her again." She sighed. "She also banned Nemo from the house. He never went along with us for any more holidays with my parents."

Evan choked on a sip of coffee. She looked at Julia with alarm. "Nemo?"

Julia nodded. "Andy's dog. He was a black, flat-coated retriever. They were inseparable in those days. When he finally died two years ago, I thought Andy would go mad with grief."

Jesus Christ. Nemo?

Julia gave her a concerned look. "Are you all right? You look like you've just seen a ghost."

Evan set her coffee down on a level bit of stone behind them. Her head was reeling, and she needed to think. Fast.

She needed to tell Julia *something*. It was ridiculous to think that she could continue to conceal all of this from her. But how much to tell her? How much was even *worth* telling her? And how would Julia react? She had no idea. But she was out of time, and out of options. Julia would leave for Paris on Sunday, and Evan wouldn't be on hand to protect her.

She shifted around and faced Julia. She took hold of her free hand. "Do you trust me?"

Julia looked even more confused. "Of course I do." She squeezed Evan's hand. "What's the matter?"

Evan took a deep breath. "It's about your accident."

Julia tilted her head. "What about it?"

Evan ran her fingers over the fading bruise that still covered part of Julia's face. "I don't think it was an accident. I think someone was trying to kill you."

Julia recoiled from her and spilled her coffee. "Damn it!" She shook her hand to disperse the hot liquid. She gave Evan an incredulous look. "What are you talking about? Why on earth would anyone want to kill me?"

Evan took hold of her hand and rubbed where the coffee had spilled. "I'm sorry. Really I am. I didn't mean to scare you. But I had to tell you. I *had* to. I spent all day Thursday poking around near the site of the accident, and I found out that someone using a bogus name and address rented the van that hit you. It wasn't a random hit-and-run, Julia. It was *intentional*."

Julia sat in stunned silence. "But *why*? That doesn't make any kind of sense. It must be a coincidence."

Evan met her blue eyes. They looked open and confused.

"I know. I wanted to believe that, too. That's why I looked into it so carefully. I wanted to be certain. And I prayed that I'd be wrong. But I don't think I am." She touched the side of Julia's face again. Julia didn't recoil this time. "If I thought there was any chance it truly was an accident, believe me, I wouldn't be saying anything to you now."

Julia leaned into her hand. "Then why? I don't understand."

Evan shook her head. "I can't explain that part. I think it has something to do with Andy and the campaign. That's all I'm really sure about right now."

"Andy? The *campaign*?" Julia shook her head and looked out across the excavation. Her expression changed from one of confusion to resignation. Then defeat. Then a bleakness, as if instead of seeing the tumbled and worn stones in front of her, she was seeing the ruined landscape of her life.

They sat in silence for several minutes. Then Julia looked at Evan with her characteristic, unreadable expression.

"It's because of the divorce, isn't it?" she asked in a flat, emotionless voice. "It's because I told him I wouldn't help him with his career anymore. It's because they're afraid that this will expose his relationship with Maya."

Evan nodded. "That's what I think, yes. But I'm not certain, and you can't be either. We don't know enough yet."

Julia gave a bitter-sounding laugh. "*Yet?* What does that mean? We wait for them to try again? Jesus." She shook her head again. Her eyes filled with tears. "James. *God.* They killed James. They destroyed the lives of his wife and children. For *what?* So Andy could win another election? My god."

Evan slid closer and pulled Julia into her arms. "I'm sorry. I'm so sorry."

Julia dug her hands into Evan's arms. Evan could feel their heat through the fabric of her jacket. "What am I going to do?"

Evan kissed the top of her head. "I don't know. We'll figure something out."

"I'm supposed to leave for Paris on Sunday."

"I know."

"I'm afraid."

Evan closed her eyes. "I am, too."

"I don't want you to leave me."

"Then I won't." Evan felt Julia tremble. She held her closer. "We'll figure something out. I promise."

They sat huddled together so long that the yellowhammers dared to edge closer and peck at the grass near their feet. A few drops of rain splattered the ground. They collected their things and made the long trek back along the Roman road toward St. Albans.

Chapter 20

They decided that Julia should cancel her trip to Paris and return to the States with Evan.

As an added safeguard, Evan asked Julia to send Andy an email, telling him that the accident had led her to rethink her future plans—and that she was putting everything on hold for the time being. It was, after all, the truth—though perhaps not the truth he would choose to take away from it.

Julia then called her parents and explained that her travel plans had changed, and that business at the firm was requiring her to return to New York sooner than she had expected.

Only she wasn't going back to New York—not just yet. Until Evan could follow through with her plans to talk with Dan—and Andy—Julia was going to stay with her in Chadds Ford. It was the only way Evan knew to keep her safe, apart from shipping her off to some undisclosed location. And *that* was something Julia flatly refused to consider.

Evan never suggested to Julia that Andy might be responsible for her accident—and for the death of Tom Sheridan. She let Julia draw her own vague conclusions about who was directing these events. All that mattered was that Julia understood the danger she was in, and that she'd agree to any course of action that would keep her out of harm's way.

There was another complication to consider, too. Stevie was beginning her fall break on Wednesday, and she would be with them at the house in Chadds Ford next week. But if Julia was going to be staying at Chadds Ford, Evan needed Stevie to understand *why*.

There were no two ways about it—it was a cluster. Evan style.

She was doing her mother *proud* with this one. The best she could hope for was that she'd somehow manage to leave less carnage in her wake.

And right now, that was looking pretty fucking unlikely.

They returned to the Brook Street flat on Saturday night and packed for their early morning departure. Julia called her travel agent and changed her return flight so she could leave from London with Evan on Sunday, instead of departing from Paris a week later. She hung up the phone and filled Evan in on the trip details.

"What the hell did that feat of aeronautical acrobatics cost?" Evan asked.

Julia shrugged and gave her a shy smile.

Evan shook her head. "Life in the fast lane."

Julia raised an eyebrow. "More like life with about four zillion frequent flyer miles."

"Ah. I see. So how many of those did you just burn through?"

"About four zillion."

"That's a pretty gargantuan price to pay for a change that probably cost British Airways less than five bucks."

"Maybe . . . but the drinks are a lot better in first class."

"You're flying back first class?" Evan tried to stifle her disappointment.

"Uh huh. So are you."

"I am?"

"You are. I just took care of that, too." Julia fanned herself with a blue and red plastic card. "This thing is pretty much worthless now." She held it out to Evan. "Got any use for it?"

Evan took it from her. "You never know." She held it up and examined it. "I might be doing a little second-story work when we get back. These things are still nature's best universal door keys."

Julia looked stunned. "You must be joking?"

"Not so much."

"Evan . . ."

"Julia?"

Julia made a grab for the card. Evan held it behind her back. Julia waved her hand in frustration. "I . . . you . . . we . . ."

Evan laughed at her distress. "I'm glad to see that the benefits of a first-class education still include verb conjugation."

Julia's jaw dropped. Evan could see the wheels turning behind her blue eyes.

"Fuck you," Julia finally said.

For some reason, Evan was pleased with that response. She loved this side of Julia, and she felt like they had just leveled their playing field—again. She held the card out to her. "Okay."

Julia tentatively took the plastic card. "Okay?"

"Sure." Evan shrugged. "I accept your terms."

"You're confusing the shit out of me. What terms are you talking about?"

"I give you the card. You fuck me."

Julia rolled her eyes. "Okay wise guy." She snapped her wrist and flung the card across the room like a Ninja throwing star. They watched it clatter against a wall, then slide down behind a couple of potted plants. "Now what?"

Evan sighed. "Well, that's a poser." She met Julia's smug gaze. Smiling, she grabbed her by the lapels of her jacket and yanked her forward. Julia sprawled across her on the sofa. "I think you fuck me, anyway."

She felt Julia's hot breath against her ear.

"I suppose there are worse ways to spend my last night in London," Julia said.

Evan smiled into her dark hair. "Now you're talking."

Julia *wasn't* talking, but she was still managing to communicate just fine. Evan closed her eyes and quickly forgot about the location of the universal door key.

Truth be told, Ben Rush wouldn't need it anyway.

They checked in at their gate, hauled their carry-on luggage to a couple of stiff plastic chairs, and settled in to wait out the two hours until their nonstop flight to Philadelphia began boarding.

Julia expressed interest in another cup of coffee and wandered off in search of anything-but-Starbucks, while Evan rode shotgun on their bags. She sat and amused herself by watching an endless throng of people roll past their gate like a fast-moving stream. This place was like a microcosm of the U.N. People in every shape, size, and color—sporting every language, every mode of dress, and every other cultural earmark—drifted by. She felt like the grand marshal at a fucking parade. The only thing all these travelers seemed to have in common was a myopic level of intensity. Coming or going, they all appeared focused on one thing: reaching their destinations *quickly*.

The other thing she noticed was the now ubiquitous use of cell phones. She chuckled when she noticed an orange-robed Tibetan monk wearing a Bluetooth earpiece, haphazardly pulling a small roller bag and having an animated conversation with someone unseen. Behind him, an annoyed-looking businesswoman in a tight-fitting suit stayed right on his ass, looking for any opportunity to break out and pass by him. Unfortunately for her, the crowds were not cooperating. She was plainly pissed, and finally just gave up—stepping out of the mêlée to lean against a steel support column and make a phone call of her own. Something about her seemed familiar to Evan.

The woman turned around to face the windows behind Evan's row of chairs.

Margo Sheridan. Jesus Christ. What the fuck was *she* doing in London?

A few moments later, Margo noticed Evan. They stared at each other across the open expanse of the gate area like Will Kane and Frank Miller in the final scene from *High Noon*.

Margo blinked first. She lowered her cell phone, walked over to where Evan sat, and stopped just in front of her.

"Fancy meeting you here," she said, dropping her eyes to take in the assortment of mismatched bags. "Doesn't appear that you're traveling light."

Evan looked her over and shrugged. "It's always hard to know how to pack for London in October. But I guess I don't have to tell you that."

"Off to Paris with Julia, I suppose?" She looked around the gate area. "Where is the poor, misguided thing? Freshening her makeup?"

Evan refused to be goaded. "What makes you think I'm traveling with Julia?"

Margo laughed. "Oh come on. Even if we managed to overlook the colossal unlikelihood of running into each other in the middle of Heathrow Airport, you could hardly suppose that Andy would've refrained from telling me about his dear wife's accident. It doesn't take a rocket scientist to connect the dots, now does it?" She shook her head. "Of *course* you'd fly across the Atlantic to be at her side."

Evan nodded. "That might account for *my* presence here. What about yours?"

"I work in London. Remember?"

"I remember everything about you, *Maya*."

Margo's fingers tightened around the cell phone that she still held in her hand. "So, how is Julia? Has she recovered from her ordeal?"

Evan raised an eyebrow. "Andy must not be keeping you in the loop as much as you think."

"What's that supposed to mean?" Margo was plainly becoming agitated.

"Just that Julia's near-death experience seems to have changed her mind about a few things."

"Such as?"

Evan sighed. "Well, you'll be pleased to know that your predictions about the tenure of *my* relationship with Julia have proved to be accurate. She no longer wants the divorce."

A trace of color spread across the skin above the collar of Margo's silk blouse. She didn't reply.

"Andy didn't tell you about that, either? Too bad. Guess we might *both* be losers."

Margo's phone buzzed, and she lowered her gaze to look at the readout.

"I have to take this. I'm horribly late." She grasped the handle of her roller bag and started to turn away. "Tell Julia I'm relieved that she survived the accident." Her tone seemed anything but sincere.

"Of course. Have a safe trip to . . . where did you say you were headed?"

"I don't believe I did say."

She turned around and walked back across the faded carpet to rejoin the fast-moving current of travelers. In seconds, she disappeared from view. Evan examined the spot where she had been standing, expecting to see scorch marks on the rug.

Jesus Christ. What the fuck was that about? And what the hell is Margo doing in London? And where is Andy?

She wondered if he really *had* been in L.A. on the night Dan called to tell her about Julia's accident. That should be easy enough for Ben to check out.

Shit. At this rate, Evan was going to make Ben Rush a very wealthy man.

She grew anxious, and glanced at her watch. Julia was taking far too long to find a cup of coffee. She was halfway out of her seat to ask the gate agent to stow their bags when she saw Julia wending her way toward her between the rows of plastic chairs. Julia was smirking, and she carried two large cups of what looked, impossibly, like Krispy Kreme coffee.

Smiling triumphantly, she walked up to Evan and held out a cup. "Searing hot, with no cream—as requested."

Evan took it from her. "Where in the hell did you find this?"

Julia reclaimed the seat next to her. "Terminal 3, right next to Burger King."

Evan rolled her eyes. "We might as well be in Philadelphia."

"We will be soon enough."

Evan nodded and took a sip of her coffee. She looked at Julia,

166

who had her feet propped up on the edge of her roller bag and was watching the passing tide of people outside their gate.

Evan decided to take the plunge. "I just saw Margo."

Julia stared at her with a shocked expression. "What? *Where?*"

"Right here. About five minutes ago. She stopped to chat before taking off on her broomstick." Evan paused. "I wonder if she earns frequent flyer miles on that thing?"

"My god. What was *she* doing here?"

"I asked her the same question. Business, she said, but who really knows?"

"Or *cares*." Julia shivered. "I'm glad I missed out on that little encounter."

"I am, too."

They sat quietly for a moment.

"Was she traveling alone?" Julia asked.

Evan gave her a surprised look. "Funny. I wondered the same thing."

"And?"

"I don't really know. She was alone when she stopped in here."

"Any interest in finding out?"

"Some. But I couldn't exactly strike out after her and leave all of our stuff unattended."

Julia nodded, dropped her feet to the floor, and set her cup down on the seat next to her. "Which way did she go?"

Evan held Julia back against the seat, preventing her from standing up. "Hold up there, Hoss. This ain't like tracking cattle-poachers on the Ponderosa."

Julia looked at her in confusion. "Which in English means?"

"I think Margo has the potential to be dangerous, and it's not in our best interest to fuck with her."

Julia winced at the choice of words.

"Sorry. I didn't mean to—"

"It's okay," Julia said. "I know what you meant."

"Look," Evan continued. "It doesn't really matter who she's with, or where she's headed."

"It doesn't?"

"No, it doesn't. Trust me, I did my best to lob a few well-aimed hand grenades over the wall of her reserve. She now thinks that you and I are on the outs, and that you're rethinking a reconciliation with Andy."

"Oh, god."

Evan nodded. "If I had to guess, she's probably on the phone with him right now." She lowered her hand to Julia's forearm. "Believe me. The more instability we can engineer between the two of them, the more time we'll buy ourselves to try and sort this whole mess out."

Julia sighed. "Remind me never to piss you off."

Evan nodded. "It's generally not a good idea."

Julia smiled and picked up her coffee. "So what happens now?"

"Now we go home, and I make a couple of late-night house calls with my buddy Ben Rush."

"Evan—"

"Julia. Trust me, okay? This ain't my first rodeo."

"I know." Julia took hold of her hand. "I just want to make certain it doesn't end up being your last."

"I'll be careful."

Julia squeezed her hand. "And what do I do while you're off sleuthing?"

"For starters, you stay away from doors and windows. And *then* you initiate a dialogue with Andy, and do your best to convince him that you have a newfound desire to put some spark back into your marriage."

"God. I don't know if I can pull that off."

"You can. I have faith in you."

Julia shook her head. "It might be misplaced."

"It isn't." Evan squeezed her hand. "Look at me, Julia." Julia raised her eyes. "This is important. We don't know who was behind your accident, but the surest way to stop them from trying again is to take away their motive."

"And what if we end up being wrong about that motive?"

Evan raised Julia's warm hand to her lips and kissed it. "One step at a time, baby. One step at a time."

◊ ◊ ◊

It was well past midnight when Evan unlocked the front door to the house in Chadds Ford. They'd been able to grab a few hours of sleep on the long flight back across the Atlantic, but they had been too keyed up to really relax and enjoy the first-class accommodations. Although Evan had to admit that the booze up front *was* a helluva lot better than what they offered back in the cheap seats.

Julia leaned against her in the small, dark foyer as she pushed the door closed and locked it. Evan stood facing the door for a moment and enjoyed the sensation. "Tired?"

She felt Julia nod against her shoulder. "Bone tired."

"Then why don't we just go on up to bed and worry about unpacking all this stuff tomorrow?"

Julia snaked her arms around Evan's waist. "Did you ever think I'd end up sleeping here with you?"

Evan chuffed. "The truth?"

Julia squeezed her arms tighter. "Of course."

"Hell, no."

Julia pulled away. "Why not?"

Evan faced her. "Because I'm a schmuck, and I have an amazing aptitude for making horrible relationship choices."

"Is that what I am?"

"No. That's the polar opposite of what you are. And that accounts for why I never thought you'd end up here with me."

Julia let out a tired-sounding breath. Evan wished she could see her eyes, but with no moon and the lights off, the house was pitch black.

"I'm not going to put up with these annoying bouts of self-deprecation forever," Julia said. "But right now, I'm just too tired to argue with you."

Evan knew she had dodged a bullet. "I guess that's lucky for me."

"Don't count your chickens before they're hatched. I just said I was too tired to *argue*—not to engage in other forms of . . . intercourse."

169

Evan smiled, took her hand, and pulled her toward the short flight of stairs that led to the second floor of the farmhouse.

"As I said . . . lucky me."

Chapter 21

Evan didn't waste any time the next day getting in touch with Dan. She took an early train into D.C. and met him at Café Europa on M Street. They sat at a small table away from the main seating area, and she quickly filled him in on the peculiar details surrounding the death of Tom Sheridan. She also told him that Andy Townsend owned a pair of yellow K2 skis similar to the ones Tom had been wearing when his body was discovered.

Dan sat chewing on the end of a plastic swizzle stick as he listened.

He dropped the mangled stirrer onto his napkin and shrugged. "What's your point?"

Evan sighed. "What do you mean, *what's my point*?"

"Come on, Evan. Why was it so goddamn important for you to pull me away from two meetings and a conference call to tell me something that has nothing to do with anything?"

"Jesus, Dan. Can you fucking *smell* the coffee in that cup? Somebody obviously killed Tom Sheridan, and right now, your boy Townsend has the word 'perpetrator' stamped all over his high-class forehead."

Dan held up a placating hand and glanced over his shoulder. "Christ. You wanna take it down a notch or two?" He leaned forward. "What the hell is the matter with you, anyway? You sound like a crazed extra from an Oliver Stone movie."

Evan sat back against the plastic chair and took a couple of deep breaths. She was furious with Dan, but hurling a drink in his face wouldn't do much to advance her cause. She needed him to hear her out, and to at least consider the possibility that she was right about Sheridan—if not about Andy.

"Okay, look. I'm willing to admit that Andy having a pair of K2 skis *might* be a coincidence. But, Andy *was* on that weekend trip with Tom Sheridan. And so was Marcus. And somebody strapped those expert skis on the feet of an inexperienced drunk who had no business being anywhere near the runs on Loge Peak. We both know that Andy was screwing the congressman's wife, and from *my* vantage point, he was the only person who stood to gain anything professionally and personally from Sheridan's death." She leaned forward. "So *you* do the math."

He stared back at her for a moment. Then he shook his head. "You're adding two and two and getting five. You've got nothing here, and, frankly, I'm more than slightly concerned that you seem to be willing to toss around these ludicrous, unsubstantiated accusations. What the hell has happened to your judgment?" He narrowed his eyes. "Scratch that. I think I know exactly what's wrong with you."

"Wrong with me? What the fuck are you talking about?"

"Oh, come on. This happens every time you lose your objectivity and start thinking with your . . . girl stuff." He waved his hand at her lap. "So, what's up?" He lowered his voice. "You worried that Andy and Julia might reconcile?"

Evan gave him an incredulous look. "What's the *matter* with you? Jesus, Dan. This has nothing to do with my feelings for Julia."

"Ah. You admit it, then?" He sat back with a smug expression. "So Marcus was right. Hot damn. I *knew* it."

Evan threw her napkin down with disgust. "I don't know why I thought talking with you was a good idea. Clearly, you can't see past your own frustrated libido."

"Oh, baby, there's not a damn thing wrong with my libido these days."

"Oh, really? You finally getting some?"

172

He laughed. "Nice try. We're not talking about *my* antics in the sack."

She pushed back her chair. "Guess what? We're not talking about *mine*, either."

He grabbed her arm. "Hang on. Don't be pissed."

"Fuck you."

"Seriously. Come on. I'm sorry. Sit down. Tell me what I can do to help out."

She eyed him with suspicion.

"I mean it." He sounded sincere enough.

She sat back down. "Okay. I want to meet with Andy—today."

"That's not possible."

She lifted her chin. "Why not?"

"Because he's in Toronto. He won't be back in D.C. until Monday."

"Monday?"

"Yeah."

Her wheels were turning. She wondered if Ben Rush could shake free tonight. "All right. Then I want to meet with him on Monday."

"Marcus won't like it."

"Marcus can kiss my white ass. You can either set this meeting up for me, or I can call my friends at the *Enquirer* and let them ask the questions."

He sighed. "Christ. Wanna dial it back a bit? I'll set up the damn meeting for you."

"Good."

"Don't get too excited. I have a couple of conditions."

"Such as?"

"I want to be there when you meet with him."

She thought about that. It probably wasn't a bad idea. Andy would feel less threatened, and she'd have a witness to anything that transpired. "Okay."

"And I get to pick the venue for the meeting."

She knew Dan. He'd want to make it someplace public, so things couldn't get too out of hand.

"All right."

Dan nodded and finished his cup of coffee. "I'll call you on Thursday and let you know when and where. And I want to get some time with Stevie, too."

He obviously knew that Stevie's fall break was this week. She pushed back her chair and stood up.

"And, Evan?"

She looked at him.

"You'd better be careful about how far you go with this bull-shit. I won't be able to salvage your reputation if you push him too far, and it blows up in your face."

She stared at him for a few moments, and then picked up her messenger bag and slung the strap over her shoulder. "I'll talk to you on Thursday about the meeting. Call me whenever about Stevie."

She left him sitting there and headed for the M Street exit.

Ben Rush was none too pleased that Evan was twisting his arm to get him to agree to an impromptu stint of B&E. It was a felony in the District—and pretty much everyplace else these days—and he'd more or less given up this kind of candy-ass crime when he started doing "special" projects for the Justice Department about six years ago. But his lucrative government assignments had slacked off since Obama took the oath of office, and money was scarce. He had two ex-wives and three kids in college, and his legit day job as an insurance investigator didn't come close to paying the bills. Evan knew that, and she waged a full-court press—with an accompanying stack of C-notes—to get him to agree to engineer her clandestine doubleheader.

She needed him to get her into *two* residences. The one in Old New Castle would be a cakewalk. It didn't even have a security system. The other? Well, that one was going to be a bit more complicated.

"You've got to be kidding me," he said, when she told him the address.

"Do I look like I'm kidding?" she said, with a raised eyebrow.

Ben shook his head. "Forget it."

"Come on," Evan said. "Where's your sense of *history*? If memory serves, you've got experience with this particular location."

He waved a hand. "Yeah, well, doing a four-year stretch in Lompoc was an 'experience' I could've lived without."

"Gimme a break. That place is a fucking country club, and you know it."

"Hey, maybe it was by the time they sent Boesky there, but it wasn't a picnic in the seventies, lemme tell you. And I have *no* desire to see how much it's improved."

Evan reached out to take back the stack of bills that sat in an envelope on the tabletop between them. "*Fine.* I'm sure I can find another porch-climber who still knows his way around Foggy Bottom."

Ben slapped his hand down on top of hers. "Not so fast. Just gimme a goddamn minute to think about this. We're talking about the fucking *Watergate*, okay? I still have nightmares about that joint."

Evan chewed the inside of her cheek. "In or out, Ben. This is a time-value offer."

Ben searched her eyes. "When do you wanna do this, again?"

"Tonight." She glanced at her watch. "In about three hours. New Castle tomorrow night—if we need to."

Ben sighed. He was in his late sixties now, and he hadn't done any bona fide breaking and entering since the mid-nineties. The closest he got these days was listening in on peer-to-peer conversations and unscrambling instant messages. And *that* he could do from his own living room wearing nothing but his t-shirt and boxer shorts.

He looked back up at Evan. Her hand was still beneath his, resting on top of the envelope full of hundred-dollar bills. He knew she wouldn't wait much longer. *What the fuck?* He needed the money, and he might as well have some fun while he was at it.

"Okay," he said. Evan pulled her hand free, and he could see a smile beginning around the edges of her gray-green eyes. "But we're going to do this *my* way. No arguments."

Evan's smile faded before it gained any traction. She narrowed her eyes. "I've got a feeling that I'm not going to like this."

Ben laughed and hauled the bills away from her. He sat back and looked her up and down. "I've got a feeling that you're going to *hate* it."

"Will you hurry the fuck up?" Ben seemed exasperated by how long it was taking Evan to walk across the pavement from the New Hampshire Avenue taxi drop-off in front of the luxury apartment complex.

"Bite me, Ben. *You* try to walk in these goddamn shoes."

"We discussed that, remember? Besides, you make a much better-looking escort than I do."

"Yeah, right. I had to be *insane* to agree to this."

He looked her over. "I don't know. You clean up pretty good."

"I look like a goddamn hooker."

He laughed. "That's the idea, love chunks."

She glowered at him.

In fact, Evan suspected that she did look pretty . . . hot. And cheap.

They'd managed to score the items of clothing they needed from an obliging set of sales racks at the Nieman Marcus on Wisconsin Avenue. The makeup was easy—Ben's daughters had the equivalent of a goddamn Sephora franchise stashed in the drawers of his guest bathroom. The shoes were a bit of a harder sell. Ben had to strong-arm Evan into trying on more than a dozen pairs before they found a style that fit the bill.

"You can't *possibly* be serious?" she said, as he held up another pair of peep-toe glitter pumps with four-inch heels. "You want me to bust my ass?"

"No, I want you to look like you *sell* your ass."

She scowled as she yanked the shoes from his hand. "You're enjoying this."

He shrugged.

"Pervert."

"Hey, I'd wear them if I could."

She gave him a smoldering look. "I really could've lived out the rest of my life without knowing that about you, Ben."

"Just hurry the fuck up. We're running out of time."

That had been over two hours ago. Now they were approaching the entrance to the main lobby of the complex, and Evan's begrudging makeover was about to pay off. She was startled every time she looked down and saw her boobs pushing out from the deep v-neck of the slinky dress she was wearing—if you could even *call* it that.

"How'd you finagle this invitation, anyway?" she hissed as they approached the doorman.

"Avery Waxman owes me. He has these little cocktail shindigs *every* Monday night. They're like little 'welcome back' mixers. Williams & Jensen foots the bill for all of it. There's no telling who you'll run into up there."

She looked at him with surprise. "We're not really going to this fucking party, are we?"

"Of course we are. We *have* to. Relax. Waxman lives on the same floor as your pigeon."

"Jesus. What happened to the good ole days when all you had to do was jimmy a lock?"

"Hey, don't blame me. I didn't pick this fishin' hole—you did."

"Christ."

"Just keep your mouth shut. I don't want to run the risk that anyone will recognize you."

"That's not very likely."

"Do it just the same, and now's a good time to start."

They approached the doorman.

Ben held out a beige card. "Hello. Ben Rush to see Avery Waxman."

The doorman glanced at the card, but spent more time giving Evan a good once-over.

"Go on up, Mr. Rush." He gestured toward the elevators behind his station.

"Thanks. Have a great night."

The doorman raised an eyebrow. "You, too."

Ben palmed Evan's jersey-clad ass. "Oh, I *plan* to."

The big steel elevator doors closed, and Evan jabbed a finger into Ben's chest. "Do that again, motherfucker, and you'll find out what it's like to sing soprano."

"Jesus. What's with the Pippi Longstocking routine? Lighten up, will ya?"

"Let's just get this *done*, all right?"

Ben flicked an index finger off the bill of an imaginary cap. "Yes, ma'am."

The elevator stopped on the ninth floor, and the big doors rolled back.

"Showtime, babycakes." He took Evan by the elbow. "Let's go sell it."

Evan had had just about enough.

Ben was making the rounds at the party, laughing and passing out his little beige cards—making sure everyone knew he was there. She was killing time, skulking behind a couple of behemoth potted palms next to the balcony doors, nursing the same god-damn martini someone had thrust into her hands as soon as they crossed the threshold of Waxman's apartment. Under normal circumstances, she wouldn't have minded—it was a good drink. Belvedere, if she didn't miss her guess. Apparently, business was good at Williams & Jensen.

The guest list at this soirée was like a goddamn index page from the D.C. *Social Register*. Evan saw half-a-dozen congressmen she knew in passing, and another three or four who once had been objects of her professional scrutiny. Keeping a low profile was harder than she bargained for. Fortunately, her ensemble was engineered to prevent anyone from looking too closely at her face, and the skimpy outfit seemed to be doing its job quite well. Ben knew his business.

She took another tiny sip from her drink and stole an innocuous glance at her watch. They'd been there twenty-five minutes. Her feet were *killing* her. She shook her head and wondered what Julia would say if she could see her. *Christ.* When she'd called

Julie earlier and explained that she'd be late getting back, there had been a moment of dead silence on the phone line.

"Do I want to know what you're up to?" Julia sounded concerned.

"No. I really don't think you do."

Julia sighed. "Evan—"

"I'll be *fine*. Just don't worry. And don't leave the house. I should be back by midnight."

"Midnight?"

"Yeah. Wait up for me?"

"Of course. Be careful?"

"Always."

"Evangeline?"

"Yeah?"

Silence.

Evan smiled into the phone. "I know. Me, too."

That conversation had taken place more than four hours ago, and if Ben didn't light a fire under his ass, it would be another fucking four hours before they got to Andy's goddamn apartment.

Over the din, she recognized a familiar laugh.

With a sick, sinking feeling, she looked toward the sound. *Jesus Christ.* This was *not* happening. *Liz.*

Liz Burke was walking in on the arm of—somebody—and she was making a determined beeline toward the makeshift bar set up just to Evan's left.

Great. Now what? Evan began to panic. If Liz saw her, she'd be totally busted. And how the fuck would she *ever* be able to explain this?

Lucky for her, Ben chose that moment to remember the reason for their presence at this goddamn party.

"Liz!" Ben called out. Evan closed her eyes and blessed God and the Holy Virgin that Ben seemed to know everyone in government—especially at Justice and State. Liz halted and turned around, giving Evan time to beat a hasty retreat. She rolled her eyes at Ben and jerked her head toward the door as she brushed behind Liz, headed toward the foyer of the apartment.

Ben joined her, and they went out into the hallway. Evan took his arm as they strolled the short distance to Andy's condo.

"What took you so fucking long?" she whispered, running her fingers through the graying hair on the back of his head. It curled over the top of his shirt collar. He needed a haircut.

Ben was doing a good job, making it look like he was fidgeting with his keys. "Quit bitching. You're just lucky I knew your girl-friend back there."

"Liz is *not* my girlfriend."

"Oh, really?" he asked. "Is there some other term for the girl-on-girl thing you got going with her?"

Ben had both picks inserted into the lock. Evan was draped over his shoulder, doing her best to look bored and impatient as she concealed what he was up to. She wanted to kill him.

Just then, another drunken couple rounded the corner and weaved past them, headed toward the elevators. Evan bent forward and kissed Ben on the ear. "Just open the goddamn door."

Ben chuckled. The pins in the lock finally cooperated, and he turned the handle. "Sweet talker."

They quickly stepped inside and closed the door. Ben fished a small, pen-sized flashlight out of his jacket pocket.

"Okay. This is your party. Where do you wanna start?"

Evan stood still for a moment, trying to let her eyes adjust to the darkness inside the apartment. "Beats me. Closets? The bedroom?"

Ben swung the tiny beam of light around the room in short, measured arcs.

"What are we looking for, anyway?"

Evan laughed. "Skis."

The blue halo of light halted. Ben turned to her. "Say what?"

"You heard me. Skis. Bright yellow ones."

Ben sighed. "Well, that sure narrows down where we have to look. And here I was all set to crack into a couple of wall safes."

"Sorry to disappoint you. We're not doing a remake of *The Thomas Crown Affair*."

Ben laughed. "Tell me about it. Besides, in that outfit, you look more like a stunt double for *Irma la Douce*."

Evan tugged at the short hemline of her red dress. "I reiterate. You're a pervert."

Evan pulled off her shoes and bent to stash them under a table next to the door. Ben swung his light around to illuminate the table.

"What the hell are you doing?"

"What's it *look* like I'm doing? These things are killing me." She straightened up and was stunned to see a familiar face staring back at her. Andy had a large, framed photo of Julia sitting atop the foyer table, next to several other family photos. Evan felt her heart miss a beat as she stared at the photo. The absurdity of her situation overwhelmed her. Not because she was dressed like a hooker, and had just violated about twenty federal laws by breaking into the apartment of a sitting U.S. senator. More because of the surreal fact that she'd managed to become entangled with the senator's estranged wife—a stunning socialite, who was as far beyond her in wealth and experience as the goddamn clothes she was wearing were beyond her in fit and fashion.

Ben flashed the beam of light toward a long hallway to their right. "Let's start over here."

They sifted through about a dozen closets. Evan had to hand it to the architects of this joint. No wonder the DNC had once picked this complex to house its offices—it was *made* for hiding shit.

The front door of the apartment opened and closed.

They froze inside Andy's bedroom. Ben clicked off his flashlight, grabbed Evan's arm, and hauled her into the guest room off the main hallway. They crouched behind a large armoire just inside the door. Someone turned on a lamp in the living room, and then an overhead light illuminated the paneled hallway. They heard footsteps headed their way. Evan held her breath, and she knew Ben was doing the same thing.

This was shaping up to be a fucking comedy of errors. What else could possibly go wrong? *Was Andy back early from his trip?* Her heart was about to pound out of her chest.

Whoever had entered the apartment stopped at the end of

the long hallway near the doorway to the room where they were hiding. Evan heard a sliding door pulled back and items being shifted around. She took a chance and strained against Ben to crane her head around the corner.

Jesus Christ. It was Margo Sheridan, standing in front of a storage closet they had just searched. *What the fuck was she doing there?*

Ben yanked Evan back and held her in a vice-like grip.

Margo finished whatever she was doing and closed the closet door. Then, they heard her retreating footsteps. The hallway light was extinguished, but the living-room light remained on.

Evan's heart rate accelerated as she remembered: Her goddamn shoes were sitting on the floor in the foyer. She stood there, frozen in Ben's grip for what felt like an hour. The light finally went out, and she heard the front door open and close. They didn't move from behind the armoire until they heard the sound of Margo's key turning in the lock.

"Who the fuck was that?" Ben grabbed a hankie out of his back pocket and swabbed at his forehead.

"*That* was Andy's girlfriend—Margo Sheridan."

Ben stopped swabbing. "Margo Sheridan? No shit?"

Evan nodded. "You heard of her?"

"Who hasn't?" He shook his head. "Your pigeon keeps pretty dangerous company."

"Yeah, well, let's just see what she dropped off, shall we?"

They walked over to the big closet. Ben slid the door open and moved the beam of his flashlight over the interior. Everything looked pretty much the same as it had earlier when they'd searched it.

"Wait a minute." Evan saw something poking out behind a rack that held several oversized garment bags. "What's that?"

Ben pushed the zippered bags apart. A long, black duffel, piped in red, leaned against the back wall of the closet.

"That wasn't there before," Evan said.

"Nope." Ben pulled it out. Near the shoulder strap was an embroidered K2 logo. "*Bingo.*"

"Jesus Christ." Evan reached around him to unzip the top half of the bag. A pair of bright yellow skis was neatly tucked inside the padded interior. "I'll be goddamned."

She ran her hand over the bottom edges of the skis—they were smooth. No wax. She stood back, shaking her head.

Ben zipped the duffel closed and stashed it back behind the hanging garment bags. "I guess our work here is through?"

Evan shook her head in amazement. "Not even close."

"Well, you got what you came here for, so let's get the fuck out of here before she decides to come back."

Evan nodded. Ben lighted their way back toward the living room and stopped in the foyer so Evan could retrieve her shoes. There was just one problem. The shoes were gone.

Evan got back to Chadds Ford at eleven-fifteen.

Her appearance had certainly raised a few eyebrows when she walked across the lobby of the Watergate on Ben's arm—barefoot. Her pantyhose were ruined by the time they got into a cab and headed back to Ben's apartment so she could change. But that hardly mattered—she really didn't think she'd need the black, crochet-striped stockings again any time soon. She left them draped over the shower rod in Ben's bathroom as a parting gift. She smiled as she hung them up. Now that she knew about the old guy's eclectic tastes, she figured he probably could find a way to put them to good use.

Her head was still reeling from the events of the evening. How fucking unlikely was it that Margo would pick *precisely* the same night she had chosen to break into Andy's apartment to return the yellow skis? And why did Margo have them in the first place? Were they the actual skis Tom Sheridan had been wearing when he had his fatal accident? That seemed unlikely—the skis had no wax on their undersides, probably indicating that they hadn't been used before.

And who in the hell tipped Margo off that Evan might be looking for them?

The whole thing smelled like a first-class cover-up, and Margo was ass-deep in the middle of it.

Evan was now fully convinced that Andy was the one who gave Tom Sheridan his fatal shove off the in-bounds run at Loge Peak.

But how could she prove it?

And how could she protect Julia?

Dan was no help. He already thought she was acting like a paranoid psycho. If she told him about her nighttime tryst with Ben, he'd probably have her ass locked up, and then sue her for custody of Stevie so fast it would make her head spin.

She had a sinking suspicion that the only way to bring all of this out into the open would be to force Andy's—and Margo's—dirty hands. That meant pushing them to make another attempt on Julia's life. But how could she risk that? It was *impossible*. There had to be another way.

An idea occurred to her. Maybe she could piss Andy off enough to make herself the target? Shift his attention away from Julia altogether. She knew Margo despised her already—it shouldn't be too hard to succeed with Andy, if she played her cards exactly right.

Evan had it on good authority that she could be *very* annoying when she set her mind to it.

Of course, she'd have to have Julia's cooperation with this scheme, and that didn't promise to be easy to achieve.

Something else nagged at her, too. Why had Margo taken the goddamned shoes?

Smiling to herself, she figured *that* happy discovery probably wouldn't bode too well for Andy.

She unlocked the big front door to her house and stepped inside. The living-room light was on, but the rest of the down-stairs was dark.

"Is that you?" a voice called out from upstairs.

Evan shook her head. "You'd better hope so."

"Wiseass. I saw you pull in." Julia stood at the top of the stairs. She was wearing one of Evan's oversized Penn t-shirts, and nothing else. Evan realized that she could stand there, in her dark foyer, and admire this view for a *very* long time.

Julia tilted her head as they continued to stare at each other. "Are you okay?"

"I am now."

Julia smiled. "Hungry?"

Evan took off her jacket. "In fact, I am."

"I'll put on some clothes and come down."

Evan didn't like that idea. "How about instead, I just grab something quick and join you up there?"

Julia thought about that. "I suppose that could work, too." She turned away from the stairs and started to walk back toward the bedroom. "When you're finished grabbing something in the kitchen, you can come upstairs and try your hand at grabbing something in the bedroom."

Jesus. This woman was going to be the death of her.

Her heart sank.

She had an eerie premonition that she might be right.

She hung her jacket up on a hook behind the door and headed into the kitchen to see what she could find to eat.

It was going to be another long night.

Evan finished her peanut butter sandwich and the last of the white grapes she'd snagged from the fridge, and set the empty plate on the nightstand. She'd also thought to bring up the rest of an open bottle of red zinfandel, knowing that Julia liked it. They sat on the bed, facing each other, as they drank their glasses of wine.

Julia's long, glorious, *bare* legs were stretched out in front of her, crossed at the ankles. Evan had a hard time concentrating on what she was saying with so much tantalizing real estate on full display.

Julia sighed and snapped her fingers. Evan looked up at her with a startled expression.

"Hello? Is anyone at home?"

"I'm sorry," Evan said, although she really wasn't. "You were saying?"

"I was *saying* that I was really getting worried about what could possibly be taking you so long tonight. I don't suppose you want to fill me in?"

Evan shook her head. "No. And before you get pissed—it isn't because I don't trust you. It's just that you're better off—legally, and in every other sense—not knowing."

Julia looked dubious. "I'm not sure I like the sound of that."

"Believe me when I tell you that you'd like it a whole lot *less* if you actually knew the details. Suffice it to say that all's well that ends well, and everything went off without a hitch."

Julia still looked worried.

Evan rested a hand on her thigh. "No worries. I promise."

"I don't like thinking that you're out there taking chances."

"Sweetheart, the biggest chance I *ever* took came and went a long time ago."

Julia looked confused. "What was that?"

Evan leaned forward and kissed her. "Ring any bells?"

Julia stroked the side of Evan's face. "I'm not really sure. Maybe you need to jog my memory a bit more."

Evan took Julia's wineglass and set it down on the bedside table next to her own. Then she turned off the lamp and crawled across the bed in the dark to stretch out on top of her.

"Is this helping?"

Julia slid her warm palms along the bare skin beneath Evan's shirt. "Oh, I think it's definitely starting to come back to me."

Evan kissed her again.

Tomorrow would be soon enough to discuss her plans for dealing with Andy.

Andy arrived at Margo's townhouse in Reston on a little before 10 p.m., and the first thing he noticed was how dark the place was. That was unusual because Margo rarely went to bed before midnight—and he knew she was at home because her black Saab was in the garage.

The second thing he noticed was that the single light she *had* left on was over the dining-room table, and it illuminated a bright red pair of . . . shoes?

He stopped and picked one of them up.

"What the hell are these?" he asked aloud, as he turned the thing over in his hands. The heels had to be at least four inches high.

"My question exactly."

Margo's voice shocked him, and he nearly dropped the shoe. He turned around to see her standing in the darkened doorway that led to the living room.

"Jesus Christ. You scared the shit out of me. What are you doing down here in the dark?"

She stared at him for a moment. "Waiting for you."

He noticed that she hadn't moved from her position in the doorway.

He held the shoe up. "What gives with these?"

She shrugged. "I was hoping you would tell me."

He tossed the shoe back down on the table. "Am I supposed to know what the hell *that's* supposed to mean?" He walked to the sideboard and turned on a lamp. Margo continued to stand in the doorway.

He sighed and pulled out a chair, thinking he might as well sit down. Clearly, whatever was on her mind didn't seem to be forthcoming, and he'd had a long day. He loosened his tie.

Margo stood there in stony silence for what felt like a full minute, before finally moving into the room and taking a seat herself. Andy noticed that she chose to sit directly across the table from him. He was certain that was by design.

"I took the skis to your apartment tonight," she said.

He nodded. They'd talked about it that morning, after he'd arranged for the replacement skis to be delivered to her office at Freedom Square. If anyone inquired, she'd just say that she was getting her own pair refurbished before her upcoming trip to Gstaad.

"Did you manage to get in without anyone seeing you?"

"Of course. I took the service elevator up from the parking garage." She picked up a piece of red glitter that had fallen off one of the shoes. "Waxman was having another one of his soirées.

187

I had to cool my heels in the corridor for a few minutes to be sure I wouldn't run headlong into half of Congress."

He laughed.

Margo wasn't smiling "I got safely into your apartment and stashed the skis." She picked up the shoes by their sling backs. "Then I found *these* beneath the table in your foyer."

He was stunned. Obviously he hadn't heard her correctly. "Excuse me?"

Her eyes were like chips of flint.

"You heard me."

He gave the shoes a good once-over. "Oh, come on, Margo. There's no fucking way you found these hooker shoes in *my* apartment."

"Oh, I assure you that I did."

"That's impossible."

"Apparently not."

He sat back against his chair. None of this made any kind of sense. Who in the hell could've gotten into his apartment—and why would they have left such a ludicrous calling card? He shook his head.

"I don't get it."

Margo sat staring at him, then she put the shoes back down on the table. "You really don't know anything about this, do you?"

He met her frosty gaze. "Of *course* not."

She sighed. "You really are a boy scout, aren't you?"

He was irked by her sarcasm. "What's that crack supposed to mean?"

She shook her head. "Never mind. If you really know nothing about these, then we've got bigger problems."

He gave a bitter laugh.

This had to have something to do with the goddamn skis—but what? Who in the hell would have done this—and *why*?

"It's about the skis, isn't it?" Her voice was cold.

He looked at her. "Why would you think that?"

She rolled her eyes. "Oh come on, Andy. It's a bit too much of a coincidence, don't you think?"

188

"I don't know *what* to think. You were there. Did it look like anything had been disturbed?"

She shook her head.

"Well. Whoever left these behind must have wanted them to be found."

"That makes *no* sense."

He was losing patience. "I didn't say it was *rational*—okay?"

She sighed. "If they were looking for the skis, they didn't find them. I arrived after they left their little present."

He thought about that.

"There's only one person who's been nosing around and asking questions about Aspen."

"Evan Reed?"

He nodded.

Margo laughed and gestured toward the high heels. "These could hardly be considered her style."

"Didn't you say that Waxman was having one of his eclectic little parties tonight?"

"Yes . . ." She looked like enlightenment was beginning to dawn. "Jesus Christ." She took a deep breath. "That bitch . . ."

He held up a restraining hand. "Relax. We have *no* idea if she's responsible."

"Then who else could have done it? And tell me something else, while we're on the subject. Why is she so interested in you and your goddamn skis?"

"We've discussed this."

"Well, maybe we need to discuss it a bit more. Maybe you need to explain to me again how it happened that Tom ended up going over a goddamn cliff wearing *your* sodded skis."

"Will you calm the fuck down? And lower your voice. I don't need for this to make the goddamn *Drudge Report*."

Margo was nowhere near calming down.

"I mean it Andy. If I find out that you *lied* to me about Tom's death, I'll—"

"You'll *what*, 'Maya'? Have one of your 'uncles' come and drag me off to the family Romper Room in Lahore?"

189

She said nothing, but her gaze was cold and unflinching.

"Face it," he continued. "You've got as much invested in this as I do. Until we know who's behind this, we need to stay *calm*."

She stared at him for another minute, then she pushed back her chair and stood up.

"Just remember what I said."

She turned and walked out, leaving him alone with the shoes.

He sighed.

Evan Reed.

And the skis. The goddamn skis.

Fuck.

Chapter 22

It snowed on Tuesday morning, a light snow that promised not to add up to much, but pretty enough to lure Evan and Julia outside after breakfast. Julia had a conference call scheduled for eleven, but they decided to take advantage of what was left of the morning to hike across the open field behind Evan's house.

"This landscape looks just like it got lifted off the canvas of an Andrew Wyeth painting," Julia said. "It's bleak, but beautiful."

Evan laughed.

"That's funny?" Julia asked. Her breath made patterns in the cold air.

They trudged along the creek bed that divided Evan's land from a neighboring farm.

"No, it's insightful. And ironic." Evan gestured behind them, at the rolling land off to the east. The snow had nearly stopped, and a single ray of sun peeked through the bare trees. "The Keurner's farm is just about two miles away, over that very rise." She bumped Julia playfully as they walked along. "I guess your gramma wasn't the only Donne gifted with a knack for sniffing out fine art."

Julia smiled. Her blue eyes were as bright as the single bit of sky visible behind the dense cloud cover.

"Flatterer."

"That's me," Evan agreed. "I'd say anything to get into your pants."

Julia lifted the front of her jacket and tugged at the waistband of the oversized pair of Carhartt jeans Evan had lent her that morning. They had belonged to her grandfather, who, fortunately for Julia, had been about a foot taller than Evan.

"Well, there *does* appear to be room enough for both of us in here."

Evan made a grand display of trying to look down Julia's pants. "I know. Lucky me."

Julia yanked the front of her jacket down and punched Evan on the arm. "Sleaze."

"I know. Lucky you."

Julia rolled her eyes.

They walked on a bit farther.

"I can't stay here forever, you know," Julia said.

Evan considered Julia's quiet words. The sun that had been struggling to break through the clouds disappeared again—almost as if an unseen special effects director had cued it to turn off.

"I know."

She supposed that now was as good a time as any to talk about her scheme to divert Andy's attention away from Julia. She was less certain about how to navigate an explanation of *how* she intended to accomplish this.

"So what are we going to do?" Julia asked.

Evan took Julia's arm as they walked along. "I got Dan to agree to let me have a sit-down with Andy on Monday."

Julia looked surprised. "What will that accomplish?"

"Nothing, if you don't do some fancy footwork on the front end."

Julia looked exasperated. "I've got a bad feeling about this."

Evan squeezed her elbow through the heavy jacket. "Don't. Remember that I promised never to coerce you into things you didn't freely consent to do."

"I know. That's what worries me."

"Meaning?"

"Meaning that if I don't agree to participate, it will end up putting you in danger."

Evan didn't want to tell her that the truth lay about one hundred and eighty degrees opposite her assessment. So she didn't.

Julia sighed. "I guess this means you want me to continue to press for a bogus reconciliation with Andy?"

Evan nodded.

"God." Julia looked at her. "What makes you think he won't see right through this? What makes you think he doesn't know where I am right now?"

"It doesn't matter. I *want* Andy to know you're . . . *involved* with me. I want him to think that I'm pursuing you. In fact, I intend to provide him—and anyone else who might be paying attention—with some pretty damn incontrovertible proof."

"Do I want to know what that is supposed to mean?"

"Probably not."

Julia waved a hand in frustration. "I'm not comfortable with *any* of this."

"I know, honey. But I need you to trust me."

"I *do* trust you. It's myself I'm not too sure of. I've never been very good at subterfuge."

"If that's true, then you're better off not knowing many details. You won't have to pretend as much."

Julia was plainly exasperated. "How can you be so calm about all of this?"

Evan smiled at her. "I try to be when it's important."

Julia stopped and faced her. She raised an eyebrow. "Where have I heard that before?"

Evan shook her head. "I simply cannot imagine."

Julia leaned her forehead against Evan's. "I have to be back in New York by Friday."

"I know that, too."

"But I can stay here with you and Stevie until then."

Evan nodded.

"Are you nervous about having me here when she comes home?"

"No."

"No?" Julia seemed dubious.

193

Evan shook her head. "Stevie's smart and savvy. She'll roll with it just fine."

"So she's used to you having overnight guests?"

Evan drew back and looked at her. Julia's demeanor seemed casual enough, but Evan thought there might be some nascent insecurity lurking behind her question.

"I don't *have* overnight guests. Ever. That's why she'll understand that this is important, and she'll be fine with it."

Julia dropped her eyes. "Isn't that asking a lot of a fourteen-year-old?"

Evan laughed. "Not *this* kid."

Julia smiled.

Evan took Julia's arm. "C'mon. Let's head back. I don't know about you, but my feet are freezing."

"Your feet are always freezing."

Evan looked down at her wet boots. Then she looked at Julia's feet.

"Yeah . . . why *is* that? You never get cold, and you're always running around barefoot."

Julia shrugged. "Hot-blooded, I guess."

"I'll say."

Julia linked arms with her as they made their way back along the creek toward the house. "It's beautiful here."

"I think so."

"I'm glad you had this—growing up. I didn't have anyplace that grounded me in the same ways."

Evan tugged her closer. "I'm sorry about that."

"Don't be. It is what it is. I managed."

"I know. I'd like for you to do more than manage."

"I'm not complaining."

"No. You don't complain, do you?"

Julia shook her dark head. "I've never found it to be terribly productive. Have you?"

"Hell, yes. I complain about everything." Evan gazed at Julia. "Are you telling me that you've somehow failed to notice this about me?"

194

Julia smiled. "I was giving you the benefit of the doubt."

"Thanks, I'm sure."

"To be frank, that's one of the things I love most about you."

"What?"

"Your . . . feistiness."

"Feistiness?"

Julia nodded.

"Jesus. You make me sound like a Chihuahua."

Julia laughed. "That would be the *other* thing."

"Gee, thanks."

"Why does that offend you? It's not like you don't enjoy sitting on my lap."

Evan thought about that. "True."

They turned away from the creek and walked up the lawn toward the house. The snow had drifted a bit in this area, and walking took more effort.

"What's going to happen to us, Evan?" Julia asked.

Evan looked at her. She knew that her answer to this question was important. "If we're lucky—nothing."

"Nothing?"

Evan nodded.

"Normally, a response like that would annoy me."

"But?" Evan prompted after a moment.

"But right now, 'nothing' sounds pretty damn good."

Evan disengaged her arm and took Julia's hand. "I'm not going to let anything happen to you."

"I believe you."

"And before you ask . . . I'm not going to let anything happen to *us*, either. Not until we decide that there isn't an 'us' to protect anymore."

"Don't hold your breath on that one."

The simple statement wrapped itself around Evan like an extra overcoat. She tightened her fingers around Julia's gloved hand. They continued on toward the house in silence.

They spent the rest of the day working from their respective corners of the house. Evan set Julia up with a makeshift office at the dining-room table, where she could have some modicum of privacy for her conference call. While Julia was occupied with that, Evan finalized Stevie's travel arrangements for her trip the next day from Albany to Philadelphia. She'd be arriving at the 30th Street Station on the twelve-twenty train.

Evan didn't really want to leave Julia alone, and she could hardly expect Julia to accompany her into the city to pick Stevie up—it was too risky right now for them to be seen together in public. Besides, she preferred to have Stevie's first meeting with Julia take place in more hospitable and inviting territory. Dan was unavailable. He'd already called to say that he wanted to connect with Stevie on the weekend, in advance of their Monday meeting with Andy.

She was trying to puzzle this out when her cell phone rang.

"Father Tim?" Evan asked with surprise, when she saw his name on the caller ID. "Whatever it is, I had *nothing* to do with it."

"Nice try. You should know by now that yours will always be the first number I'll call."

"In that case, what do I need to atone for now?"

He laughed. "You're not on the hot seat this time. I have to be in Kennett Square tomorrow, and I wondered if you wanted to grab some lunch. You know, maybe see what it's like to meet in the daylight?"

"Now there's an interesting idea." Evan thought about it. *Why not kill two birds with one stone?* Tim needed to meet Julia at some point, and maybe he could help her out with Stevie. "What time do you need to be over here?"

"Mid-afternoon—any time before three. I've got to make a condolence call, and then stop by the hospital there. Why?"

"Stevie is coming home on the twelve-twenty train from Albany. Feel like picking her up on your way? I can explain why later."

"Sure," Tim said. "I'd love to see her. And this will give the

196

three of us time to grab some lunch together before I have to head out."

"Yeah. About that." She hesitated.

"Okay. This sounds ominous. What's up?"

"Remember the woman I told you about?"

"The married one?"

Fuck him for picking *that* fact to zero in on. "Yeah. The *married* one."

"What about her?"

"She's here."

The line was silent for a few seconds. "Here—as in *there?*"

"Right. Here."

"Evan—"

"Before you jump to conclusions, it's not what you think." In fact it was probably *exactly* what he thought, but that was beside the point. "I can explain everything, and I *will*—once you get here with Stevie." She paused. "I need you to trust me, Tim. I would never do anything reckless where my kid is concerned."

He sighed. "I'll probably live to regret saying this, but I do believe you."

"Thanks, *Father.*"

He chuckled. "I know I'm in for it whenever you start tossing out the honorifics. Will you let Stevie know I'll be picking her up?"

"Yeah."

"Okay, then. See you tomorrow." He hung up.

Evan set her cell phone down on the desktop.

"Thanks, Father?"

Evan swung around in her chair to see Julia leaning against the doorframe.

"Jesus, you startled me."

Julia raised an eyebrow.

Evan shrugged. "That was Tim . . . my, um . . ."

"Priest?"

Evan shrugged.

197

Julia crossed her arms. "Everything okay?"

"Yeah. He's going to pick Stevie up for me and drop her off here. I, uh, asked him to stay for lunch."

Julia nodded. "Lunch. Okay."

Evan was embarrassed. "Look, I know this is bizarre, but Tim is more than my . . . he's really a friend—a *good* friend. We sort of raised each other." She hesitated. "He wants to meet you."

Julia looked amused. "He knows about me?"

"Well. Yeah."

"Interesting."

Evan stared at the floor. Then she stole a look up at Julia, who was trying hard not to laugh. "You're enjoying this."

Julia nodded. "Immensely."

"Well, thank god my angst can serve some useful purpose."

Julia laughed. And Evan smiled, although she was trying hard not to. "How'd your call go?"

Julia walked into the room and sat down in an upholstered chair next to the desk.

"Okay." She picked at a stray thread that dangled from the sleeve of the lightweight fleece jacket Evan had lent her. The snow had stopped, but it was chilly in the house. "I also talked with Andy."

Andy? Evan was shocked.

"How did that happen?"

"I called him."

"And you *got* him?"

"Of course." Julia's tone was sharp. "Why wouldn't I? He's in Canada—not on Mars."

Evan didn't say anything.

Julia sighed and closed her eyes. "I'm sorry."

"It's okay."

Julia laid a hand on Evan's knee. "No, it's not. You didn't deserve that."

Evan remained silent for a few moments and then put her hand over Julia's. "What did you talk about?"

Julia shook her head. "Nothing. Everything." She looked up

to meet Evan's eyes. "He's going to stop in New York on his way back to Washington on Friday. We're going to talk about our situation."

Evan nodded. The thought of Julia with Andy made her half sick with worry—and dread. "Where are you meeting him?"

"At my office. He'll only have about forty-five minutes, then he'll take the train back to D.C."

Evan's wheels were turning. "What time will you have to be back in the city?"

"I'll need to be there by noon for a lunch meeting. Andy will be there between two and two-thirty—if his flight from Toronto is running on time."

This might just work out, Evan thought. She could drop Stevie off at Dan's office on her way.

She leaned forward in her chair. "I know this will be difficult, but it needs to happen."

Julia leaned forward, too. "I hope you're right."

Evan kissed her and stroked the side of her face. "I know I am."

In fact, she was never less certain of anything, but she knew it was a risk they had to take.

Early that evening, Evan got a text message from Ben Rush.

> Did some poking around and made an interesting discovery about Ms. Yellow Skis.

Evan quickly typed back.

> Where are you?

In short order, Ben wrote back.

> Reston. Will call you in 5 minutes.

Julia was upstairs showering, but Evan carried the phone out to the back porch just to be certain she wouldn't overhear their conversation.

In exactly five minutes, her phone rang.

"Ben?"

"Yeah."

"Talk to me."

"So, it turns out that your girlfriend, the Black Widow, went on a little shopping spree the other day."

"Meaning?"

"Meaning that she dropped about a yard and a half at Willis Ski & Snowboard in Fairfax. Care to guess what she bought?"

"Jesus Christ."

"Exactly."

Evan drummed her fingers on the porch rail. "I'm curious about something."

Ben laughed. "I was sure you would be."

"Why did she do this herself? I mean, why not job it out? Make it harder to trace?"

"Fuck you, Reed. What makes you think she *didn't* job it out? I just happen to be very good at my work."

Evan sighed. "My apologies, Ben. I'm sorry I underestimated you."

"That's more like it."

"So who actually made the purchase for her?"

"Beats the fuck outta me. Some joker named . . . hang on a minute." She could hear him fumbling around with some papers. "Here it is. 'D. Nemo.' Ring any bells?"

Evan thought she was going to be sick. "Are you serious?"

"Yep. That's the name. It was an online purchase, but the stuff shipped to Sheridan's office in Reston."

Christ almighty. "Yeah. I'm familiar with the name. Thanks, Ben. Great work."

"No problem. Oh, and, Reed?"

"Yeah?"

"Thanks for the little present you left hanging in my bathroom. *Not.*"

"What's wrong, Ben? Not your size?"

"Fuck you. I had a date last night, and she wasn't any too pleased when she came back from taking a piss."

"*Oopies.* So sorry, Ben."

"I repeat—fuck you."

"I'm sure you'll find a way to make me pay for it when you bill my ass."

"Count on it, love chunks."

He hung up.

Jesus, Evan thought. Now she knew for certain that Margo was in this with both feet.

But what was she going to do about it?

Everything was starting to move fast now. And that worried her. She needed to slow things down. Get Andy and Margo to relax and take their jumpy feet off the accelerator. She needed to buy some time. And she needed to buy it *now,* before Julia got caught in their crosshairs again.

She'd have to play her hand exactly right on Friday, which was shaping up to be her only shot at turning this mess around. She had no idea how Julia would react to her performance, but she didn't have a choice. The less Julia knew in advance, the better.

She walked back inside the house. The water wasn't running. That meant Julia was out of the shower, and would likely be back downstairs soon. Dinner was already in the oven, and would be ready within the hour. She glanced at the refrigerator. She still had a good bottle of champagne left over from her birthday. Dan had given it to her, jokingly, in a big box with a bottle of Don Julio tequila and a note that read, "For old time's sake."

Evan had long since re-gifted the tequila, but the champagne was something she'd been saving for the right occasion.

Since she thought there was even money on the likelihood that Julia wouldn't be talking with her again after Friday, she decided that tonight was the right time to open the bottle of Veuve.

She got out two glasses, and then walked into the living room to lay the fire.

With any luck, their last night alone together would be one for the memory books. She hoped so—especially since she had no confidence that she'd ever get a shot at another one.

After dinner, Evan and Julia lounged on the floor in front of the big stone fireplace and drank the last of the bottle of champagne.

Julia's arms were wrapped around Evan, who sat propped against her chest. Stevie's red throw was spread out across their legs.

Evan's fire was burning well. She'd built it earlier, using an assortment of cherry and apple-wood logs that she'd salvaged from trees that had fallen during an ice storm two years ago. The slow-burning hardwood filled the room with warmth and a heady aroma that was mildly intoxicating. It smelled like winter and spring, all at the same time.

Julia took a sip from her champagne glass and set it back on the coffee table beside them.

"I could get used to this."

Evan smiled. "It *is* pretty good hooch, isn't it?"

Julia kissed the back of her head. "Yes, it is, but I wasn't referring to the champagne."

"No?"

Julia tightened her arms around Evan. "No."

Evan smiled.

"I think maybe you knew that," Julia said.

"Maybe."

Julia kissed her head again. "I'm going to miss you when I leave on Friday."

Evan closed her eyes. "Me, too." *More than you know.*

"Come and see me in New York?"

"I will if you want me to," Evan said. She didn't like the direction this conversation was taking. She wanted to stay in the moment, and not look beyond tomorrow.

"Of course I'll want you to." Julia's mouth was close to Evan's ear. "Why wouldn't I?"

The hot breath against her neck was making it hard for Evan to think straight.

"Oh . . . I don't know. Outta sight—" *Ohmygod.* Julia's hands traveled over her body. "Outta mind."

She felt a gentle nip on her earlobe. Julia's warm hands slipped beneath her shirt. She licked and kissed along the side of Evan's neck.

"Outta *what*?" Julia's voice was low and husky.

Jesus god. Evan pulled free and pivoted within the circle of Julia's arms.

"My *mind*," she muttered against Julia's mouth. "I'm outta my mind."

Julia kissed her back as they dropped to the floor together. "Then we're both crazy."

She got no argument from Evan as they quickly lost themselves in each other, and in the sweet, hypnotic heat of the fire.

Chapter 23

Tim arrived at Evan's house with Stevie in tow at nearly one forty-five. The big redhead unloaded Stevie's oversized blue duffel bag from the back of his Subaru wagon. Evan realized that this probably was a bad omen—hinting at the fact that Stevie hadn't done any laundry in a while.

Stevie walked over to her, smiling, and Evan pulled her into a hug. She stroked her head and smiled into her blonde hair. She didn't want to let go of her. The weeks since she'd last seen her felt like a couple of lifetimes.

"Hi, Mom," Stevie said into her sweater. "What's for lunch?"

Evan laughed. "I missed you, too."

Stevie drew back and shrugged. "I *tried* to get Father Tim to stop at Dunkin' Donuts, but he said no." She looked over her shoulder at Tim, who stood just behind her.

Tim reached around Stevie to kiss Evan on the cheek. "Yeah. I told her that *one* munchkin in the car was enough."

Stevie sighed and rolled her eyes. "He's hilarious."

Evan swatted her on the butt. "Show some respect."

"I *am* showing respect. *You'd* just tell him to fuck off."

Evan looked at Tim.

He shrugged. "Hard to argue with that."

Behind them, Evan heard Julia's low laughter. She stepped aside to make the introductions.

"Stevie and Tim, I'd like you to meet my very good friend,

Julia Donne. Julia, this freakishly tall person is Tim Donovan—one of my oldest and best friends. I figure the two of you will soon see eye-to-eye on most things—literally, if not metaphorically." She looped an arm around Stevie's shoulders. "And *this* vertically-challenged victim of Tourette's Disorder is my daughter, Stephanie. As you have, no doubt, already determined, she takes after her father."

Julia smiled and stepped forward from the doorway.

She shook hands with Tim, who seemed to be looking her over with surprise and admiration. Evan felt irrationally pleased by that.

Then Julia faced Stevie. *The moment of truth.*

"Hi," Julia said. "I'm really happy to meet you. And I confess that I like donuts, too. So, selfishly, I wish you *had* stopped for some on the way." She held out her hand. Stevie took it without hesitation. She smiled shyly at Julia, then looked at Evan with a raised eyebrow.

Evan looked between Tim and Stevie. They stared back at her.

All that was missing from this goddamned scene was an overlay of cricket noises.

What the fuck?

She sighed. "Okay. Let's just get it out there and move on." She stepped back toward the open door and took Julia's hand. "Yes. She's my *girlfriend*. Okay? Any other questions or concerns will have to wait until lunch. I'm starving, and I'd rather not stand out here in the cold any longer."

Julia looked stunned. Tim and Stevie started laughing.

They all made their way from the yard into the house.

Stevie dropped her backpack on the floor of the foyer and announced that she needed something to drink. She pulled off her jacket and made a beeline for the kitchen.

Tim dropped the bulging duffel bag near the bottom of the steps and turned to Evan and Julia. "Well. At least we don't have to kill time talking *around* anything." He smiled at Julia, who still seemed nonplussed.

"I guess not," she said.

Tim laid a hand on Julia's shoulder. "Don't worry. I'm used to her unorthodox style."

Julia smiled. "You're a few steps ahead of me when it comes to that, I guess."

Evan held out both hands to Tim. "*Hello?* In the same room and standing right in front of you."

Tim looked at her. "Deal with it, Evangeline. You're the author of this little drama."

Evan started to unleash a stream of expletives, but Julia clamped a hand across her mouth.

"Stop it. He's a *priest*, for crying out loud."

Evan pulled Julia's hand down. "Oh really? And what tipped you off? The dog collar?"

Tim laughed. "I think I like this woman, Evan."

Evan looked back at him. "Now *there's* a newsflash. You always were a sucker for blue eyes and a good set of gams."

Tim shrugged. "I *am* still a man."

Evan leaned closer to him and lowered her voice. "Don't worry, Timbo. I won't tell anyone."

Stevie walked back into the living room, carrying a can of Diet Coke. "What are you all still doing in the foyer? You look like you're expecting a tornado or something."

Evan rolled her eyes, started toward the kitchen, and stopped to grab Stevie by the arm. "Come on. You can help me carry the food in."

Julia still looked slightly shell-shocked, so Tim took her by the arm and led her toward the sofa. "Come on, Julia. Let's sit down and get better acquainted while Evan gets the food up."

Julia just nodded and followed him into the living room.

Tim sat down in the armchair next to the couch. "So, I know a little bit about your . . . situation."

"My *situation?*" Julia asked.

"Well. I'm reluctant to run the risk of inaccurately characterizing your relationship with Evan," he said. "What I mean to say is that I know a bit about how the two of you met, and a little bit about the complicated dynamics of your personal situation."

Julia raised an eyebrow. "You should be a politician."

He smiled. "Don't think it hasn't occurred to me. The wardrobe choices are a lot better."

She smiled at him. The muffled voices of Evan and Stevie laughing and arguing came from the kitchen.

Julia dropped her gaze. "It's true that I am still married to Andrew Townsend, but we've been estranged for some time now. This—this *thing* with Evan . . . this relationship—it wasn't planned. For either of us." She looked up and met Tim's eyes. "It just happened. And I'm not sorry it did."

He laid a hand on her forearm. "You don't owe me any explanation."

"Yes I do. You matter to Evan. I want you to know that I'm not using her, or leading her on."

Tim gazed at her for a moment. "I believe you." He inclined his head toward the kitchen. "She's a handful. You sure you've got the stamina to keep up with her?"

"I honestly don't know. I hope so."

Tim nodded. "Well in that case, my best advice is to tie a knot and hang on."

She smiled at him. "I had planned to do just that, but thanks for the heads-up."

Stevie put some pre-sliced cold cuts and raw veggies onto a large plate. "What's with the rabbit food, Mom? I was really hoping for something home-cooked."

Evan handed her a plastic container. "Quit complaining. I got this for you at Wawa."

Stevie snatched the container out of Evan's hands. "No way. Is this a Hot Turkey Shorti?"

"It's *most* of one. You have to supply your own bread. I didn't want it to get soggy."

"Sweet." Stevie looked up with a hopeful expression. "But you'll still cook something tonight, right?"

"I might be persuaded—if you don't do or say anything to embarrass me."

"Oh." Stevie set the container down on the countertop. "Right. Not in front of your girlfriend. Jeez, Mom. When did *that* happen?"

Evan crossed her arms. "It hasn't 'happened.' It *is* happening." She watched Stevie for a minute, trying to gauge her reaction to the revelation. Stevie looked calm enough—unmoved, even. "So, are you okay with this?"

"This?"

Evan exhaled. "Yes. *This.* Julia. Me. *You* and me. You and *we.* All of it."

Stevie picked up a carrot stick and bit it in half. "Sure. Why wouldn't I be?"

"Are you being serious?"

"Yeah. I mean, it's about time. You haven't even gone out with anybody since Cruella."

Stevie meant Liz.

They had actually met once—accidentally—the previous spring when Evan took Stevie to a concert at Wolf Trap. Evan remembered how awkward she felt, introducing Stevie to Liz— who was hardly discreet about the nature of her interest in Evan. She shook her head at the recollection of how mortified and dirty she felt—how shallow and exposed.

"Julia's not like Liz," Evan explained.

Stevie rolled her eyes. "No kidding. She's *nice*, and gorgeous."

Evan was surprised. "You think so?"

"Duh? Now who's not being serious?"

Evan shrugged. "I guess she is."

Stevie gazed at her with an amused expression. "How long will she be staying here?"

"Only until Friday morning." Evan hesitated. "Is that okay with you?"

Stevie nodded. "Does Dad know?"

"About Julia?"

Stevie nodded again.

Evan thought about how to answer. She decided that less was more. "Yes and no. Honey, you need to know that Julia is married to Senator Townsend."

Stevie's eyes grew wide. "No way."

Evan sighed. "Way."

"For real?"

"Yes. For real."

Stevie chewed on this detail for a moment. "Wow. Am I going to, like, see your photo on the cover of *People* magazine or anything?"

"I certainly hope not."

"Does Senator Townsend know?"

Evan nodded. "But he and Julia are separated right now."

"Because of you?"

"No. Not because of me."

Stevie looked toward the living room. She lowered her voice. "Does Father Tim know?"

Evan looked over her shoulder, and cautiously leaned toward her, making a grand ceremony of whispering into her ear. "Yes."

Stevie drew back and socked her on the arm. "You *suck*."

Evan laughed. "So I've been told."

"Mom, that's just *gross*."

"You said it, not me."

Stevie looked up at the ceiling. "Why'd I have to be the one tagged with the lesbo mother?"

"Beats me. Luck of the draw, kiddo."

Stevie sighed. "Do you really like her?"

Evan was trying hard not to blush. It wasn't easy. "Yeah. I do."

"That's okay, then." Stevie picked up the tray of cold deli meats. "Let's eat."

She turned around and walked toward the dining room.

Evan stood there and watched her go, feeling like she'd just won the lottery—twice.

The conversation during lunch bounced around from religion, to politics, to yesterday's surprise snowfall. The four made short work of the platters of cut-up meats and cheeses. Stevie even generously offered to share part of her Turkey Shorti sandwich with Julia. Clearly, the teenager was making an effort to reach out to her mom's new girlfriend.

Julia seemed to notice, and more than once, she met Evan's eyes with a quiet smile.

Tim cleared his throat. Evan looked at him with a guilty expression.

"I was *saying*," Tim repeated. "Is there any way to coerce you into making some coffee?"

"Sure." Evan pushed back her chair. "Coming right up."

Tim stood up, too. "How about I help you?"

They collected plates and silverware before heading into the kitchen.

"I just don't get all that Mormon jazz," Stevie said to Julia, continuing their conversation about the questionable popularity of the entire *Twilight* series of books and films.

Evan pushed open the door into the kitchen, shook her head, and smiled.

Behind her, Tim pushed the swinging door closed.

Evan suddenly felt like she'd been caught smoking cigarettes beneath the bleachers at school.

Tim set his stack of plates down and leaned against the countertop, facing her.

Here it comes, Evan thought.

"So," he began, "not what I expected."

"No?" Evan asked.

"No. Not even close."

"I'm sure you've seen photos of her before."

"I'm not talking about how she *looks*—although may I just say, *wow*?"

Evan felt her cheeks get hot.

Tim laughed. "No. What I meant was that she's just so much more . . ."

"Poised?" Evan suggested.

"Yeah, that. But really . . . just . . . *more*."

210

"More?"

He nodded. "More. Isn't that how she first hit you?"

Evan thought about it. "No. I'd have to say that how she first hit me was more like having a ton of bricks dropped on my ass."

Tim smiled. "I can see that."

"I bet you can, you old letch." She started setting up the coffeemaker.

"Hey." Tim held up a hand. "Hold off. I've never once resented you for *any* of your girlfriends—until right now."

"High praise, Tim."

"Yes, it is." He smiled smugly. "Stevie seems to like her."

"You think so?" Evan took three mugs down from an overhead cabinet. She tried to sound casual.

He nodded. "I'd say so. She's enough like you and Dan that she doesn't pull any punches. If she didn't like Julia, I think you'd know it."

"I guess that's true."

"So, what happens now?"

"With what?"

He sighed. "With you and Julia. Where are you going with all of this? I'd assume that having her here to meet Stevie is a pretty big step."

"It's a step," she agreed. "How big it ends up being remains to be seen."

"What about her husband?"

Evan was growing impatient with this line of questioning. "What about him?"

"Come on. Does he know about you two? Is he going to step aside?" He paused. "Are you?"

Evan lifted her hand and made rapid slashing motions across the base of her neck. "You wanna give the inquisition a rest? We're not in the confessional right now, and I'm not really feeling the urge to wax prosaic about my future relationship prospects."

"Okay, okay. Forget I asked. But, Evan . . . I know you. And there's no way you'd be this far down *any* road if you only saw diminishing returns."

"Is that so?"

"Yeah, that's so. And you know it, too."

She sighed. "I'll keep that in mind."

"Just do me—and yourself—a favor, and be careful. I'm not sure what all is going on here, but it's clear that you're involved in something . . . ominous."

She looked at him in amazement. "Just how in the hell did you come up with that idea?"

"As much as I'd like to pretend that I'm psychic, I have to confess that Dan called me."

What the fuck? "*Dan* called you? When?" Evan was furious.

Tim shrugged. "Two days ago. He was pretty bent out of shape after you met with him on Monday."

"Jesus Christ! So he calls my fucking *priest?*"

Tim laid a calming hand on her shoulder. "No. He called your friend."

She fumed for a moment, while she tried to collect her thoughts. *What the hell was Dan up to with this bullshit?* It had to be about Julia. Goddamn it to hell. He was *jealous*. She *knew* it. This happened any time she showed serious interest in someone.

Not, she reasoned, that she showed serious interest in anyone all that often.

She sighed. Maybe he really was just concerned about her acting like some out-of-control, conspiracy-mongering whack job.

Great. She hated it when she was forced to pull back and think about things rationally.

Well, it was all about to get a lot worse. After Friday, Dan would have the guys with the butterfly nets all spooled up and ready to haul her ass off. This was all working out just *fine*.

First she'd lose Julia, then she'd lose her job and her credibility. It probably wouldn't be long until Dan tried to take Stevie away, too. Then what would she be left with?

From the dining room, the silvery sound of Julia's laughter floated in above the noise of the coffeemaker. Evan dropped her head and stared at her shoes.

Julia would be safe and alive. That's what she'd be left with. And then Evan could return to her life of self-imposed solitude. *Julia will be safe, and I'll be alone.*

The solution wasn't perfect, but she'd find a way to live with it. Just like she always did.

Evan felt like they'd been playing this damn game for about six hours. She stole another glance at her watch.

No, it wasn't that bad. Yet. But it sure as shit *felt* like it.

Stevie's turn—*again*—and Evan couldn't believe the level of intensity her daughter was applying to Scrabble. Stevie loved games—always had. That amazed Evan, because she never had the patience to enjoy them, or the inclination to try and acquire it.

She looked across the table at Julia, who was wearing an expression that mirrored Stevie's. She was studying the board with textbook intensity. Watching her, Evan got a clear sense of what it must be like to face this woman across a boardroom table.

Not something, she realized, that she'd ever want to do.

Evan tapped a tile against the tabletop. It was the fucking "z"—*of course*. She'd drawn it about five turns ago.

The board was filling up. There were precious few open spaces left. And Stevie wasn't helping. Evan had had just about enough.

"You planning to make a play during this life, kiddo?"

Stevie lifted her gaze and looked at her. "Jeez, Mom. You got a train to catch or something?"

"No. I'd just like to wrap this up before my first Social Security checks start rolling in."

Stevie rolled her eyes and looked back down at her row of tiles. "I'm not taking *that* long. Just chill."

"Chill?" Evan sat back. "You're kidding me, right? I think the Hanging Gardens of Babylon were finished in less time than this damn game is taking."

Julia laughed. "Will you just relax? Go and make us all something to drink."

Evan brightened at that suggestion. *Why not?* It was after four.

"Okay." She pushed her chair back. "Whatcha want, kiddo?"

213

Stevie didn't lift her head. "A mojito, please."

"In your *dreams*, munchkin. Wanna make another selection?"

Stevie sighed. "Diet Coke."

"That can happen." Evan stood up and started for the kitchen.

Julia raised her eyes. "Hey? Aren't you going to ask me what I want?"

"Oh," Evan said. "I already *know* what you want."

Julia blushed.

Stevie looked back and forth between them, then sighed as she laid her tiles down on the board. "*Gross*. Why don't you two get a room?"

Evan thumped her on the head as she passed by her chair.

"We *have* a room."

Stevie shook her head and started counting up her score. "Okay . . . that's five, six, eleven, twelve, thirteen—and triple word score makes thirty-nine."

Evan stopped and turned around. "Thirty-nine? Are you kidding me?" She looked at the board. "What the hell is a *fakir*?"

Stevie met her gaze. "Are you challenging me?"

Julia sniggered.

Evan sighed. "Oh, the two of you *royally* suck. I don't know why I agreed to this."

She walked on into the kitchen to make the drinks. Behind her, she could hear Julia and Stevie laughing.

In her wildest dreams, she never would have imagined that they would get along so well. It was incredible. *Surreal.* What were the odds?

And now that she'd experienced it . . . how would she ever adjust to life without it?

She yanked open the door to the freezer and filled Stevie's glass with ice. Rhetorical questions like this didn't accomplish anything. They just made her feel cranky and hopeless.

And she didn't need any more incentive to be cranky. Tomorrow would take care of that. Tomorrow, she'd go and do what she had to do. She'd take care of business, because, after all, that's what everything came down to at the end.

And after she took care of business? Well. She'd have plenty of time to sit alone and sort through the detritus of her life.

She grabbed a bottle of Seghesio and two glasses. Why not lend some elegance to life's misfortunes? Wasn't that what Jane Austen said? *Hell.* She could deliver a credible enough imitation of Mr. Bennet and sit quietly in her study, sifting through the ashes that filled the coal bin of her life—searching for stray diamonds. They were there, certainly. Some she'd made, and some that came her way just because they did.

There was plenty of time for all of that. *Plenty.*

Right now, though? Right now, Stevie was calling her because it was her turn to play. It was her turn, and she had nothing to put down that would add up to any kind of winning score. Not here, and not anyplace else in her life, either.

She loaded the drinks onto a wooden tray and went back into the dining room.

Julia raised her eyebrows when she saw the bottle of wine. "Are we celebrating something?"

Evan handed Stevie her Coke. "You might say that."

"What's that, Mom?" Stevie asked. "You finally come up with a way to play that 'z' you've been waving around for the last hour?"

"Smartass," Evan said, as she reclaimed her seat. "I *knew* I shoulda taken that morning-after pill."

Stevie just laughed at her. This was not a new exchange between them. "You know what hindsight is worth?"

"In your case? About sixty grand in tuition payments, and never being able to watch what I want on TV."

Stevie stuck her tongue out at Evan. "It sucks being you."

"Sometimes it does."

They smiled at each other.

Evan sat forward and got serious about groaning her way through another turn. This was really hopeless.

Then she saw something. *No way.* She checked her letters. Then checked them again.

Well, whattaya know?

With great deliberation, she laid out her tiles, and did her best imitation of Stevie.

"That's ten, fourteen, sixteen, seventeen, eighteen, nineteen, and triple word score makes fifty-seven."

She sat back, curled her hand in front of her mouth, and blew across her nails.

Julia and Stevie stared at the board.

"You have *got* to be kidding me with this." Stevie was hunched over the board, recounting the point values of the tiles.

"Zygote?" Julia asked, with a raised eyebrow.

Evan winked at her, as she poured herself a big glass of wine. "What can I tell you? I'm a sucker for cleavage."

Julia gave her a dramatic eye-roll, but had a hard time concealing her smile.

Maybe, Evan thought, *these damn games really are okay—once you get the hang of them.*

She smiled back at Julia.

Even losing wasn't half bad, if you had a good time getting there.

Chapter 24

Julia left early on Friday, having called for a car the night before. Evan protested, but Julia insisted. She said that leaving was going to be hard enough, and she didn't want to eat into any more of the time Evan had at home with Stevie.

Shortly after seven, they stood in the dark foyer saying their goodbyes.

"I'll miss you," Julia said.

Evan pressed her face into the side of Julia's neck. She wanted to memorize her smell—create an intimate link between it and her memories of the last few days. She took a deep breath. *Lavender*—heir of the ancient oil used to ward off evil. It was the same libation used by the sister of Lazarus when she washed the feet of Christ.

The scent of hope and calm, and it clung to Julia like a second skin.

"I'll miss you, too," Evan said. *Probably forever.*

"Call me tonight?" Julia asked.

Evan nodded.

Julia drew back and looked down at her. "You okay?"

Evan shrugged. "I hate this kind of thing."

Julia smiled at her. "I don't care for it much myself. But it's not forever, just for a bit."

Evan nodded again.

Two short blasts sounded from a car horn. Julia's car had arrived.

Julia kissed her, then stepped back and took hold of her roller bag.

Evan opened the big front door. "Bye."

Julia laid a hand on Evan's forearm as she passed her. "I love you."

Evan's throat felt tight. She wasn't sure she could get the words out. "Me, too." She shrugged. "Love you."

Julia smiled at her discomfort. "You're a nut."

Evan didn't disagree.

"Call me later." Julia squeezed her arm and walked outside to the waiting car.

Evan stood in the open doorway and watched her go.

Dan was surprised but not unhappy when Evan called about dropping Stevie off earlier in the day—much earlier. He had a morning appointment in Philadelphia anyway, so he agreed to meet them at the 30th Street Station, where Evan was catching the noon Metroliner to New York. Andy was due to arrive at Julia's office sometime between two and two-thirty, and Evan wanted to make certain she arrived plenty of time in advance.

Stevie was going to spend the night with Dan at his apartment in Philadelphia. This would give her the chance to see her grandparents before he brought her back to Chadds Ford on Saturday afternoon. Evan and Stevie would have another full day together before Stevie's break ended and she had to head back to Emma Willard.

For once, Evan's train pulled into Penn Station right on time.

She took her time on the short walk to Julia's office building on Madison Avenue, trying to compose herself and prepare for what was about to happen.

Once inside the massive high-rise, she found a convenient seat in a remote corner of the lobby—one that gave her a clear view of the Madison Avenue entrance.

Andy was easy to spot. He arrived a few minutes after two and crossed the lobby with the ease and confidence of someone who never questioned his right to be wherever he was. He looked handsome and self-assured. He was alone, and Evan said a quiet prayer of thanks for that. She looked at her watch and decided to give herself fifteen minutes before she followed him up to the thirty-eighth floor offices of Donne & Hale. She was banking on the hope that Julia would not be running behind schedule.

Evan pushed open the big door that led into the lobby area of Julia's offices, and was relieved to see a different woman behind the reception desk—one who would not recognize her. She held up the FedEx Letter Pack that she had brought along to use as an alibi and approached the harried-looking woman, who seemed to be struggling with a fax machine. She barely looked up when Evan entered.

"Hello, there," Evan said. "I'm Senator Townsend's assistant, and he asked me to deliver this letter to him as soon as it arrived. I believe that he and Ms. Donne are waiting on it."

The woman glanced up from her awkward position, hunched over the fax machine. "Oh. Of course." She started to put down the package of toner cartridges she was holding. "Just give me a moment, and I'll call Ms. Donne's assistant."

Evan held up a hand. "No need to trouble yourself. I know the way. And the senator asked me to deliver this to him personally."

The receptionist looked like she was going to protest, but Evan just smiled at her and quickly started down the long hallway that led toward Julia's office. She heaved a sigh of relief when the woman didn't try to stop her.

So far, so good.

The door to Julia's private office was just ahead. Evan stopped outside it and took a deep breath, then she dropped the bogus letter pack to the floor and pushed open the door.

Julia was seated on the small loveseat, and Andy was close beside her, holding her hand. They looked up in surprise when she entered, then their expressions quickly changed from recognition to amazement.

"Evan? What on earth are you doing here?" Julia asked in a low and anxious voice.

Andy stared back at Evan with narrowed eyes and an expression that showed more curiosity than anything. He didn't speak. He didn't release Julia's hand, either, and that fact pissed her off.

A lot.

Maybe this little performance wouldn't be as hard to pull off as she had feared.

Evan gestured toward Andy. "I could ask *him* that same question."

Andy looked back and forth between Julia and Evan, and then he faced Evan.

"What do you want, Reed?" His tone was not very charitable.

"Isn't that kind of obvious? I want the same thing you want."

"Evan—" Julia started to stand up, but Andy pulled her back down—a little too roughly to suit Evan.

"I think you'd better leave . . . before this goes any further," Andy said in an icy tone.

"Fuck you, Townsend. You have no idea how far it's *already* gone." She leveled her gaze at Julia. "Tell him, Julia. Go ahead and tell him how *far* we've gone. I want to hear you explain it in plain words that even I can understand."

Julia looked shell-shocked. "Evan, what are you *doing*? This won't help you."

"Oh really? What will help me, Julia? Watching you hop back into bed with *him*? Is that what I need to 'help me' get over you?"

Julia looked incredulous. "Why are you *doing* this? This isn't what we talked about."

Evan laughed. "No. It isn't. *None* of this is what we talked about. But you just couldn't leave your gilded little cocoon, could you? Tell me: What was I, Julia? Just another little science experiment—like *Margo*?"

"That's enough." Andy jumped to his feet. "You need to leave—*now*. Don't make me call my security detail."

Evan took a step closer to him. "I'll leave when I goddamn well want to. I'm not finished yet."

Andy pulled out his cell phone and punched a button on its keypad. "Oh, trust me, you're *beyond* finished here. And unless you want to be finished everyplace else, too, you'll go—*now*."

Evan poked a finger at his chest. "You slimy motherfucker, don't think I don't *know* what you've been up to."

"Are you threatening me?"

Julia stood up. "Stop it. Just *stop* it." She stepped between them, and stood with her back to Andy. Her eyes were like chips of ice. "Evan. You need to leave. Now. *Please*."

Andy took hold of both of Julia's arms as he stood behind her. Even as ridiculous as the circumstances were, Evan couldn't help noticing what a perfect-looking couple they made. They were like models for one of those pairs of figurines that topped wedding cakes.

She exhaled. "Sure. I'll go. It's pretty clear what the lay of the land is here." She turned toward the door, then stopped and faced them. "You were a good fuck, Julia. Just like Margo said you'd be." She shook her head. "I should've listened to her. She told me you'd never stick around."

Julia slapped her—hard. The sound seemed to reverberate off the walls of the office. For a moment, the three of them stared at each other in silence. Stunned, Evan raised a hand to the side of her face.

"I've had enough of this—" Andy tried to push past Julia, but she barred his way.

"Stop it, Andy." She looked at Evan. Her expression was stoney. "Let her *go*."

Game. Set. Match.

Evan nodded. "Yeah. Let me go. *She* can help you out with that one, Senator. She's a *pro* at it."

She turned around, walked out, and slammed the door behind her. Her face hurt like hell. Julia packed one hell of a wallop.

Evan felt dazed and half sick as she weaved her way back down the long hallway toward the lobby. She just hoped she'd be able to get out of there before Andy's goons arrived. She knew she was unsteady on her feet—she struggled to even walk a straight line. Her head was pounding, and she felt like she might throw up. But she needed to keep moving—just until she could get out of the fucking building and get some fresh air.

She left the firm and crossed the hallway just as the big steel elevator doors opened and two large men exited. They pushed past Evan without a second look and walked rapidly toward the entrance to Julia's offices. Evan got quickly into the car they had vacated, pushed the lobby button, and sagged against the wall as soon as the doors closed.

It had all gone *exactly* the way she had hoped it would. Better, even.

Andy had more of a hair-trigger than she realized, and he had taken the bait. Judging by the murderous looks he was giving her, he'd taken it hook, line, and sinker.

And Julia?

A wave of nausea washed over her.

Yeah. Julia had taken it, too. Evan had made certain of that.

It had all gone *exactly* according to plan.

And she had nobody but herself to blame for her success.

Evan had nearly an hour and a half to kill before she caught her train back to Philadelphia. She was miserable.

She thought about hitting any one of the dozen bars she passed on the walk back to Penn Station. But why add insult to injury? All she'd get for her trouble would be an express pass to waking up tomorrow with a hangover, and she knew she didn't need that on top of everything else. Instead, she dropped down into a chair in the lounge at her platform, and stared at the other travelers—trying not to think too hard about how well her little drama had just played out.

It was going to be a long night. And when she got home, Stevie wouldn't be there to take her mind off the damage she'd just done by tossing a monster-sized hand grenade into the center of her personal life. But if it worked, and it got Julia out of Andy's crosshairs—even temporarily—it was a price worth paying.

Still, it hurt like hell, and she was having a hard time extolling the virtues of selflessness in service to the "greater good."

Maybe she could give Tim a call?

No. That wouldn't work. He knew too much, now. And she'd

never be able to blow smoke up his ass if he tried to pin her down about Julia, and she was positive he would.

She sighed and slid lower into her chair. The lounge was filling up. A kid with one of those obnoxious toy lawnmowers filled with plastic, popping balls kept running back and forth in front of her row of chairs. Evan wondered if the kid's parents would notice or care if she tripped her the next time she passed by.

The lights were too bright in this joint. She closed her eyes against the glare and tried to empty her mind.

Her seat jolted when someone sat down right beside her.

Jesus Christ, she thought. *What the fuck is up with people?* There were at least a dozen other empty seats in this damn lounge. She'd just have to move.

Then she caught a scent of something familiar.

Lavender.

She opened her eyes and turned to face the person who had just claimed the seat next to her.

A pair of blue eyes stared back at her.

Julia.

And she didn't look very happy.

"That was some performance." Her voice was flat. Atonal. "Just what in the hell were you trying to accomplish?"

Evan was stunned. "You *can't* be here."

Julia gave a bitter-sounding laugh and crossed her arms. "Apparently, I *can*. Now. Will you do me the honor of explaining what that little costume drama was all about?"

Evan's head was spinning. The kid with the damn lawnmower made another lightning pass in front of them, barely missing their feet.

"Performance?" She felt like she was struggling to keep up.

Julia nodded. "Did you think I took *any* of that seriously?" She shook her head. "I was furious with you. But as horrified as I was about your behavior, I was angrier that you would pull a stunt like that without telling me about it beforehand."

"Stunt?"

Julia sighed. "Should we just sit here a while until you can recall how to string an entire sequence of words together? You sure weren't having any problems with that an hour ago."

"You can't *be* here. I'm not kidding."

"Why not?"

"Because it will ruin everything if Andy finds out."

"Oh, I think things with Andy were pretty much ruined before you decided to explode through my door with both guns blazing."

Evan sighed. "That isn't what I meant."

"I know what you *meant*, Evan. Andy isn't an idiot, and neither am I."

"What's that supposed to mean?"

"It means that even if you were successful in getting him to take your bait—and that's a stretch, at best—I certainly did not. And I won't. So it's going to go better for you in the long run if you start dealing more directly and honestly with me." She paused and gazed at Evan for a moment. Then she raised a hand and stroked the side of Evan's face. "I'm sorry I slapped you. I can't believe I did that."

Evan laid a hand over hers, and then slowly lowered their hands to rest on the arm that separated their chairs. "I deserved it."

Julia nodded. "I won't disagree with that."

"Still. I never would've pegged you as the violent type."

"Really? You've just never seen me react when something I care about is threatened."

Evan was growing exasperated. "Julia, I'm trying to *save* you, not threaten you."

"Save me from what?"

Evan lowered her eyes.

Julia sighed. "That's what I thought." She squeezed Evan's hand. "Look at me."

Evan raised her eyes and met Julia's steady gaze. Her expression was still unreadable, but at least looked less menacing.

"I don't need you to save me. If you can't find your way to accepting and honoring that—in every sense—then there won't be much left for us to talk about. Ever." She took a deep breath, and then exhaled. "I don't need a protector. I don't need a security detail. And I sure as hell don't need a lover who can't grasp the simple concept that I'm a big girl who can take care of herself."

Against her will, Evan smiled. "You're a big girl?"

Julia smiled. "Last time I checked."

"Jesus." Evan chuffed. "This sure as shit didn't pan out the way I thought it would."

Julia squeezed her hand again. "Is Stevie with Dan?"

"Yeah. Until tomorrow."

"Come home with me," she whispered.

Evan felt her toes curl up inside her shoes, but shook her head. "No dice. We can't be seen together now."

"Why not?" Julia asked. Evan rolled her eyes, and Julia held up a hand to stop her. "Never mind. Forget I asked."

After a few moments of silence, Julia withdrew her cell phone from her bag.

"What are you doing?" Evan asked, as she watched her punch in a sequence of numbers.

"The firm maintains a suite at the Plaza for out-of-town guests. I think you qualify."

Behind them, a loud wail rose over the din of the waiting area. Evan turned her head to see that the aspiring groundskeeper had somehow managed to get her mower wedged between a large trash receptacle and a vending machine. She stomped her feet in front of it, crying and tugging at its plastic handle in frustration. It wouldn't break free.

No one seemed to be in a hurry to help her out, either.

As she watched the girl, Evan thought about the obvious parallels to her own situation. Then she smiled. *Quit struggling, kid. There are worse ways to be stuck.*

Julia was finished with her call. She stood up. "Are you ready?"

Was she?

The seconds they stared at each other felt like several lifetimes.

Evan grabbed the strap of her messenger bag and stood up. "Yeah. I think I am."

They left the waiting room and headed for the nearest street exit, and its accompanying sea of taxis.

Chapter 25

"Just what the fuck do you think you're doing?"

Dan was furious with her, and he wasn't trying to hide it.

She sighed. "Hello, Dan. Enjoying the cooler weather?"

"I mean it. You went too far this time."

"*This* time?"

"Yeah. This time. Which, loosely translated, means you're fired."

Evan glanced down at her watch. She'd only been back from New York about thirty minutes—they hadn't been in a hurry to vacate the suite that morning. News certainly traveled fast.

"It didn't take him long to call you," she said.

"What the fuck did you think he would do? And he didn't call *me*—he called Marcus. Jesus. You're just lucky he didn't take out a goddamn restraining order."

Evan remained silent.

"This is serious, Evan. Marcus can make it impossible for you to work in this town again."

She snorted. "What a tragedy *that* would be."

"You think this is *funny?* You think I'm kidding?"

She exhaled. "I know what I'm doing. I need you to trust me."

"*Trust* you?" he asked, sounding incredulous. "When you're running around acting like Glenn Close on crack? Jesus, Evan."

"It's not like that."

"It isn't? *Really?* You fuck the wife of a sitting U.S. senator—

one you're being *paid* to investigate—and then you flip out and go all *Fatal Attraction* on their asses? What the hell do *you* call it?"

"Doing my job."

"You really have lost it."

"I mean it. I need you to trust me."

"How can you ask that of me when you're behaving like a lunatic?"

"I know what I'm doing," she repeated.

The line was silent. Then she heard him sigh.

"Then how about cluing me in so I can understand it, too?"

"I tried to explain it to you already. You just didn't want to hear me."

"Oh, come on. You're not still talking about that Aspen bull-shit, are you?"

Evan picked at a loose thread on the cuff of her shirt as her exasperation grew.

"Evan?"

"Yeah. I'm here." She decided to shift gears. "When are you bringing Stevie back?"

He sighed again. "I thought I'd run her over around three-thirty."

"Why don't you plan on staying for an early supper? We can talk then."

He thought about it. "Okay. I suppose that could work."

"Good. I'll see you both around four."

"Evan?"

"What?"

"I can't fix this for you. You're on your own with this one."

"What else is new?"

She laughed and hung up the phone.

After they finished dinner that evening, Stevie disappeared to Evan's office to watch online episodes of *Glee*, and probably text a couple dozen of her friends. Evan and Dan sat on the back porch, drinking iced coffee and watching her neighbor's Jersey cows mill around near the tiny stream that cut across the back half of her property.

"You really are making me crazy." Dan still sounded concerned, but less exasperated than he had been earlier.

She looked at him in the fading light. He really was a good-looking man. Too bad they couldn't make a serious relationship work. But she couldn't change the way she was wired, and she wouldn't want to, even if she could.

And besides, they had Stevie. They couldn't get much more serious than that.

"I know I'm making you nuts. It's one of the perks of the job."

"Not funny . . . and if you'll recall, you don't *have* a job anymore."

She shrugged and set her glass down on a small table next to her chair. The table was mostly a distressed white, but still had one dark red leg—a carryover from the day many years ago that Stevie decided it would be fun to paint the porch furniture with some of the Rustoleum Evan had been using to refurbish an old lawn tractor. At first, she left the table untouched as a kind of wages-of-sin object lesson. But as the days and weeks passed, she grew fond of its peculiar appearance, and decided to leave it alone—free to sport its singular blemish with impunity.

"Is she really worth it?"

Dan's voice was so low, Evan wasn't sure she'd heard him correctly.

She gave him a perplexed look. "Excuse me?"

"Julia. Your . . . *thing* with her." He waved his hand. "Is it worth all of this?"

"My thing?"

"You know what I mean." He gestured toward the inside of the house, where Stevie reposed in what he plainly assumed was blissful ignorance. "Don't make me spell it out."

Evan looked at him like he was some kind of bizarre museum exhibit. "You don't have to speak in code. Stevie knows about Julia."

"She does?" he asked, surprised.

228

Evan rolled her eyes. "Of course she does. I don't hide things like this from her."

He raised an eyebrow. "Things like this?"

She nodded and met his gaze. "Things that are worth it."

He was silent for a minute. "Just for the sake of argument, let's suppose that your suspicions about Aspen have some merit."

Evan widened her eyes in surprise.

Dan held up a hand. "I said, *suppose*—so don't get excited. I'm not saying I believe *any* of this. I just want to know what you expect to gain by it."

"For starters, I want to stop him from hurting anyone else."

"Him?"

"Andy."

Dan got up and strode across the porch. "This is *insane*. You're talking about a U.S. senator, for Christ's sake."

"I'm aware of that."

He faced her. "Are you? I don't think so. You make a mistake here and, believe me, it won't be *his* career that goes down in flames. There'd be no coming back from this—not for either of us."

"What are you talking about?"

"Oh, come on. You don't think Marcus is going to continue to sit idly by and let you smear shit all over the party's poster boy, do you? These are high stakes . . . with high rollers. And they play for keeps."

"I'm not afraid of Marcus."

"No? You should be." Dan shook his head. "I thought you were smarter than this."

Evan drained her glass and snagged an ice cube to crunch. She knew the sound made Dan crazy. "So tell me. What's Marcus gonna do? Un-friend me on Facebook?"

He watched her as she chewed on her ice. "Fine. Yuck it up. It's clear that I'm wasting my breath on this." He finished his drink and slammed the glass down on the table. "Send me your final expense report tomorrow. Thanks for dinner. I'll find my own way out."

He stormed back into the house, undoubtedly headed toward the study where Stevie was watching TV.

Evan picked up her glass and spit out the crumbled chunks of ice.

She knew that Dan was telling the truth about Marcus. That slimy motherfucker would never take something like this lying down.

The whole thing was one hell of a shell game, and she was struggling to keep up with how fast the pieces were moving. But she had no choice—not now. She'd set everything in motion, and it would all play out the way it would play out. She just hoped that Julia wouldn't be the one caught in the crosshairs.

From inside the house, she heard the sound of the front door slamming. Then she heard the dull, grinding noise of Dan's old Chrysler. The big V-8 finally stopped protesting and turned over on the fourth try. He really needed to ditch that piece of shit. But he loved the damn thing and babied it like it was something precious.

Well. He was right about one thing. There was no way to predict what you'd end up caring about.

She got up and went inside to join her daughter.

Chapter 26

Julia arrived back at her Park Avenue apartment shortly after eleven on Saturday morning.

She was tired. The three-way tango she had been doing with Evan and Andy was exhausting her. She'd never been good at subterfuge, and she didn't know how much longer she could keep the deception going. Sooner or later, it was all going to come crashing down around them, and they'd be left with one hell of a mess.

It was a mess already. Why not stop pretending that a better outcome was possible? The chips would fall where they would fall, and there'd be nothing left to do but work to minimize the damage. Why forestall the inevitable?

She shook her head.

Why? Because Evan was persuaded they *had* to in order to keep her safe.

But safe from *what*? Safe from whom? *Marcus?*

She tossed her keys onto the sideboard, kicked off her shoes, and headed toward the kitchen.

It wasn't that she had a hard time believing Marcus capable of menacing behavior. But her dislike of him had never extended far enough for her to imagine him capable of *murder* . . . and Evan's discoveries about Tom Sheridan's death were beyond disturbing.

And then there were all those questions surrounding her accident in London. What if Evan was right about that, and someone *had* been trying to kill her?

She shook her head. All this crazy cloak-and-dagger stuff was making her jittery. It was like being tasked with one of those annoying math problems where you're expected to solve for "x." But this equation *had* no "x"—therefore, no possibility of arriving at an outcome that made sense.

It was impossible.

She opened the fridge and pulled out a bottle of lime soda.

She thought about yesterday afternoon. What on earth prompted Evan to storm into her office like that? God, she had flown off the handle like the jilted lover from a B-movie. That over-the-top performance hadn't fooled Julia for a second. But she had to admit that she'd never seen Andy quite that angry before. Even after Evan left, he seemed unable to calm down.

She carried her cold drink back toward her study, intending to collapse into a chair and try to make some kind of sense out of the last twenty-four hours—especially the changes in her relationship with Evan. For, certainly, some kind of tectonic plate shift had occurred there.

Well. Things seemed to have changed for *Evan*. Julia had already been sure of her own feelings. At least, she had been sure since the day she opened the door to her parents' London flat, and saw Evan standing there—wearing that shy and embarrassed expression.

That had been Julia's moment—that split-second when she knew that everything in her world had shifted. It seemed to her that Evan's moment had come yesterday afternoon, while they sat next to each other in that noisy train station, saying nothing, but saying everything.

At least, she *thought* so. They didn't talk much once they got to the suite at the Plaza. She smiled. Not in conventional ways, anyway.

She entered the study and flipped on the light switch next to the door. This room faced East 71st Street, and it tended to be darker in the mornings.

"Sleep well, dear?"

The voice came out of nowhere, and it scared her half to death.

She nearly dropped her open bottle, managing to catch it by the neck just before it slipped entirely from her grasp.

Andy.

He was seated on a small settee by the window. He didn't appear relaxed, and he certainly didn't look happy.

"I wondered when you'd make it back," he added.

She set the sweating bottle down on her desk blotter and shook her wet hand to try and dry it. Her pulse was racing.

"Good god, Andy. What are you doing here?"

He uncrossed his legs. He looked awful. Unkempt. Unfamiliar. He needed a shave.

"I live here," he said.

She leaned back against the desk and crossed her arms, trying to regain her composure.

"Correction. You *used* to live here. And I don't appreciate having you show up unannounced like this."

He laughed. "Why not? Afraid I might disrupt some of your extracurricular activities?"

She could feel her face growing hot. "Did you intrude on me like this just to insult me?"

"Oh, come on, Julia. Do you think I don't *know* about your sick little tryst last night with that common dyke, and at the *Plaza*, no less? A little out of her league, wouldn't you say?"

She was too shocked and annoyed by the suggestion that he'd been following her to react to his crude slight against Evan.

"I refuse to be goaded by you, Andy. I can't imagine what you hope to achieve by this brutish behavior."

"Oh, really?" He leaned forward and picked up a cut-glass tumbler, half full of amber liquid. Probably Scotch. In some other set of circumstances, she would have been concerned that he was drinking this early in the day. "A bit too realistic for you, darling? And here I thought maybe you'd developed a taste for the gutter—at least in terms of your bedmates."

She dropped her arms.

"I think you need to leave. *Now.*"

"Oh no. Not until we clarify a few things."

"I have nothing further to discuss with you." She turned around and started to leave the room. "You can let yourself out—but, please, leave the key. You won't be needing it again."

He stood up.

"Not so fast, Julia. You're still my *wife*."

She turned to him. "You certainly picked an odd time to remember that."

He took a step toward her. "Unlike you, I've never *forgotten* it. We had an agreement, and you're going to hold up your end."

"I *held* up my end—even when you mortified me and everyone else in our acquaintance by your shameless involvement with Margo Sheridan."

He laughed. "Am I supposed to be impressed by this display of virtue? Or are you just still pissed that I got to fuck her first?"

She raised her hand to slap him, but he caught hold of her wrist.

"Let go of me," she hissed.

He tightened his grasp. "You don't get it, do you? I won't *ever* let go of you—not now. Not until this campaign is finished."

"Fuck you, *and* your selfish aspirations!" She forced her arm free and stepped away from him. "Get out, Andy. It's over. *We're* over. I'm seeing my attorney on Monday morning to file for divorce. And, frankly, I no longer *care* how you manage the headlines."

Julia could see him struggling to regain control of his temper. He was silent for a moment. Then he slowly reached into an inside pocket of his jacket, withdrew a brass key, and set it down atop an end table.

"Marcus won't like this." His voice was flat. "You need to reconsider."

"Marcus can go to hell."

"This is a mistake. I won't be able to control the outcome if you go ahead with this."

She shook her head. "It's over, Andy. You don't need me any-more."

He met her eyes. "You're wrong about that."

She sighed. "Fine. I don't need *you* anymore. I don't need *this*, Andy, and I don't want it."

He stood there, flexing the fingers of both hands as they continued to stare at each other. Then he squared his shoulders and headed for the door.

"Goodbye, Julia."

She stood rooted to the spot, listening to the sound of his retreating footsteps until she heard the front door to the apartment open and close. Then she dropped into a chair, and started to shake.

Chapter 27

On Sunday morning, Julia called Evan to fill her in on the disturbing encounter with Andy.

Evan was incredulous—and more than slightly pissed off about this turn of events.

"Why did you wait so long to call me?" she demanded.

The line hissed with dead air, then Julia sighed. "Because I needed some time to process it for myself—without any filters."

"Is that what I am? A *filter*?" She knew it was a petty response, but she couldn't help herself.

"Stop it, Evan. You know what I mean."

"No, I'm not sure that I do know what you mean. This isn't a game. These people play for keeps. My filter might just be the only thing that keeps you from becoming the next casualty in this sick little drama."

There was more silence on the line.

"I think you're overreacting. Yes, Andy was . . . upset, but he'd never do anything to hurt me."

Evan silently counted to five before allowing herself to speak. "Sweetheart, I think you're underestimating the Marcus factor."

"No, I'm not. I have no illusions about what that man might be capable of."

"Then I'll ask again: Why did you wait so long to let me know about this?"

"I'm letting you know about it now."

"Twenty-four hours later?"

"Evan . . ."

"I *mean* it, Julia. One day can be a lifetime when you're dealing with a scumbag like Marcus."

"I don't even know how to respond to a comment like that."

"Well, I don't either, and that's why we need to make use of every second."

Julia exhaled. "All right. What do you think we need to do?"

Evan relaxed a little. *At least she said "we." That has to be a good sign.* "Let me get a few things squared away on this end, and I'll call you back." She considered. "Where will you be for the rest of the day?"

"I was going to go into the office for several hours. If you'll recall, I didn't get much work done on Friday."

Evan felt her face grow hot. She was glad that Julia couldn't see it. "Right. Good idea. Go on to the office and stay there until you hear back from me."

"Okay."

"Julia?"

"Yes?"

"I mean it. Stay there until you hear from me."

Julia sighed. "Okay. But will you please calm down? Your tone is scaring me more than *any* suppositions about what Marcus might do."

Evan sighed. The truth was that she needed Julia to be scared. But she needed her to be smart, too—and careful. "I need you to trust me."

"I do trust you."

"Then I don't see that we have a problem."

Julia gave a laugh of resignation. "I guess not. Call me later." She hung up.

Christ. Now what?

Evan opened her desk drawer and pulled out her stack of timetables. Stevie's train for Albany was leaving at two thirty-five. She could catch the three-ten for D.C. and be at Marcus's office on M Street by five. She knew he'd be there. The scumbag had no life, and he always found other goons to do his dirty work.

She shook her head. "Too bad I can't buy stock in fucking Amtrak."

She stuffed the timetables back into the drawer and closed it.

She looked toward the doorway to be sure that Stevie was still upstairs gabbing on her phone. She waited until she heard the muffled sound of her laughter, then walked over to the bookcase and picked up a small ceramic mug. It was misshapen and haphazardly decorated with gang symbols in bright, primary colors—a craft project she had made years ago, when her grandfather forced her to attend one of those lame-ass CYO summer camps. The only reason she got away with the design was because the nuns were so fucking clueless. But she recalled that Tim, who had been at the camp with her, just shook his head and told her that she was begging for it.

Not much had changed since those days.

She took the small brass key out of the cup, walked back to her desk, and unlocked its big bottom drawer. Beneath a stack of fat file folders sat the wooden box that contained her handgun. She kept the ammo in a box on the top shelf of her closet.

She hadn't fired the thing in about two years—not since she spent that weekend with some pals at Quantico. She hoped she could still shoot straight.

She pulled the box out of the drawer and opened it.

But that was one thing about a Glock . . . it was *very* forgiving of a limp-wristed shot.

And that was just the kind of insurance policy she needed right now.

Chapter 28

Marcus was losing patience. He hated repeating himself, and it was clear that this conversation was going no place fast. He'd already made his decision, and he never changed his mind. Never.

He tried again to make his position clear.

"I've already told you that I can't undo *any* of this. It was all set in motion long before the former first lady took her playmate to the Plaza. Calling me about it now is pointless, *and* dangerous. I suggest that you don't do it again."

He started to hang up the phone.

"Don't you *dare* hang up on me, you bloodless asshole. You're the one who got me into this mess in the first place." The voice on the other end of the line was desperate now—he found himself vaguely amused by that. Especially since it was coming from someone who was renowned for being such an icon of restraint.

"Are you threatening me?"

"You're goddamn right I'm threatening you. I want to know what the fuck you intend to do to short-circuit this catastrophe?"

He exhaled. "Not my problem. All the dogs in this fight appear to belong to *you*—not me."

"Is that a fact? You seem to forget that if I go down, you go down with me."

"I beg to differ." He glanced at his watch. This was taking up too much time. Time he couldn't afford right now. He had plans

239

to set into motion. The damage control from this one was going to be Herculean. He might even need to add staff. "May I remind you that this whole little scenario was *your* enterprise—not mine? It was *your* bankroll that set the ball rolling. Or have you forgotten about that?"

The line was silent for a moment. "No. I haven't forgotten that. I have all those pesky deposit slips as affectionate reminders. They should make good reading for a grand jury—don't you think?"

He was unfazed. "I don't know what you expect me to do. In this situation, it seems that you'd be better served by consulting with your friend, Mr. Nemo."

"Goddamn it, I've *told* you what has to happen. You're just not hearing me."

"Wrong. I heard you perfectly. I'm just not interested, or able to help you."

"Jesus, Marcus. I'm telling you that this mess is out of control. You have to stop it before it goes any further."

He sighed. "The only thing I'm stopping is this conversation. Don't call me about this again."

He hung up and sat with his hand resting on top of the receiver for a moment, then he sat back in his chair and tented his long fingers.

One way or another, tomorrow's headlines promised to be *very* interesting.

The phone on his desk buzzed. He leaned forward and tapped the speaker button.

"Yes?"

"Evan Reed is here to see you."

He shook his head. Of *course* she was.

"Send her in."

Chapter 29

Margo was making a concerted effort not to panic. She refused to panic because Andy was panicking, and they couldn't *both* be out of control. There was too much at stake. Everything she'd been working toward since Tom's death was starting to unravel at lightning speed.

If Julia met with her attorneys tomorrow, that would be *it*— the death knell for Andy's presidential aspirations. For certainly, once the lurid details of their affair became public, the party leadership would lay a patch running in the opposite direction. Not because of his infidelity, of course. The American public was bored and jaded enough now that it no longer applied those arcane, *Ozzie and Harriet* values to its celebrities. And that's what national politics was all about these days—celebrity. Who had it, and who didn't. In today's drag-and-drop world, attention spans were like cheap gum that lost its flavor after the first two minutes. And presidential campaigns were won and lost on the cover of *People* magazine, not on the editorial pages of *The Washington Post*.

So it wasn't a pending messy divorce that would bring Andy's potential candidacy to a grinding halt. No. It was his backdoor involvement with an *Arab*.

Of course, she wasn't an Arab, but that wouldn't matter. She was from Pakistan, and that, as far as the rank-and-file American was concerned, was guilt by association.

She sighed with disgust. The average American probably couldn't find Pakistan on a map—assuming, of course, that they even knew where to look to *locate* a map.

It didn't matter. Her accidental relationship to two suspected terrorists would be enough on its own to ruin any shot Andy had at national office. That was the *real* dust Evan Reed would bring to light—not anything related to her husband's untimely death, or her own sexual involvement with both of the Townsends.

Correction: Evan Reed would never reveal *anything* about Margo's dalliance with the sainted Julia.

But Tom's death . . . something about that still stuck in her craw. She had long suspected that something other than an unfortunate accident had transpired on the slopes in Aspen that day. But as many opportunities as she gave Andy to tell her the truth, he continued to deny it. And the perversity of it all was that she really didn't *care*, either way. After all, Tom had turned out to be a terrible disappointment—both to her, and to the agency. He'd squandered the potential he'd shown early on and cashed in his one shot at political success to join ranks with a bunch of two-bit, Greenpeace ambulance chasers. It was pathetic.

But Andy? Now *he* was another matter—smart and savvy, and tinged with just enough ambition to make him malleable. But there was a problem: Andy was lying to her. She was certain of it. And if he lied to her about *this*, there would be no way to predict what *else* he might lie to her about. And that uncertainty made him dangerous. It meant that she couldn't control him—and if she couldn't control him, then she couldn't count on him. He was a liability—both to her, and to the boys in Lahore.

Just like Evan Reed.

And Julia.

Marcus was right about Julia. As long as Andy remained tied up in knots over his twisted push-me, pull-you relationship with her, he'd be worthless to them both. Something had to give. She knew that Andy was near the breaking point. She hadn't been able to calm him down when he had called her that morning from Manhattan. He was irrational, and running scared. He was acting out, and she didn't trust him. She knew that if she didn't step in and sort things out—*soon*—there'd be no salvaging *any* of this. She might as well pack her bags and head back to a life of anonymity in Punjab.

Enough was enough. She picked up her cell phone and punched in the speed dial code for JetBlue.

Fuck Marcus.

It was time to take matters into her own hands.

Chapter 30

Where the fuck is she?

The illuminated watch dial showed that it was now after 10 p.m.

I can't keep sitting in here. Sooner or later, I'm going to have to get out and move around.

It was a hell of a time to have a bout of claustrophobia.

The utility closet in Julia's apartment was larger than most New York walk-ups. Still, it was small and dark—but it was the *one* place Julia would be unlikely to visit when she got home from . . . wherever in the hell she was.

The watch now read five after ten.

Christ.

It was hard not to feel a little hysterical. A sweaty palm was making it hard to retain a good grip on the goddamn gun. It was hefty. That was a surprise. This thing was supposed to be quiet, and clean. No history.

You paid extra for that. A lot extra.

Fire it, and drop it. That was the way it worked. Let them think it was a robbery gone bad.

Shouldn't be hard.

In the last two months, there'd been a slew of them in these Gold Coast high-rises. That was helpful. Even the cops thought it was an inside job—someone who was familiar with the terrain.

Well. They'd be right about this one, wouldn't they?

The quiet inside the apartment was disrupted by the sound of the front door opening and closing.

Lights. Camera. Action.

This little soap opera was about to end.

With a bang.

It was after 10 p.m. when she finally unlocked the door and stepped inside the dark apartment. She saw no reason to turn on any lights—she was going straight to the bedroom.

She was emotionally exhausted.

This was one day she was glad to see the back end of. It had been fraught with frustration over Andy's sudden, disturbing appearance there yesterday, and the ensuing, seemingly endless disputes about how she could best manage a response.

They'd argued for a solid hour about her right to return there for the night. It was ridiculous. She was a grown-up with an advanced degree in competence—and she certainly knew how to take care of herself. She didn't need a nanny, and she didn't need a nursemaid.

And she didn't need company. Not tonight.

This was her bailiwick. She knew better than anyone how to navigate it.

She entered the bedroom and kicked off her shoes. She didn't waste time getting undressed. She went to the bed and folded back the coverlet. Nothing mattered to her right now but being here, in precisely this exact spot—*alone.*

It was going to be a long night.

Twenty minutes later, it seemed safe to exit the closet and move toward the bedroom.

The quiet in the apartment was the worst part. But marble floors were very forgiving. Crepe-soled shoes helped out, too.

The bedroom door was open.

Good.

There was a bit of ambient light streaming in from a large window at the end of the hallway. But that should only make this easier—less opportunity to miss.

It was a bit easier to see inside the bedroom. Blue light from a bedside clock was casting freakishly large shadows on the walls.

The shape on the bed was unmistakable.

It was time.

Make the shot. Drop the gun. Grab the bag full of jewelry and loose change stashed in the utility closet. Leave by the back door, and ride the service elevator to the basement—where a change of clothes was waiting. Exit on 71st St. Take the subway to Midtown, then a cab to Grand Central.

Q.E.D.

Problem solved.

But it was important to be a step or two closer to the bed. No margin for error that way.

The dark would make it simpler—no eye contact. No chance to rethink it.

But goddamn that fucking blue light. It was distracting.

So was the fact that the shape on the bed was moving.

The bedside light came on. It was hard to see in the sudden blaze of yellow light. But it wasn't hard to hear.

"You sure as hell took your time. I nearly nodded off waiting on you."

Jesus Christ.

It was Evan Reed.

And she wasn't alone—she had a big goddamn gun in her hand.

And it was pointed right at him.

His eyes were starting to work now. But his breathing was so labored that he was having a hard time thinking through his options.

There weren't many—and none of them were looking very good.

Evan Reed looked like the picture of calm, sitting there in Julia's bed, holding that big-assed gun.

She was talking again.

"Why not put your weapon down, Andy? You're not getting out of here anytime soon. And it's not going to help you if we *both* end up dead."

He needed to buy some time until he could figure out his next move. He tightened his grip on the gun. "You won't shoot me. You don't have the guts for it."

"Really?" she pulled back the slide on her gun. The click it made was deafening. "I beg to differ."

He tried to remain calm. It wasn't easy.

"You're a chickenshit, Reed. I'm not buying it."

"Suit yourself." She shrugged. "This thing is semi-automatic. Which means that right now, my dick is a *lot* bigger than yours. I can turn your preppy ass into a high-priced slab of Gruyere before you can get off a single shot. And trust me—I could do it, and *still* sleep like a baby tonight."

"Fuck you."

"*Ding!* Wrong answer, Senator. Wanna try again?"

"You're bluffing, Reed."

She sighed. "Why not drop the gun and pull up a chair, Andy. You're the one who doesn't have the stomach for this."

He didn't budge.

"She won't stay with you. She never stays with *anyone*. Ask me. Ask *Maya*."

For a split-second, he thought he saw her waver. All he needed was an opening. Just *one*. He needed to keep her talking.

"Admit it, Reed. You were sucked in by her just like we were. She's using you, too. That's why you're here right now. You're a stooge—a *pigeon*. You're dispensable—just like me. Once I'm out of the way, she won't need you anymore."

Evan sat there staring at him. Her expression gave nothing away, but he could tell she was seething. It was palpable—a giant elephant had just entered the room and stood there right between them.

"Since you're in such a mood to chat," she said, "why don't you fill in a few blanks for me about someone *else* who proved dispensable? What really happened to Tom Sheridan?"

He laughed. "You're kidding me. *This* is what you want to talk about?"

"Why not? There's no TV in here . . ."

He shrugged. He had nothing to lose now.

"Tom got in the way."

"Meaning he found out about you and Margo?"

He nodded.

"So you killed him, and made it look like an accident."

He snorted. "You make it sound like a *Lifetime* movie plot. It wasn't quite that simple. Tom was a drunk and a buffoon. He persuaded me to go with him that day, against my better judgment. No matter *what* you choose to believe, Reed, I didn't want him to get hurt. But once we were alone on the slopes, he confronted me about Margo. He was crazy drunk and he threatened me. He said he'd ruin me—*and* my chances to run for the senate."

"So you were already in cahoots with Marcus?"

He laughed. "*Cahoots?* You read too many dime-store novels."

She said nothing. But she wasn't lowering the gun yet, either.

"Yes. I had already hired Marcus to help me manage my career. Why not?"

Evan said nothing.

"I tried to calm Tom down, but he kept at me. It escalated, and finally, he took a swing at me. I hit him back—then he really went crazy." He paused. "I had no choice. It was self-defense."

"You killed him."

"It was self-defense."

"If it was self-defense, then why work so hard to cover it up?"

He gave a bitter laugh. "Are you serious? I thought presidential politics was supposed to be your goddamn *raison d'etre.*"

"Fine. So you swapped skis with him and pushed him over the cliff on the out-of-bounds run. Then you skied back down and stayed quiet until three days later—when you could safely step up and offer solace to the grieving widow."

He shrugged. "More or less."

"And you had Marcus on hand, to manage the details."

"No comment."

It was her turn to laugh. "No comment necessary. I'm sure it's no accident that you announced your candidacy for Art Jacobsen's senate seat a week later."

"Do you need me for this conversation, Reed?"

She nodded. "Tell me about Mr. Nemo."

He was stunned. "Nemo?"

"Yeah. Nemo. The name you used when you rented the van in London that was supposed to kill Julia. The name you used when you bought the replacement set of K2 skis. The name you probably used when you bought that gun in your hand. You know . . . *Nemo*. Named after your favorite dog?"

He could feel himself starting to tremble. "Goddamn you. There's no *way* you can prove any of that."

She laughed. "Oh that's the beauty of this, *Senator*. I don't have to *prove* anything. I just have to pick up the phone and give Sean Hannity a call. He'd salivate to get his mitts on a story like this. As you said—presidential politics is my specialty—and I'm awfully goddamn good at it."

"You fucking bitch."

She nodded. "That's me."

His heart was hammering so hard he could hear it. There was a roaring in his ears. His hand was sweating to the point that he thought he might drop the damn gun. He raised his hand and squeezed it tighter in a desperate attempt to retake control of the situation.

Time seemed to stop when the shots rang out. He was vaguely aware that Evan Reed had slumped forward on the bed.

A hefty stream of blood was making its way across the floor. He stared at it.

"Is that mine?" he asked.

His vision clouded over, and he dropped to join the expanding red pool at his feet.

Margo stood in the doorway behind Andy's unmoving body.

Evan was barely clinging to consciousness. One of the bullets had passed through Andy, and tagged her on the shoulder. It was bleeding like a sonofabitch. She grabbed a small throw pillow and crammed it against the wound. She still held on to her own gun.

Margo looked at her without emotion. "You don't need that now." She gestured at Evan's gun.

"Yeah? Well, forgive me if I don't take your word for it."

Margo laughed. "I've already taken care of the only business I had here tonight."

Evan was starting to feel light-headed. She fought to remain upright. "You expect me to believe that? Why would you cap your own goddamn meal ticket?"

Margo glanced down at Andy's body. "He lied to me about Tom." She shrugged. "He fucked up, and he panicked. Then he tried to kill Julia." She met Evan's eyes. "He was a rogue. And we don't work that way. We can't afford to."

Evan was starting to shake. "Who the fuck is 'we'?"

Margo shook her head. "The 'we' that just saved your ass. Don't look a gift horse in the mouth, Reed." She lowered her own gun. "Now, if you'll excuse me, I've got a plane to catch."

She turned to leave the room.

"Wait a goddamn minute." Evan was going to pass out—she could feel it coming. She tried to swing her legs over the side of the bed to stand up, but all that did was make things worse. A huge wave of nausea washed over her.

When she could finally raise her head again, Margo was gone. *Fuck me.*

She heard a loud scuffling in the hallway outside the bedroom. There was a crash, and the sound of glass breaking, followed by a couple of loud thuds. Then it grew quiet again.

"Jesus Christ. What now?"

She managed to stand up—barely. The throw pillow covering her shoulder was soaked with blood, and more was running down her arm and dripping onto the floor.

She took a couple of shaky steps toward the door and ran headlong into Ben Rush.

He was breathing heavily. He stopped and looked her up and down. Then he saw Andy's body on the floor. He met her eyes.

"Christ, Reed. You look like *shit*. What the fuck happened here?"

"Where's Margo?" Her voice was barely a whisper.

Ben jerked a thumb toward the hallway. "Out there cooling off. She's not going anyplace for a while."

"Jesus Ben. You killed her?"

"Fuck no. I just knocked her ass out." He rubbed his jaw. "That bitch has some left hook, lemme tell you."

Evan staggered back toward the bed and sat down. "What the hell are you *doing* here?"

He shrugged. "Dan called me."

"Dan?"

"Yeah. He told me to follow your ass—seems like he was worried that something like this might happen."

Dan called him? Dan *believed* her?

Jesus. Go fucking figure.

She really felt like she was going to puke. She needed an ambulance.

But there were things to take care of first.

"You have to let her go."

"Who?" Ben looked confused.

"Margo. You have to wake her up and get her out of here."

"Are you *nuts*? How do you intend to explain *this*?" He waved a hand toward Andy's unmoving body.

"I don't *intend* to explain it. Get Margo out of here and call Marcus."

"Marcus? Marcus *Goldman*?"

"You heard me."

"Why the fuck would I do that?"

"Because this is all *his* mess, and the slimy fucker has a cleaner spooled up and ready to manage it."

Ben stood there thinking. He still looked unconvinced. "Are you sure?"

She nodded. "The only bad guy in this drama is right there on the floor. It won't do any good to hand Margo over to the cops. She has diplomatic immunity. Trust me. Wake her up and make the call. Marcus is in New York at Julia's office, and he's waiting to hear from me."

Ben looked at her like she had two heads. "Are you *shitting* me? You planned this whole fucking shindig with him?"

She gave him a weak smile. "You wanna catch a fish, you learn to think like a fish."

She looked down at Andy's body, and her smile faded. The down side to this theory was that you usually ended up *smelling* like one, too.

Ben shook his head. "I'll be goddamned."

He turned back toward the hallway.

"And, Ben?"

He looked back at her.

"Tell Marcus I need a goddamn ambulance."

Then she did pass out—right after she vomited all over Julia's polished marble floor.

Ten days later, Evan was still at home, recovering from her shoulder wound.

Julia stayed with her for the two days she was in the hospital, and then accompanied her back to Chadds Ford. Julia had only returned to the apartment on Park Avenue long enough to gather some clothes and her toiletries. Immediately after learning about Andy's death, she declared that she would never return there to live. It would be up to her parents to decide what *they* wanted to do with the coveted, now infamous, property.

Evan didn't doubt her assertion. She was already well acquainted with the core of determination that ran through Julia's character like a vein of iron.

Predictably, a circus of media coverage followed the shocking news of Senator Townsend's accidental shooting death during a robbery attempt at his wife's Manhattan apartment. But within a week, the news frenzy tapered off. Already the story had dropped from its prominent position above the fold and listed toward the inside pages of the nation's leading newspapers.

TV outlets were the first to move on. With no shooting suspect in custody, there was no allure of a prime-time perp walk, and, thanks to Marcus, there was an impressive dearth of salacious detail.

Internet coverage, with the exception of a few chat-room zanies who were hot on the trail of the latest government conspiracy, had all but abated, too. Although Evan had to hand it to a few of the more prolific wing nuts: This time they were closer to the truth than even they realized.

But Marcus did his job very well. And to the causal observer, Senator Townsend's untimely death was simply a tragic accident. It even provided an opportunity for the party to make some political hay by touting its agenda to impose tighter restrictions on the regulation of handguns. This reignited the national pissing contest on gun control, and both sides poured millions of fresh dollars into ad campaigns. No matter which side of the second amendment you came down on, guns were big political business, and lots of people were cleaning up on the rhetoric that fueled the debate.

So it appeared that Andy managed to hang on to his poster-boy status, after all. Even in death, he remained a hot commodity that paid dividends to special interests.

Fortunately for Julia, his funeral was a private affair—carried out quickly and quietly in Delaware, with no members of the press in attendance.

Marcus managed that, too.

And now? Now it would just take as long as it would take for these events to completely fade from the national memory.

Evan shook her head. *About five minutes—that's how long it will take.* Another scandal would spool right up to fill the limelight. The mainstream media hated a vacuum even more than Mother Nature did.

From inside the house, she heard the clatter of what sounded like a pan lid hitting the floor, followed by the muffled, but distinct, sounds of cursing. Julia was in the kitchen, and it was anybody's guess what kind of unrecognizable food creation would be likely to emerge.

Evan sighed and looked out across the pasture. She loved having Julia there, but she knew that this idyllic respite they were enjoying wouldn't last forever. Right now, they were like bugs in amber— frozen in the moment. But real life would intrude soon enough. Julia would have decisions to make—and so would Evan.

They hadn't talked much about the future. For her part, Evan was just starting to get used to the idea that they might *have* a future. For now, that was enough. The rest would sort itself out in time.

She shifted her weight on the chaise and watched a couple of cows make unhurried progress toward the stream that bisected her property. They moved as if they had all the time in the world.

Vacuums. It was incredible. One way or another, the holes in your life got filled.

And it was impossible to predict who would end up wielding the shovel.

Epilogue

Thirty-six thousand feet above Chadds Ford, Evan's "shovel" ordered another dirty martini.

The Townsend mess had been one hell of a sticky wicket. But all the loose ends had finally been tied off, and Marcus was on his way to Brussels. The U.S. envoy to NATO was going rogue with some badly timed public comments about one of the administration's Middle East initiatives—again. And he was being dispatched to discuss the wisdom of adjusting the envoy's viewpoints.

But first, he'd have a well-deserved week in Paris.

It wasn't like him to take time off, but these could hardly be considered normal circumstances. None of the events leading up to Townsend's neutralization had unfolded according to plan. Too many players had too many ideas about how it should go, and none of them seemed to give a flying fuck about the effort it would take to contain the damage.

Evan Reed, in particular, had been like a bull in a china shop.

Not, he reflected, that this was any kind of behavioral departure for her. She was fractious and impossible to manage on her best day. That made her . . . liaison with Julia Donne even more of a curiosity. On the night of the shootings, he had been stunned to see Donne's implacable veneer of indifference shatter like cheap windshield glass. And it didn't occur when he told her about Andy's death—it happened when she learned that Evan Reed was unconscious, and being taken by ambulance to Mount Sinai with a gunshot wound. He had a hard time restraining her until the car arrived to take her there.

He shook his head and sipped from his drink.

What fools they were—behaving like dogs in heat.

He'd had to shift gears midstream and have Andy's body transported to Sinai, too—just so Julia's presence there would make sense once the story of the break-in hit the news wires.

Fortunately, the mainstream media already regarded Townsend's wife as a recluse. So her unwillingness to appear publicly in the aftermath of her husband's shooting death just seemed like consistent behavior.

Dan Cohen had been almost as difficult to manage. That little stunt he pulled with Ben Rush nearly ruined everything. If Reed hadn't still been conscious when the fat gumshoe blundered his way into the middle of everything, Margo would now be in the hands of the Feds, and he'd be on his way to Paris with a shitload more baggage in the cargo hold.

Fortunately, Ben Rush was a reasonable man, and twenty-five thousand dollars in cash bought a lot of cheap gin—and silence.

And as far as Evan Reed was concerned? He didn't have to worry about her. They had an agreement, and she had got what she wanted. All things considered, his arrangement with her was the least expensive part of the cleanup process. She and her reward were down there right now—hiding from the media in the middle of that field of cow shit she called home.

He took another sip from his drink.

Stupid. And shortsighted. It would never last. But that wasn't his problem.

Not anymore.

The plane jolted and dipped when it hit a pocket of unstable air. He had a hard time keeping his drink from sloshing over the rim of the glass.

The woman in the seat next to him stirred and opened her eyes.

"Where are we?" she asked, stretching out her legs. Her voice was husky from sleep.

The first-class compartment was mostly dark, but he could still see her eyes.

"Someplace over the Atlantic," he answered.

"How long was I asleep?"

He glanced at his watch. "About an hour." He held up his glass. "Want one of these?"

She shook her head. "I hate martinis."

"You hate a lot of things," he reminded her. "But you've been known to change your mind." He ran a long finger across the exposed skin of her forearm. She didn't flinch.

"You know I have to go back to Pakistan."

"Have to?" He smiled at her. "Someone with your unique skill set could work anyplace."

She looked at him without emotion. "I know this is a paradigm that doesn't resonate for you, Marcus, but some of us do what we do for reasons that transcend personal gain."

He laughed. "Nice speech. Is that what you're going to tell your friends in Lahore?"

She was unfazed. "I don't regret what I did, and neither do you."

"Still, it begs the question about your motivation, doesn't it?"

She shrugged, then pushed the call button above her seat.

"Maybe I'll have that drink, after all."

He chuckled. "I don't know which one of them you thought you were saving."

She met his gaze. "What do you care? You got the result you wanted."

He rested his open palm on her knee. "True."

The flight attendant appeared and took Margo's drink order. He decided to join her.

Why not?

They had another six hours to kill, and when they got to Paris, they'd have a week to take care of other business.

He looked at her. She was cold and indifferent. He didn't trust her. And he was fairly certain that she despised him.

They had a lot in common.

He smiled. He could live with that.

About the Author

ANN McMAN is the author of seven novels and two short story collections. She is a recipient of both the Alice B. Lavender Certificate for Outstanding Debut Novel (*Jericho*) and the 2017 Alice B. Medal for Outstanding Body of Work. Her novel *Hoosier Daddy* was a Lambda Literary Award finalist. Her books *Sidecar* and *Three* won Golden Crown Literary Society Awards for Best Short Story Collection, and *Backcast* was awarded the Silver Medal for Fiction in the Independent Publisher Awards (IPPYs) for the Northeast Region. *Backcast* also received the Rainbow Award for Best Lesbian Book of 2016. A career graphic designer, Ann is a two-time recipient of the Tee Corinne Award for Outstanding Cover Design.

Ann and her wife, Bywater Books Publisher Salem West, live in Winston-Salem, North Carolina, with two dogs, two cats, and an exhaustive supply of vacuum cleaner bags.

Acknowledgments

Dust was written during a particularly difficult period for me, and I would never have been able to finish it without the love and unflagging support of my family of choice. Jenny, Cap'n, Tini, and Midway—you kept me sane, and you helped me feel safe and warm during one of the darkest times in my life. Dee Dee—I never want to be here without you. Luke—thank god we know we can always make it hanging sheet rock if this writing gig doesn't pan out. Trent—I wish you were a woman, so I could not marry you . . . you know what I mean. W. Grier—you're a steadfast friend and the best partner in cyber-crime a gal could have. Hayes (a.k.a. PornStar)—you'll always be my personal GPS. Bagel and DeLovely—you're living proof that a wounded human heart can always make room for one more . . . or two.

I love you all.

As always, thanks to the wonderful authors and staff—my friends and family—at Bywater Books. I think I'm ready for my close-up now. . . .

Bywater BOOKS

At Bywater Books we love good books about lesbians just like you do, and we're committed to bringing the best of contemporary lesbian writing to our avid readers. Our editorial team is dedicated to finding and developing outstanding writers who create books you won't want to put down.

We sponsor the Bywater Prize for Fiction to help with this quest. Each prizewinner receives $1,000 and publication of their novel. We have already discovered amazing writers like Jill Malone, Sally Bellerose, and Hilary Sloin through the Bywater Prize. Which exciting new writer will we find next?

For more information about Bywater Books and the annual Bywater Prize for Fiction, please visit our website.

www.bywaterbooks.com